Pop Stars and Playbooks

Pop Stars and Playbooks

A Love Story

Juliet Rhodes

Thomas Nelson
Since 1798

Pop Stars and Playbooks

Published by Thomas Nelson, 501 Nelson Place, Nashville, TN 37214, USA. Thomas Nelson is a registered trademark of HarperCollins Christian Publishing, Inc.

Thomas Nelson titles may be purchased in bulk for educational, business, fundraising, or sales promotional use. For information, please email SpecialMarkets@ThomasNelson.com.

HarperCollins Publishers, Macken House, 39/40 Mayor Street Upper, Dublin 1, D01 C9W8, Ireland (https://www.harpercollins.com)

Library of Congress Cataloging-in-Publication Data

ISBN: 978-1-4003-5939-4 (trade paper)
ISBN: 978-1-4003-5939-4 (epub)
ISBN: 978-1-4003-5941-7 (audio)

Cover Design: Carolina Marando
Interior Design: Chloe Foster
Football, microphone, and scarf art: Copyright © Adobe Stock

Printed in the United States of America

26 27 28 29 30 LBC 5 4 3 2 1

For the girls who are learning the difference between being wanted and being chosen

Chapter 1

Griffin

It's a common misconception that professional athletes are too tough for the likes of an Aria Wilder concert—or pop music in general—but Griffin Hayes, tight end on the Chicago Wardens, is the perfect rebuttal to any such claim. He could've gotten the luxury box seats the team has first dibs on, but Griffin wanted floor seats. Closer is better for seeing his celebrity crush perform for the first time.

"Want anything from concessions?" Elliott calls over the thumping bass of the opening act.

Griffin turns to look, and his best friend gestures with his thumb toward the stairs he's about to take. Elliott's girlfriend, Cassandra, hovers at his side, tapping her foot as she eyes her watch.

"But Aria's about to come on," Griffin says.

Elliott grins. "I'll be fine if I miss a song or two."

Griffin shrugs. "I'm good, man, but thanks." The water beside him is the only thing available for purchase that's approved for his in-season diet. His personal trainer would have his head if he ordered one of those icy beers or the bag of buttery popcorn that were both calling his name. Soon enough, at the end of the season, he'll indulge.

"Can you grab me a Diet Coke, please, hon?" Cassandra asks Elliott. "I'm going to hang with Griff. I don't want to miss her entrance."

Elliott nods once and takes off up the stairs in bounds toward the concession stand. Griffin turns back to the stage, the lights flashing, the band growing sweaty and red nearing the end of their set, and he sways gently to the music. His teammates had poked fun in the locker room earlier, calling him the third wheel to Elliott and Cassandra's date, but there's no amount of ribbing that would keep Griffin from this concert. He might have a healthy crush on Aria, but it's also nice to momentarily leave behind his role as professional football league tight end hero and the heavy pressure to perform and win. To get lost in the music born of another person's creativity. He's often wondered what it would be like to be a musician. The one conclusion he can draw is that it's worlds away from playing football—the one thing he knows. The thing at the very center of him.

Griffin has always been a football player, for so long and so intensely that he has to wonder if he came out of the womb and immediately caught a football thrown his way. In a family of overachievers it only seemed natural that he'd cling to the thing he was good at, and in all fairness, it has brought him great success.

The opening act finishes their set, and Griffin claps along with the cheering crowd. In the quiet that follows, the lull before Aria takes the stage, Griffin can't help but wonder what else there is to him besides the sport. If he'd measure up without football. Sure, he's at the height of his career, but every athlete knows football doesn't last forever. Griffin got a hefty dose of that reality when he suffered an ACL injury five years ago. Fortunately, he rehabbed the injury and returned in full strength. Well, "full strength" if he doesn't count the fact that his knee has started to act up occasionally. Without football, who is Griffin Hayes? It's something he'll have to figure out eventually.

Suddenly the lights cut to dark, the crowd erupts, and Aria's voice echoes through the arena, an alternative melody playing alongside her most famous lyrics.

"Girl meets boy,
Boy meets girl,
Hearts aflutter,
Forever love."

The crowd screams—all 250 pounds of Griffin Hayes included—and fireworks explode across the stage in neon pink and purple. A shadowed figure in a power pose, a fist toward the sky, chest held high, lowers from the ceiling, and the crowd chants, "Aria! Aria! Aria!"

Spotlights flick to the backup dancers who rise onto the stage on hidden platforms from below just as Aria's feet meet the stage from her aerial descent, and she immediately launches into her megahit, the one she teased, "Girl Meets Boy."

Griffin loses himself in the music, dancing and singing, clapping to the beat. His eyes never stray far from Aria's mesmerizing figure on the stage. He is entranced.

Elliott steps back to glance around Cassandra's position between them and throws him a look.

Griffin raises his palms and shoulders as if to say, "*What?*"

Elliott laughs to himself and shakes his head.

Sure, the guys in the locker room will give him a hard time when Elliott, a running back also on the Wardens, recounts the story after practice tomorrow, but Griffin doesn't mind. It won't come as a surprise to any of them. Griffin's always been the guy who turns down the celebrity party invites, the one who likes to cook for himself rather than head to the latest hot restaurant where all the other celebrity types hang out. He's the one who will stay longer to make sure every kid gets a signature from him postgame.

Revealing the depth of his true Aria Wilder fandom won't come as a surprise. Though for now, he'd like to keep his secret crush under wraps. *That* would be another level of teasing from the guys he'd rather avoid.

Griffin nods his head as Aria transitions into a lively hit about girls running the world, even mouthing a few words here and there. Cassandra beside him is dancing, arms in the air, belting out lyrics, and Elliott stands beside her with his arms crossed and body still, but moving his head almost imperceptibly. Cassandra is a model, and she and Elliott have been together for two years now. The press calls them "The Beautiful Couple"—a topic that's already been covered to a great extent in the locker room.

Next comes the opening melody for Aria Wilder's "Glass

Heart," and the stage lights all come to center where Aria stands confidently, feet planted as she holds the microphone out and belts the notes powerfully into it, her words flowing to her adoring crowd.

Griffin is close enough to see the power in Aria's face, to feel the impact of the lyrics and song, and it's all he needs to release the weight of life's expectations and worries that he carries with him. He forgets that he has a professional team who banks on him, fans who expect him to win. He forgets his worries about being enough without the game. He forgets that his knee needed extra icing after last weekend's game.

Griffin closes his eyes and pulls his hands to his wide, muscular chest. At six foot four, he's easily two heads taller than most of the crowd, but he lets go of his inhibitions. The breakup anthem lands with him—that familiar feeling of not being enough—and he sings along, loud and unapologetic.

He opens his eyes and Cassandra—and even Elliott—let out whoops and applause in his direction. Griffin smiles ear to ear. He lifts his hands up, even pumping them in the air gently as he sings along about heartbreak and finding true love. He sways and nods his head, not wanting the song to end—it's such an escape to lose himself in the rhythm. He forgets that he's not alone, that he's surrounded by the public.

But as the beat slows, the notes returning to a final iteration of the main melody, he comes slowly back down to earth.

He smiles to himself as he lets his hands drop to his sides and opens his eyes.

To his surprise, a few concertgoers have made their way to the aisle, their phones now trained not on Aria but on him.

The young women giggle conspiratorially, and all Griffin can do is smile, wave, and shrug.

"You know what that means, dude?" Elliott drags his eyes pointedly to the women who have cut their recordings and since gathered into a clump to review whatever is on the screen.

Griffin lets out a breath and nods. "Fingers crossed it's a big news day."

Cassandra drops a hand on Griffin's shoulder. "Hate to break it to you, Griff, but a big, burly football player like you singing your heart out to Aria Wilder can rise to the top of any news cycle nowadays."

As the next chart topper kicks off, Griffin turns back to the stage. This time he's more measured in his enthusiasm, no-nonsense claps or head bobs. Stuff the guys on the team would do if they were here with their girlfriends. Still, he's no dummy. He knows it'll only be a matter of hours—or minutes—before that footage is somewhere online.

Chapter 2

Aria

Aria's home is spread out in a wooded area she lovingly calls "the country" despite its proximity to the city. You can take the girl out of a small town, but her heart will always be country. It's a strange thing to imagine her hometown, the folks there who never would've fathomed the stardom and fame she's achieved. She set them right, it would seem.

At the bottom of her basement stairs, Aria flips on the lights to her studio. Having her own recording studio at home has been one of the best things her success has afforded her. When she bought this house several years ago, she had the music industry's top sound tech design and outfit it for her.

Despite it being her—and every other musician's—dream to have this state-of-the-art equipment at her fingertips, today it falls flat. Aria crosses the room to the comfortable sofa—the spot where she brainstorms lyrics and plucks out melodies and harmonies on her beat-up acoustic guitar. It was her very first one. She sets her coffee mug and phone on the small table in front of the sofa and pops open the guitar case. It's not fancy, but it's consistently the source of her inspiration. As she slumps onto the sofa, the awards that line the walls loom over her—Billboard charts, Grammys, music awards for best album year after year. They're all reminders of the bind she's in.

Aria picks up her guitar and strums, tuning the strings that went unused while she traveled for events last month. She owes her record label another album, and for the first time since she started on this journey, back when she blew up as a teen, she feels hollow inside.

At first it was exciting when her songs hit the top of the charts. In fact it was better than exciting; it was exhilarating, thrilling, otherworldly. But year after year, tour after tour, eventually it started to feel like copy and paste. It was supposed to be different this time. She was supposed to get to negotiate a new contract. She was supposed to make it clear that she wanted to take a new approach—to be real and honest, raw in her songwriting.

Instead, her label hid a clause in the existing contract requiring one more "commercial album," and despite her agent, Monroe's, fastidiousness, Aria owes them another copy-and-paste pop album or she will see them in court. For a while she considered that option—that's how strongly she feels—but ultimately Monroe talked her out of it with her reasonable points: It would result in a massive gap in her album releases; she would be burning bridges with the most connected record label; and was it really worth it over an album she could create in her sleep?

Aria strums harder on the guitar, mentally noting how pinned down she feels, and at her roughness, a string breaks. It snaps back with a *boing*.

"Maybe they just don't think I have what it takes to be anything else. Maybe I believe them," she whispers to herself. "Maybe *this* is the only thing the fans want from me."

The fans—her true heartbeat. If there's one thing more important to Aria than following her own desires, it's making the fans happy. They're the only reason she's come this far. She has to do things right by them.

Aria sets the guitar lovingly back in its case, making a note to replace the string once she's gotten some work done. She closes the lid and pats it, as if tucking it in to sleep. Back when she was a kid, when she was new to the instrument, she slept beside the thing. Despite her mother's protests, fretting that she'd roll over and break it, Aria curled up beside her guitar, and first thing every morning, she would wake, find it, and strum whatever her favorite song was that week.

Remembering her younger self, her pure passion for music, her heartfelt dedication, feels like remembering a different person entirely. Aria can't pin down when exactly things changed. It probably happened gradually over time. That, as her fame and prominence grew, the pressure to be Aria Wilder, Pop Superstar and America's Darling, mounted until who she was before—a small-town girl with a heart for song—was eclipsed.

Aria whirls around, unable to look at the guitar case and swim in her thoughts any longer. She owes Worldwide Records another album, and if she's putting something out with her name on it, she's going to make it exceptional—perfect, ideally.

Aria sits down at the piano and starts playing with a major chord, working out a new melody. Something new but also familiar. She remembers what the rep told her.

"We want 'girl meets boy, boy meets girl.' The listeners love that stuff. It needs to be easy-listening, turn-the-radio-up songs. There's no need to mess with something that's working."

Despite her tinkering with the piano keys, Aria's mind wanders back to her own desires for something new. A fresh take on her own music. Not an overhaul, just a makeover. What if the folks at Worldwide are right? What if the fans don't want anything different from her? What if she's trapped forever in the bubble she created as a young twentysomething almost a decade ago?

After a few minutes of messing around on the piano, a familiar rumble of footsteps comes from the stairs before Bailey, beaming wide, appears at the bottom step, eyes trained directly on Aria.

"Sis." Bailey marches across the room in long, measured strides, phone in hand. "You *have* to see this."

"I'm guessing from the look on your face it's something good?"

It comes with the territory of being a well-known pop star that all sorts of things are shared in the press and on social media about Aria. Some of those things are incredible—generous compliments from fans, their own creative work she's inspired, teary statements about how a song brought them through a hard time. But just as often, if perhaps more frequently, less palatable stories are posted. Rumors about her being rude to waitstaff (false), rumors of her taking off with a married actor (false), articles picking apart her physical appearance (just plain mean), or "gotcha" photos of her sneaking to the grocery store in sweats looking worse for wear (true).

Bailey squeezes in beside Aria on the piano bench, and at the touch of her little sister's shoulder to hers, Aria feels the tightness in her unwind. Bailey always has a calming influence on her. Even if she's the younger sister, having Bailey at her side during tours or here at the house just living life grounds and calms Aria.

"This is from last night." Bailey holds out the phone, and Aria takes it.

She taps the icon to turn on the sound, and immediately she knows it's "Glass Heart" playing. She sang it for the crowd last night, but perhaps even more so she sang it for herself, for her own hurt feelings over being pigeonholed for a whole new album.

Aria dismisses the thoughts about her own heartache as the video zooms in on a big, burly guy singing along to the music. Her mouth lifts into a smile as the shot captures his face, shouting the lyrics passionately toward the stage, his fists gripped emotionally as he sways to the beat.

"You know who that is?" Bailey asks, eyes wide, her long lashes batting.

"Looks athletic. It's already got a million views." A wrinkle forms between Aria's brows as she thinks it over.

"Only Griffin Hayes, tight end for the Chicago Wardens."

Aria is still smiling as she holds the phone out for Bailey to take back. "I knew I had all sorts of fans, but a professional football player might be a first."

Bailey nudges the phone back toward Aria. "No, you didn't even see the best part. He reposted. See what he said."

Aria navigates back through the app until she finds his account. She taps on his share of the viral video and reads the caption out loud.

"'Guess the secret's out! I'm Aria Wilder's number one fan. Don't we all know a little something about a glass heart?!'" By the time Aria finishes reading, her cheeks are warm. She hands the phone back to Bailey.

"The internet has now also taken to calling him your 'number one fan,' by the way. That's why he mentioned it. Isn't that so sweet?"

Since the news of the hidden clause hit, Aria's been feeling like she's been walking around cast in slight shadow, but seeing this athletic powerhouse of a man go all emotional and adorable over her song feels finally like stepping under the rays of the sun.

"It is. It's super sweet."

Across the room, Aria's phone rattles on the coffee table. She hands Bailey's phone back, gets up, and retrieves hers. She swipes to accept the call.

"Kelsey. To what do I owe this pleasure?"

Kelsey has been Aria's publicist since before she made it big, believing in her from the start. Back then, Kelsey had multiple singer-actor types, but once Aria's career took off, she signed her on full-time.

"Well, good afternoon to you too, Pop Superstar and America's Darling."

Aria tsks-tsks playfully. "Are you buttering me up?"

Kelsey laughs. "Have you seen the internet?"

"The video of the football player?"

"'The football player'? Aria, this is Griffin Hayes, only the top tight end in the league. He's absolutely killing it. Not to mention the fans adore him."

"It was a cute video, but why does it have you calling?"

She clears her throat. "Well, I spoke to Monroe, and we both agree that we should really take advantage of the moment. Seize the organic positive press."

Aria pauses. She's not always the biggest fan of the PR activities that are pitched in her direction. Aria has always wanted to be genuine and personal, and sometimes the publicity efforts leave her spinning so much she feels icky. This time—the organic moment with Griffin, accidentally caught on camera—she has fewer qualms.

"What did you have in mind?"

"Well, we were thinking you could invite him as a special guest to the next concert tomorrow?"

Special guests are not a new thing to Aria. The record label often brings in folks, people they're attempting to woo. Or fans who win competitions. Occasionally kids with serious illnesses fulfilling their wishes granted by Make-A-Wish.

"I guess it could be interesting to meet him."

"Great! And I'm glad I caught you, because we were thinking it would be fun if you invited him publicly. Maybe share his post, and in your caption invite him? The fans would *love* it, and I know they're your top priority."

Aria can't stop the laugh that pops out. Never before has a PR activity felt fun like this. And, Aria must admit, this Griffin guy has her interest.

"You got it," Aria says. "I'll do it now."

"You're fabulous. I'll be waiting for your post and continue to monitor."

Aria says goodbye, hangs up, and navigates over to socials. She opens her account, the one with several million followers, and looks up this Griffin Hayes. She taps on his post, the one she just read out loud with Bailey.

"What's going on?" Bailey asks from over at the piano.

"Oh, just the silly game that is being a public figure. PR stunts left and right." She sighs, but she's smiling at the same time.

Aria hits Share and types her caption.

"Hey @GriffinHayes, love the enthusiasm! We can always use that kind of energy on show nights. Care to be my guest of honor tomorrow? Have your people call my people."

Aria taps to post. Immediately the likes start pouring in, and she walks the phone over to her sister. Bailey waits, mouth slightly agape, and takes the phone. She reads and squeals.

"Oh em gee, we get to meet him!" Bailey wiggles like the excitement is bursting from her of its own accord.

Aria pulls her sister under her arm. "What can I say? Your wish is my command."

"Like with so many things."

"Not that I had 'Wardens tight end concert drop-in' on my bingo card. Nothing seems to be out-of-bounds—pun intended—for your world anymore. What's next, a circus collab?"

Bailey laughs as she squeezes Aria around the middle, and Aria can't help but consider the truth in her statement. A professional football player in her orbit? There really don't seem to be any limits to the scope of the Aria Wilder universe these days.

Chapter 3

Griffin

The day after the concert, Griffin and Elliott are the last ones in the locker room after practice. Oftentimes they stay late to get in some more reps or additional recovery activities. Today Griffin wanted to hit the ice bath, and Elliott decided to stay too. Afterward in the locker room, they change clothes and pack their bags.

"Oh, shoot." Elliott pats around his pockets, then his bag. "I think I left my phone in the weight room. Be right back."

Griffin nods as he drops onto the bench seat and pulls out his own phone that he's left unchecked since before practice. It's one of many small rituals he's built into his life to protect his dedication to football. When the phone is stowed away, his focus is entirely on his work.

When the screen lights up, Griffin is surprised at the thousands of social media notifications that've come in—far more than usual.

"Ah," Griffin whispers to himself as it dawns on him.

The Aria Wilder concert.

Of course he played along with the viral meme moment. It was all done in good fun, and almost all the comments were good-natured. As a professional athlete, he gets a significant amount of attention online already—or at least what he *thought* was a significant amount—but these responses to the concert clip are on another level. An Aria Wilder level.

He opens his email, and there is a message from his agent.

Griff—

Hey, man. All this stuff with Aria Wilder is fire for your PR spin. You see the response from Aria about making an appearance at the next show? We really think you should go. This is a new angle for you outside of the usual sports stuff. You know the athletes who do best in the long run diversify. Football can't be forever.

Call me when you get this.

Mike

Griffin darkens the screen and turns it face down in his lap. He bites his lip. Even if Mike thinks this is a good idea, Griffin isn't quite convinced. He's comfortable with postgame interviews, the special events the team volunteers the players for, signing for fans after the game. But a concert with a hugely talented singer? That's miles out of his comfort zone. He can't wrap his head around what good it would actually do for his career either. Hanging out with Aria Wilder, as adorable as she is, won't lead the Wardens to the Super Bowl, and he's not anywhere close to aging out of the league yet.

Elliott walks in, his phone held out in front of him. "Dude! You're mega-viral! And Aria Wilder—"

"Wants me to come to the concert tomorrow," Griffin says with a glum look.

"Are you for real?" Elliott throws his hands out to the sides incredulously. "The world's biggest pop star is sending an invite your way, and you're bummed about it?"

"Since when have I ever been into these things?"

Griffin shouldn't have to say more. Elliott said almost these exact words when the team was invited to the holiday party of a reality television personality turned online influencer and Griffin sent his regrets. The same conversation was had when they were invited to a movie premiere. This sort of spotlight—outside of his comfort zone on the field and at the end of the postgame camera lens—isn't his thing.

"But Aria Wilder is your celebrity crush." Elliott drops his hands to his sides and narrows his eyes.

"What? How do you know that?" Griffin's eyes dart around.

"Come on, man. We've been buddies for a while now. You're not a 'night on the town' sort of guy, but you came third wheel with me and Cassandra to the concert. You wanted close seats so—and I quote—you could 'really see the contours of her face.' I'm not a rocket scientist, but I'm also not a total idiot."

Griffin sighs. "You got me there."

"So, what do you have to lose by going tomorrow?"

"Distraction from the season. Being off in the game the next day."

"Those sound like excuses to me."

"Mike wants me to do it." Griffin's leg bobs up and down nervously. "And I guess it'll just be a onetime thing. The concert itself was incredible, so I'll get to enjoy that again. Then it'll be all said and done."

Griffin gets to his feet, and Elliott slaps him on the back. Both men grab their gym bags and head for the exit.

"You're right, man. Gotta take the opportunities when they float by. Who knows when you'll get another special invite from a pop star," Elliott says.

Likely never if Griffin is taking history into account. This is the first and only time he's crossed into other spotlights. Other players—especially the ones who have famous girlfriends—flit in and out of other highflier circles. Take Elliott, for example—he routinely attends New York Fashion Week and has made enough contacts that designers dress him for events.

Even the sound of that makes Griffin want to run for the hills, but a night spent watching the world's most enchanting pop star from the wings, well out of sight? *That* he can manage.

By the next evening, when Griffin gets to the backstage entrance at the venue, he's glad he accepted Aria's invite to the concert. He was excited for the first show, but this experience is like a VIP version of the last one. The fan in him is buzzing over the experience, the insights. Backstage he sees all the nuts and bolts of the world-class production that unfurls onstage. He's observer of the frantic backstage managers barking into their headsets, hair and makeup artists chasing after performers with brushes and sprays. The amount of tech professionals in attendance to make sure the right smoke machine and levitating platform go off at the right time—and don't maim any performer—seems comparable to the crew assembled for the moon landing. In many ways, the inner workings of this production feel akin to putting a human on another planet.

Eventually Griffin is escorted to a nook in the wings that affords him a decent view—though admittedly lower quality than he had the other night. Not that he would complain after getting the backstage pass. But tonight he won't be able to see a single contour of Aria's face.

The music sounds different in the wings too. The speakers are set up for the people out in the audience, but Griffin watches happily, swaying a little, humming along, cautiously enjoying the music, while simultaneously keeping an eye peeled for a camera-toting member of the public ready to film him again and keep this circus going.

Griffin smiles to himself as he hears the opening notes to "Glass Heart." He's starting to feel grateful for this silly social media moment. Elliott was right that he might as well enjoy the fun chances that swim by him in life. They're once in a lifetime.

But just as Griffin is making his peace with his moment in Aria's orbit, he hears his name in the monologue Aria speaks to the crowd.

"You guys know I invited the famous Griffin Hayes tonight, right? Anyone see that online?"

The crowd goes wild. Griffin's cheeks turn hot pink.

"He might be a beast on the field, but he's a softie at heart, right?"

Lots of female cheers bubble up.

"Well, he's here tonight, and as a thanks, I'd love to invite him onstage! Griffin? Come on out!"

Suddenly, a stage manager, a more junior one who seems less harried, arrives at Griffin's side and clips a mic to his shirt, then hands him the electronic dock that goes with it. "You can slip that in your pocket then head out. Just a quick wave and hello!"

Griffin does as he's told, gulps audibly, then steps hesitantly out onto the stage. A telltale heat creeps up his neck, and he prays his blushing is drowned out by the stage lights. Aria skips up to meet him, her golden curls bouncing in the stage lights. The tassels on her cowgirl boots sparkle in the stage lights. Despite the fear welling in Griffin, he can't miss the fact that she looks sort of angelic.

"Well, if it isn't Griffin Hayes! Everyone, let's give him a warm welcome."

The crowd cheers.

She lingers before him, her lips parting gently into a playful grin that feels as if it's entirely for him. Griffin's heart picks up, his gaze glued to her. In the moment before she lifts the mic, she winks and it practically stops his heart.

Aria turns to the crowd and talks with miraculous ease. "I didn't have a chance to meet Griffin before the show, but I've been looking forward to it ever since I saw the video. So, what's the final verdict? *Are* you my number one fan?"

She reaches out a hand to bridge the gap between them and dances her fingertips down his shoulder. A shiver runs down his arm, and Aria's glow eclipses the crowd behind her.

Griffin holds her stare, and his smile grows. After a beat,

he looks away and laughs, and it surprises him when he hears it broadcast across the venue. "Guilty as charged." He grips his chin, massaging it bashfully as he sneaks another close-up look at her. "And thank you all for having me. You can trust me when I say backstage is not for the faint of heart."

Aria throws her head back and laughs, and her fans join her. Griffin cannot take his eyes from her; she's magnetic.

"Well, well, you should take a spin in my hair and makeup chair, Mr. Hayes."

Honestly, in the middle of this moment that feels very much like being under a spell, he might be convinced.

Eventually he finds his wherewithal. "Only if you play Sunday's game against the Panthers."

Aria puts a finger to her cheek and taps playfully as if she's mulling it over. "No thanks! I'll keep the sparkles and the blisters from these killer boots."

The crowd goes wild.

"You do it well, so I can't imagine you wanting to change course."

Aria fans herself playfully. "Well, thank you, I might just have to invite you to every concert to keep my spirits high."

Griffin extends an arm to acknowledge the crowd, and when Aria slips under it and pulls him into an embrace, he's covered in warmth. She looks up and holds his eye, and Griffin's breath catches. Stage fright, nerves of being called out unexpectedly, most likely. Definitely not the effects of this enchanting woman he's so lucky to have become entwined with.

Aria slips away from his side and turns back to her fans.

Griffin feels the heat of his face as his pulse picks up, and he seizes the moment to bow out.

"Thank you so much, Aria. And all of you." He waves to the crowd, then turns and ducks back into the wings.

He unclips the mic and hands it off to the waiting stagehand as quickly as he can manage. *One and done*, Griffin tells himself. And it wasn't all that bad—or it won't be once his flaming red cheeks cool off.

Chapter 4

Aria

Only five songs remain in the show after "Glass Heart," but Aria is surprised by the energy that thrums through her. Every dance step has an extra bounce and every note a perfect roundness to it. Perfection is always her goal, so pulling a professional football player onstage during her down-to-the-minute planned show was a gamble she wouldn't usually entertain. But after all the online chatter, the crowd would've been disappointed if Griffin didn't make an appearance—onstage or on a big screen—and Aria didn't want to let them down. Nevertheless, she'd worried about him coming out straight-faced and rigid like an athlete trained to buckle down for battle when the lights go on in the stadium. Sunday football games might be a performance, but they certainly weren't the type she put on.

Despite a few audible gulps and the flush that filled his cheeks, Griffin had been charming when he stumbled onstage.

The postgame interviews were probably good training for the moment—reporters tossing hardball questions his way after hours of pushing his body to the limits.

As the final song ends, a great applause erupts and Aria lets the microphone drop to her side. She beams at her fans, her chest rising and falling quickly from the exertion of dancing and singing at a rapid pace. As the cheers quiet, she lifts the microphone once more.

"Thank you, Chicago! You are always a safe bet for a good night."

The crowd cheers.

Aria turns to the wings. "And thanks again to Griffin Hayes for being such a good sport. Good luck tomorrow. Go Wardens!"

Aria gives one final big wave as she turns and marches off the stage and into the wings. Backstage she greets the staff and calls out, "Great job, guys! It went off without a hitch, as usual!" Aria high-fives the audio tech closest to her and gives the lead a wink. She is only as good as the team around her, and even though it's her name in the headlines, Aria understands how many good people it takes to pull off productions of this quality. It's one of the reasons she's known as a generous bonus giver in the industry.

Aria ducks into her dressing room, closes the door behind her, and lets out a tired sigh.

Bailey looks up from her phone screen, where she sits on a rolling desk chair in the corner. "Another great show, big sis."

Aria drops into a chair that matches Bailey's and starts pulling off her boots. "Thanks. I didn't love 'After the Storm.' I couldn't get the power behind it."

"I didn't notice a difference." Bailey gets up to open the

mini fridge. She stops at Aria's side with a bottle of water and cracks it.

Aria groans. "Thanks. You're a godsend."

Bailey laughs. "I've got to earn my keep around here somehow."

Aria smiles, then pulls down a hearty gulp of the icy drink. Bailey may worry about whether she's making a contribution, but Aria doesn't. She's told her—at length, on many occasions—how much Bailey does for her. Bailey is the listening ear Aria needs when she's faced with a hard decision. Bailey is the comfort person when Aria has problems in a show. Bailey is the shoulder to cry on when unkind rumors are spread online about her. What Bailey gives is far more valuable than being her personal beverage concierge.

In fact, Aria has worried more than once if *she's* the one holding Bailey back. Being her tour buddy is an easy choice for Bailey, but if that hadn't been an option, would she have pursued something more meaningful for herself? Is Bailey really getting what she wants out of life by living on tour or backstage? Aria worries that she's being selfish by keeping Bailey at her side.

"You don't have to earn your place here with me. But if the day comes when you want to spread your wings and leave me behind in the dust, I won't be anything but happy for you."

Bailey wraps her arms around Aria from behind and drops her chin onto her shoulder. Her hair tickles Aria's cheek, teasing the corners of her mouth into a smile.

"I know I'm not chained here, sis. I just love it."

Aria reaches up and squeezes her sister's hand. "Me too, Bails. Me too."

Bailey releases her arms and pulls herself upright. She heads for the sofa along the far wall of the room and flops down onto it. Aria spins her rolling chair to the mirrored wall on the opposite side, and in the reflection she notes not a speck of her makeup has budged.

Aria reaches for her makeup remover and gets to work. "I'll tell you what, the hair and makeup team are killing it. Hours of sweating my rear off onstage, and every bit of this is intact."

"You'd better keep them on staff. Remember Dallas?"

Aria shudders at the memory. She was a newbie back then, a teen with big dreams and big curls and little else to show for herself, but through sheer will she'd landed a spot at an outdoor country festival. At that point, all she could afford was drugstore makeup (some of which she still swore by) and a setting spray. As it turns out, no setting spray can go toe-to-toe with the Texas summer sun, and by the time she was five minutes into her set, heavy makeup was running in ravines down her face and into her eyes, stinging them as she strummed her guitar. It was the only time she counted herself lucky to have had a short set.

"I'll only ever do indoors in Texas now. Lesson learned."

Aria and Bailey laugh. As Aria scrubs what feels like permanent makeup from her face, Bailey pulls out her phone and scrolls.

"Dang. People are talking about Griffin again," Bailey says.

"I'm so relieved bringing him onstage didn't flop."

"Honestly, I think the crowd would've loved it even if he'd just stood there. But the two of you together? That was next level."

"What do you mean, 'the two of us together'?" Aria turns slowly to face her sister, her eyes narrowing.

"The two of you were so natural together. Like you'd known each other forever. Or like it was staged."

"Well, it *was* staged."

"You know what I mean—as in you'd practiced the lines. Sure, the setup was planned, but the rest was . . . just the two of you."

Aria shrugs and whirls back to the mirror. He'd made for a fine side act, she wouldn't argue that fact, but there also wasn't any point in harping on it. Griffin was a blip on the Aria Wilder timeline—a nice one, but nothing that would last.

"I'd do anything for the fans. We all know that. So this little stunt is my pleasure."

Aria just about has the makeup scrubbed off when a knock comes at the door.

"Come in!" Aria calls, then turns toward the door.

The door squeaks as it's pushed open a crack, and Kelsey appears in the gap, her chestnut-brown eyes sparkling like they do whenever an idea strikes. "Hey! Got a second?"

"Sure thing. Come on in. I didn't know you'd be here tonight." Aria waves, and the door swings open into the room, Kelsey entering in jeans, boots, and a bedazzled coat. Somehow the statement is nineties mom fashion but also entirely contemporary chic at the same time.

Kelsey drops into the second rolling chair and props her elbows on her knees.

Aria swallows. She knows this stance, and it usually entails far more than the "second" of time Kelsey asked for. Aria doesn't mind the publicity work. She enjoys the spotlight like any other performer, but as her career and success have grown, so has the pull to make appearances and give interviews. That in combination with the fact that Aria now owes another album of a variety she'd rather not pursue, it feels like another force pulling her from what she wants so badly: to reconnect with the joy of making music, the thing that kicked off this career all those years ago.

"Okay, so we have an idea." Kelsey grins wide, enthusiasm bubbling in every syllable.

"Okayyy." Aria pulls out the word to make it sound like an invitation to go on.

"This Griffin Hayes thing. It's wildfire. It hasn't even been an hour since the concert wrapped, and the clip of you and Griffin bantering onstage has already been shared thousands of times. By the morning, there's no question this will be another viral moment." Kelsey reaches out and gives Aria's knee a squeeze. She wiggles her eyebrows.

"Okay, and?" Aria asks gently. She could guess what was coming next, but she knows the song and dance, so she lets Kelsey make her pitch.

"We'd love to keep this thing going. Stage a 'friendship' between the two of you. It'd be beneficial to you both. For him, he's getting off-field press, and all those guys want to diversify these days. They can only play so many years before their bodies give out, but if they've got their hand in something else? Easy transition. For you, we're between albums. Of course, *all* of yours are megahits, but this will keep the fans close until the next classic Aria Wilder album hits. In this day and age, everyone has to stay relevant."

Aria swallows the sigh she wants to release at the mention of the next album. She slowly crosses her arms and leans back in her chair to consider this proposal. Admittedly, Aria doesn't love it. The idea of a fake friendship doesn't fit with who she is at her core: someone who wants to be genuine, to show her real self in her life and work. It's the same desire that lies at the heart of what she wants to do musically by taking a new approach. However, it's also true that the friendliness between her and Griffin itself wasn't staged. Bailey was right that although they were intentionally put together, the fun that bubbled up between them in that moment onstage was organic. Griffin Hayes might even be someone she could genuinely enjoy spending some time with.

Aria presses her lips together. "What are the specifics? I don't want this to take away from the music or the performances I have lined up."

Kelsey's head bobbles as she nods. "Oh, of course! Trust me, there's nothing we want less than to put a barrier in the way of getting *more* Aria Wilder hits! We'd keep it simple. Some shared appearances, social media, maybe a brand collab."

Aria's gaze goes across the room and finds Bailey. She sits upright, leaning in toward the conversation.

Bailey lifts her eyebrows eagerly and shrugs, as if to say, "*Why the heck not?*"

Aria lets her face relax, and it falls into a soft smile. Bailey is a reliable source of good advice, and Aria doesn't have a good reason to dig her heels in on this one.

"Okay. I'll do it. Just don't let it get out of hand."

Kelsey claps, then pumps a fist in the air. "Yes! Excellent. Now that we've got a green light from you, we'll pitch his team. I don't think we'll have problems getting a yes. I mean, your star power way outshines his. But I'll be in touch with deets as soon as I know."

Kelsey leaps to her feet, and as she passes Aria, she squeezes her shoulder. "And killer show tonight. As usual."

"Thank you. As usual. And for everything," Aria says.

Kelsey calls a goodbye over her shoulder, then pulls the door shut gently behind her.

Bailey smiles wide. "I guess we'll be seeing more of this Griffin Hayes character after all."

An incredulous laugh pops out of Aria. "Sounds like it." She gets to her feet and starts gathering her belongings into her bag. "Let's work on getting out of here. I could murder a cheeseburger."

Bailey hops up and grabs both of their coats from the hooks. "I thought you'd never get us out of here."

Chapter 5

Griffin

The Wardens beat the St. Louis Panthers 28–21 on Sunday, and Griffin walks off the field with his head held high, proud of his performance. The Panthers sure put up a fight, and that's how Griffin likes it: a fair match. All of his fellow players in the league put in just as much work as he does. Extra training, weights, good nutrition, and appointments with sports medicine, all on top of the existing demanding schedule. It might look glamorous on Sundays, but it's all the hard work behind the scenes during the week that makes it possible.

As Griffin leaves the field and passes into the shade of the tunnel that leads to the back halls of the stadium, a friendly palm lands on his shoulder before Elliott says, "Griff, nice work today, man."

Griffin slows his pace to allow Elliott to fall into step beside him, and together they weave through the cement-walled passageways toward the locker room.

"And two touchdowns for you isn't too shabby." Griffin reaches out and returns the slap on his buddy's back.

As the pair traverse the hallways, Griffin is stopped several times by staff—one asking for an autograph, one a photo, and a maintenance staff member calling out his congratulations.

"You know, for the guy who made two touchdowns, I'm starting to think I'm invisible." Elliott laughs. "Guess that's just the Griffin Hayes golden-boy effect."

"Or it's all a figment of your imagination. Probably people just know that I'm approachable."

They make it to the locker room door and file in, Griffin first. Many of the players are already back—some changing, others sitting and catching their breath on the bench. Jerseys have been stripped off. The usual postgame sweat smell pervades the room, and despite the stink, Griffin relishes the post-win locker room. The guys are worn out—some with scrapes and bruises, himself included—but he revels in the satisfied feeling that always follows a job well done.

Griffin stops at his locker, and Elliott slots in beside him at his own.

"Of course, you always have people stopping you like that, but I'm starting to wonder if people aren't also a little excited about your new friendship with Aria Wilder."

Griffin turns away. If he starts to blush, he cannot let Elliott see it. Or the other guys. Truth be told, his mind has wandered back to Aria more than once since the concert last night. He might've been thrown off by being pulled onstage—and very out of his comfort zone—but something about being there with *her* made it all feel . . . fun. Surprising in the best way.

He's even more intrigued by Aria now that he's gotten a glimpse of the special shine that comes only from being up close and in person. Admittedly, most of the world also believes that Aria is special, begetting the continued chart toppers and sold-out concerts, but what Griffin noticed the night before was not all of that. It was the wit in the words she threw his way onstage. The sharpness softened by her playfulness. The warmth and generosity in the way she pulled him, a stranger thrust upon her by the PR crew, into her moment. Griffin can't help but suspect that there is more to this woman than her public image.

"Eh. I think the Aria thing is just going to fade out of internet relevance from here. I mean, how long does any viral moment keep up its momentum these days?" Griffin says.

Despite his interest in Aria being piqued—admittedly the woman is gorgeous—Griffin wouldn't mind taking a reprieve from being the subject of internet obsessions.

"Fair enough." Elliott pulls off his jersey, grabs his water bottle, and sits on the bench. "I'm going to grab a shower. Wonder what they've got for dinner."

Attached to the locker room is a space where the team is catered dinner after every game. The Wardens are militaristic about making sure their players stay well fed.

"I've got to ice before anything." Griffin doesn't say it, but it's mostly for his knee. "Depending on what they've got, I might eat back at the condo."

Griffin loves his penthouse condo, and even more so at

night. His floor-to-ceiling windows allow him a dazzling city view, and at night the lights look like a sea of stars. The guys gave him a hard time when he hired an interior designer to help him outfit the place, but he took it on the shoulder. It's no secret that he's a homebody, so why wouldn't he hire a professional to make the space comfortable like he wants it?

"I swear if you could play the game at your condo, you might never leave."

Griffin laughs. "Football will always be worth stepping out for."

Elliott hops up and stows his water bottle back in his locker. "All right, I'm hitting the showers. See you tomorrow at practice."

Griffin waves a hand. "Night, man."

On his way to the recovery room, Griffin stops to chat with some teammates, congratulating them for their performances, hyping them up for the next game, commiserating over a fumble. Eventually he enters the recovery area where there are high benches for massage and chiropractic services or physical therapy. A couple of ice baths are set up, as well as an open area for stretching.

Charlie, one of Griffin's favorite athletic trainers, stands by as he enters. "Hey, Griff. Great game. Want any assistance getting a good stretch?"

Griffin pauses. "Thanks, but I think I'm just going to ice."

Griffin takes a dip in the ice bath, then heads to the shower to warm back up. When he returns to his locker, his muscles feel slightly better, tension released, and he's ready to get dressed and head home. He's got his favorite chicken, vegetables, and rice meal prepped at home—thanks to his nutritionist's plan—and he'll take that over the catered meal any day.

Just as he's about to get toweled off, Griffin's phone starts buzzing on the metal shelf of his locker, sounding more like a pesky mechanical issue in an industrial engine than a small electronic device. He snatches it up to stop the sound.

Mike, his agent's name, appears on the screen.

Griffin brings the phone to his ear. "A game day call means something's happening. Good or bad?"

Mike's slow, deep laugh fills the space. "You don't miss a thing, do you? It's good news today, so no need to worry."

Griffin turns around and leans back on the locker. He took his time in recovery and the shower, so by now only a few of his teammates remain, many of whom are in the process of making an exit, gathering belongings, slamming lockers, and heading out.

"Lay it on me."

"Aria Wilder."

Griffin's heart does a small leap. "Yes?"

"Her team wants to keep this thing between you guys going."

"What thing?"

"You know, the staged friendship. The fans love it, and when the two of you come together you get major attention online. It's a win-win for both of you. Great press. Shows your human side. And for you, Griff, there's nothing better than showing your fandom of a pop star to reach a new audience. People who have never watched professional football a day in their lives are following you online, waiting for your next Aria Wilder pop-up."

"Hmm." Griffin chews on his lip. He can't argue that attention from new fans isn't objectively a good thing in this business—in any business—but this sort of attention is so far from his thing.

He can take the spotlight on the field. There he has a job, and he knows how to do it well. He prepares and trains. There are timers and buzzers, plays and plans, and when all of that runs out, he can hit the showers and head home for a quiet night. Being pulled onstage or secretly filmed is not something he's practiced for.

Sure, the concerts have been a blast. And Aria is electric, but is continuing this—and in the context of a fabricated friendship—really a good idea?

"What do you think?"

Griffin chuckles. "I think you can probably guess that this is *definitely* not my cup of tea."

"I know, but remember: Football isn't forever. The more you build up your brand by doing things like this now, the more prepared you'll be when it's eventually time to retire. We made the plan from the start that we wouldn't let you be one of the guys who blows his NFL earnings on poorly managed real estate or a fleet of fancy cars. We're planning for the long run, and becoming friends with Aria Wilder is definitely good for that."

Admittedly, Griffin rears back at the reminder that football will eventually end for him—even if he's glad Mike is looking out for his future. Griffin tries to imagine himself without the sport, but the only picture that comes to mind is him as some underwhelming, lame version of himself. A has-been who takes every chance to relive his glory days. There's not much else he's good at, not much else he has to offer.

Griffin pushes the thoughts away. For now, he's still a professional player, and he's just been pitched a PR opportunity.

He's not clamoring to say yes. But if Aria's team pitched the setup, that means Aria sees it as valuable, so he wouldn't be taking advantage. Griffin's heart picks up a little when he thinks of Aria—his crush—his interest in knowing more about her, getting more glimpses of her behind the scenes.

That moment onstage, though initially terrifying, felt like opening up something new. Aria's presence was powerful yet warm, witty and endearing. *That woman* has his interest. Spending time with her would be enjoyable, and although Griffin isn't convinced the plan is error-proof, the pros probably outweigh the cons.

"I guess I'll give it a shot. But first—what did they have in mind exactly? I can't be her prop onstage every night. Especially with games and training."

"No, no, no. An appearance or two that we've planned and agreed upon in advance. Social media stuff. It sounds like they've already gotten an ask for a commercial, but it's still being discussed. Of course, you'd be compensated for such work."

"So no going onstage?"

"Doesn't sound like it. To be fair, I don't think she needs you as a backup singer or dancer."

Griffin smiles. "That works for both of us then. Yeah, I guess sign me up. But Mike? Let's try to keep this whole thing simple, okay?"

"You got it! Trust me, this will be great for you."

Griffin hangs up after saying goodbye and stows his phone away. He's ready now more than ever to get himself dressed and on the road to go home. He pulls on his fresh clothes, dumps his towel in the laundry basket, and throws his gym bag over his shoulder. He calls out his goodbyes to the staff that remains in the back areas and takes the familiar path through the maze of his hometown stadium's hidden tunnels to the players' parking lot.

As the cold night air hits the back of his neck, he picks up his pace.

Griffin slips into his car, a moment in which he usually relaxes with the knowledge that his work is done as he makes for home, but his thoughts go back to Aria Wilder.

The woman who keeps dipping into his life whether he likes it or not.

Chapter 6

Aria

Not even a full week passes, and Kelsey has the first engagement for Aria and Griffin set up. The Chicago Animal Society is hosting their annual fundraising gala, and the pair have been invited to attend as celebrity guests. The event takes place at a charming, historic hotel downtown that promises an enjoyable evening for all.

Two hours before it kicks off, Aria stands in her walk-in closet at home wearing a robe, assessing the gown options her stylist sent over. The first is a ruby-red satin halter-neck dress that dips low in the back. The second is long-sleeved, midnight blue with sparkles arranged in an ombré pattern of sorts. The final option is a billowing floral-print cupcake-style gown with small puffy sleeves.

"I don't think any of these are a bad choice," Bailey says.

Aria grabs the red satin option and holds it in front of her before the mirror. "I like this one a lot, but I'm worried I'll be cold with the low back." She replaces it on the hanger and takes the long-sleeve option. "Maybe this one."

"It brings out the blue of your eyes," Bailey says. "Plus that sparkle is so you!"

Aria decides to wear the blue dress, but not because of the sparkle. Because she knows she'll be comfortable in it too. Aria isn't sure how much longer sparkle and happily-ever-after songs will be considered "her" when she wants to dig deeper lyrically. Then again, when aren't sparkles appropriate? She could write a heartfelt song all her own, one true to her heart, and still rock a sparkle.

Aria slips into her bedroom to lay the dress on her bed.

Tonight will be interesting. She and Griffin have been chosen as the mystery celebrity guests at the gala, so to begin, they will stay under wraps in one of the hotel's downstairs meeting rooms while the guests mill at the bar with a few adoptable pets in attendance. This is the time the guests will stop by the silent auction, get their cocktail of choice from the bar, and make their annual pledges to support the animal shelter's efforts. Once the guests take their assigned seats in the ballroom, she and Griffin will make an entrance and introduce the official programming.

Aria is good on her feet—thanks to a lifetime of being a performer—but she's not sure how the two will pass the time backstage.

"*Can we get separate rooms?*" Aria had asked Kelsey.

"*You really want to? They've suggested you wait together, and I think it could work so you can warm up to one another before going on. Real friends would want to be together, right?*"

"If you think it's important."

"I think it'll help this whole setup for you to get to know each other a bit. And no one likes a diva."

Aria had sighed, then acquiesced. All in the name of good PR.

Before long, Aria has applied her makeup—including her signature red lipstick—and styled her hair. Her hair and makeup are done so often by the professionals before shows that she actually looks forward to doing it herself when the occasion allows. It feels nice to have more input on her own look. Take some chances with makeup.

An hour before she is due at the gala, her driver pulls up in a black car and idles as Aria makes her finishing touches. In a final sweep, she grabs her silver clutch, wraps a silky scarf around her neck, and takes Bailey into her arms.

"Have fun," Bailey says. "I bet Griffin will look great in a tux."

Aria gives her sister a squeeze, then releases her. "My only goal is to make it out of there with a cute PR moment—oh, and make some money for the sweet animals, of course."

Aria walks out, taking the steps carefully in her heels, and loads into her ride.

On the drive there, she mulls over what Bailey said about Griffin in the tux. The thought hadn't crossed Aria's mind until her sister mentioned it, but she doesn't disagree. Griffin would probably look nice in a tux, but then again, that has nothing to do with her.

Aria pulls out her phone and starts jotting down ideas for song lyrics as the car slowly makes its way toward downtown.

Aria arrives first at the hotel and is snuck in through a back entrance that leads into a small hallway. Almost at once, the door to the room appears, and she's ushered in by an event volunteer.

"We stocked a full bar with snacks from your requested list sent by PR," the waiter says, folding his hands at his waist. "But there's also a call button here if there's anything you need that is not stocked. Mr. Hayes should be here shortly." He nods his head and ducks efficiently out into the hall.

Aria hates these lists she's asked to send so places have the right food and drinks. She's genuinely flexible when it comes to that stuff, and it makes her feel like such a snob to make demands. Rumor has it that some artists will demand candies be picked out of a mix for imperfections or beverages be flown in from overseas.

Taking a quick glance at the bar, it appears Griffin doesn't fall into that category either. Much to her relief.

Then, with a gentle *click* of the doorknob and the swing of the door, the man himself appears. He stops short before fully entering the room, as if there's some confusion over whether he's in the right place. Aria smiles and waves, and he walks tentatively in and pulls the door shut behind him.

"Just wanted to make sure I wasn't barging in," Griffin says.

He wears a classic black tux, one that spans the gulf between his shoulders but tapers at his waist. His pants must've been heavily altered—his thighs thick and muscular.

"It's not a dressing room, Griffin! Just a hangout spot for us 'friends.'"

He smiles as he props his hands on his hips and takes in the room. "I hope it won't be too painful getting through the evening together."

"I think we'll get along just fine."

"Me too," he says. "Assuming they only keep us onstage for a bit."

Aria cocks her head, then slips onto a barstool. "Am I hearing a hint of stage fright?"

Griffin takes the lapels of his jacket and adjusts them, even though they don't need any adjustments. "Guess I'm sort of a one-trick pony. I can play tight end, and that's it for me."

"Can I grab you anything from the bar?" Aria reaches over and takes a Coke for herself.

Griffin wanders over to the bar and slides behind it. "Hmm, the pickings are good, but in season, it's pretty much water or Gatorade for me, as lame as it sounds." He reaches over and takes the can of Coke from Aria's hand. "Allow me?"

Griffin takes the scoop from the ice bucket, fills a plastic cup, pulls the can tab, and attentively pours the soda, monitoring the fizz level to make sure it doesn't run over.

"You look like you've got some experience with sodas there." Aria grins at him.

He's quite the gentleman looking out for her like this. You never know with celebrity types. Some of them are all charm while the cameras are rolling, making sure they're only captured in their best light. But behind the scenes—in a situation much like this—it's upturned noses, demands being made, and all cold shoulders. Aria feels her mood lift slightly. Maybe Griffin is the sort of person she wouldn't mind being friends with after all.

"I come from a long line of health-conscious medical professionals, so let's just say that when the chance came to get a soda, you didn't let it spill."

He sets a beverage napkin down on the bar and then places the cup on top.

Aria takes it and sips. "Thank you. This might be the best poured Coke I've had this year."

Griffin pulls a hand to his chest in mock thrill. "Well, I'll be."

Aria giggles. "I don't drink much of it either. It might come as a surprise, but the length of the sets I do onstage is like my own version of a football game. A dancing and singing marathon."

"Oh, I believe it. Don't forget I've been close to the action on two occasions recently."

Aria nods. "I appreciate you playing along with this. I can't see how it helps when you're at the top of your football career, even if your publicist thinks it's a good opportunity."

He shrugs. "It's all part of the gig. It's funny—all of us go into it with a passion for something, but soon enough it starts to morph into something all its own."

Aria nods. If only he knew how deeply she can relate. Back when she was a teenager with a decent voice and unruly curls, a cheap guitar, and a relentless work ethic, she was razor-focused on the craft of making music. She begged her parents for lessons and practiced as instructed as often as she could. She played for free—begged to get a set in front of a crowd. Sometimes when Aria looks back, she wonders if that's the closest she's ever been to the art of it all. Back before it became big business. Back before she was a household brand.

"It's all about the 'brand' nowadays."

Griffin cracks open a bottled water. "Don't I know it."

"Though I guess these are problems I'm grateful to have."

It's Aria's canned follow-up comment whenever she mentions any of the downsides of fame. She is genuinely grateful for the opportunities she's had, and she knows a line of aspiring musicians would gladly take her place. Aria never wants to come across as being ungrateful. It's just that there are also real challenges to the fame, to becoming a brand. A brand that boxes you in.

"I hear you. It's all right to acknowledge the bad parts too. I get it. It's not all parties and fancy outfits. There's real sacrifice that goes into it."

Aria sucks in a breath, her reply already on the tip of her tongue. Griffin is right, and she has so much to add. But before she can get the words out, a knock comes at the door.

A woman wearing a headset peeks in, clipboard held before her at the ready. "Hi, there! Ms. Wilder and Mr. Hayes, we're so thrilled you're here, and we're ready for your grand entrance."

Griffin goes still behind the bar, his easy, down-to-earth demeanor evaporating. He tugs at his collar. "Yes, of course. What all is involved?"

"I'll be there with you the whole way until you go onstage. And then just a natural and very brief exchange between the two of you—thank the guests, express your belief in the mission, and then we'll roll the fundraising video on the big screen."

The color leaks slowly from Griffin's face as the woman describes the bit.

Aria reaches out and pats his arm. "Don't worry, I'll take the lead. You follow?"

Griffin nods.

"I've been training for this my whole career." Aria winks at him before getting to her feet and walking with purpose toward the woman in the headset. When Griffin doesn't budge, she waves for him to follow her.

It's actually sort of cute to see him freeze at the mere mention of an appearance.

The woman begins power walking, clipboard bobbing, and Griffin takes a few loping steps to catch up. When he arrives at Aria's side in the hallway, a hint of cologne arrives with him.

"Thank you. For taking the lead," he says. "You're such a natural."

Aria smiles to herself. "It's my pleasure."

Nothing feels quite as satisfying as using her natural talents for good.

Chapter 7

Griffin

The idea of a petite, curvy blonde coming to the rescue of a six-foot-four, 250-pound professional athlete is laughable to some, but to Griffin Hayes, it's his reality in the moment he and Aria Wilder are nudged onstage. As their names are announced, the gathered crowd claps in a contained but enthusiastic manner appropriate for the formal affair.

Aria's eyes glint in the lights, matching the sparkle on her gown, but Griffin looks away. Now is not the time for admiring her beauty. He's about to be thrust into the spotlight and out of his comfort zone again.

Aria reaches out and squeezes his forearm. They lock eyes, and she winks. "Trust me, this crowd is child's play. Just smile and it'll be over before we know it."

Griffin gulps. Didn't Mike promise him that the engagements that would be part of this setup would be easy and low-key? Granted, he wasn't being asked to deliver a keynote speech, but Griffin would much prefer cleaning out the cat litter boxes at the shelter than this. Believe it or not, he'd take the pooper scooper over the tuxedo any day.

Aria accepts a microphone from the A/V tech and bursts through the small velvet curtain they've set up behind the stage. Griffin takes the matching microphone that's been pressed into his hand and follows, smiling and waving. Sweat prickles at the back of his neck.

"Well, hello, fellow animal lovers!" Aria cries. The crowd claps. "I've got my buddy Griffin Hayes—aka my number one fan—in the house to help me kick off this fabulous fundraising event for the most vulnerable of animals in our great city. Truly, I could not be happier to partner with such a devoted organization. What about you, Griffin?"

He resists the urge to tug on his collar. "Oh, definitely! Thank you all for having me here and your dedication to keeping our canine and feline friends off the street."

The crowd claps. Maybe Griffin's starting to get the hang of this.

"Now," Aria says as she props a fist on her hip, reminding Griffin of how she looks before she starts a song onstage—powerful. "Before we start the video that will detail all of the wonderful ways the Chicago Animal Society is working in our communities to keep animals off the streets and get them into safe homes, I have to make one final plea." Aria looks to Griffin in the pause. "Are you thinking what I'm thinking?"

A smile creeps across Griffin's face, and for a moment he forgets that he's on a stage in front of hundreds of people.

"Hmm, are you thinking that the great and well-adored Aria Wilder is about to make a pledge of generosity?"

Aria aims a finger at him and winks. "Bingo! Friends, I am prepared to match donations as high as $200,000 this evening with the help of my friend Griffin, so please be generous when getting out your checkbooks."

The crowd claps loudly, and several of the organization leaders off to the side swell with eagerness. Apparently Aria is ad-libbing this donation. Griffin would be happy to split the match with her, even though she didn't run it by him in advance. His salary is public knowledge, so it wouldn't be showing off to announce the amount of his donation.

"Happy to split the check, Aria," Griffin announces with a grin.

"And what if we're at a fancy restaurant?" Aria replies.

"I'd have to cover the whole thing."

Aria's eyes glint before she pulls her gaze from Griffin's and turns to the audience. "You heard it, ladies and gentlemen. The friend you want to go out to eat with is Griffin Hayes!"

The crowd laughs and claps again. Then the emcee steps in and thanks them both for their support. The large screen that hangs over the stage behind them leaps to life with an intro segment showing ill, injured, or homeless animals, with a voiceover reading the mission statement of the Chicago Animal Society.

The woman with the headset returns and warmly shepherds Aria and Griffin offstage. As soon as he hands off the microphone, Griffin's shoulders drop, and he wipes the beading sweat from his forehead.

"I really owe you one," he says to a cool and collected Aria at his side.

"You were great out there! I don't know what all your fussing is about." She turns and throws him a playful look.

It only helps pull Griffin back to reality, and he follows Aria back through the halls to their room.

"So, is this it?" Griffin asks. "This is our whole deal tonight?"

Aria pops the door open and strides into the room. "Yup! They told us they'd keep it short and sweet for us. I mean, we both know that clip of us is going to be online in the next hour. Unless you want to stop by the lobby for a puppy?"

"Only if it's living at your place."

"Kitten?"

"I'm already Aria Wilder's number one fan. Add a kitten and I lose all street cred in the locker room." Griffin leans in close, catches a hint of floral perfume, and whispers, "Unless we keep it our little secret."

When Griffin pulls back, Aria is grinning mischievously. "What's another secret?"

"So you agree to shared custody?"

Aria laughs. "We only just met. Isn't that too much?"

Griffin shrugs. "It's nothing between friends."

"Fair enough." The words come out of Aria like a slow exhale, and her eyes scan the room. "Fair enough."

Aria walks to the bar, retrieves her clutch and her scarf, which she tucks into the crook of her arm.

"You heading out?" Griffin asks.

Aria passes by him to exit, but she stops to pat his upper arm. Despite the bulk of muscle that covers it, the touch of her hand draws Griffin's attention magnetically. "I travel far too much for a pet, so it seems it's time. But the cats are really tempting."

Griffin turns and follows behind Aria, feeling clumsy compared to her grace. "Don't we have to check out with someone or anything?" he asks.

"Your green is showing, newbie. There's no cooldown or massages here, no locker room chat. It's in and out. Check off the job, then onto the next."

Aria pushes out of the back doors into the chilly night, and Griffin catches the door and walks out behind her.

"I need to text my driver," Aria says, her breath turning white in the cold air. She takes her phone from the clutch, then very quickly groans.

"Everything okay?" Griffin asks, genuine concern flexing in him.

Aria sighs. "My driver got sick. Food poisoning, he thinks. He said he could send his other—"

"Come with me," Griffin says.

"Oh, I couldn't. Where do you even live? I'm out in the boonies." Aria begins to type rapidly.

"It's no problem, and I'm not going to leave you here to wait alone. Not with all those dangerous animal lovers inside. Who knows, they might ply you with *two* kittens at gunpoint."

Aria laughs, and when she tosses her head back, Griffin realizes he hasn't seen her do that before. The times he's seen her laugh onstage, she never wore this real happiness. It's like a glimpse into the rest of her—the woman who's hiding behind the Aria Wilder brand.

Aria's eyes flick left then right as if she's thinking.

"We'll go to your house first, drop you off, and it's farewell until our next engagement. No weird stuff," Griffin says.

"You're being so nice."

"I try to be a decent guy."

Aria blinks long and slow. "Okay, fine. And thank you. I genuinely appreciate it, because rolling the dice with new drivers—or god forbid a rideshare—is risky. Me traveling alone is a genuinely unsafe option."

"I imagine," Griffin says. He's already taking his phone from his pocket, knowing his driver is idling around the block. He sends a quick text. "Vic is just around the corner."

"I owe you one."

"Let's just say we're even after you saved my butt out there."

Aria folds her arms tight across her chest, shivering slightly. Griffin wonders if he should offer his coat. Usually he would in a situation like this, but after insisting on the ride, would it be too much? This is a PR operation, and the last thing he wants is Aria thinking he's hitting on her in the context of a professional arrangement. Sure, they do get along pretty well. He genuinely enjoys her company. And yes, there's that small issue of the long-standing crush on his end, but that wouldn't have anything to do with it. Maybe it would be the right thing to do to offer his jacket. A *friend* would offer, and them acting like friends is part of this.

"Would—"

The beam of headlights shining into Griffin's eyes interrupts him.

"Oh, is that Vic?" Aria points.

"Should be," Griffin says.

"Sorry, what were you going to say?" Aria turns back to Griffin.

"Nothing. Nothing important."

As the car pulls up, Griffin reaches around Aria and opens the door. She hops back as if surprised by the gesture, and Griffin internally kicks himself. Maybe he is leaning too hard into being kind. Maybe he needs to relax. Once Aria is in, Griffin closes the door and rounds to the other side of the car.

He climbs in and tells Vic, "Let's drop her off first, and then take me to the condo, please. I appreciate you being flexible."

"Yes, thank you so much!" Aria rattles off her address and thanks Vic a second time. She looks over to Griffin and offers him the warmest smile, one that presses her eyes into a delighted squint. "And thank you for being so generous. You know this isn't a for-pay gig, right?"

"Oh, it isn't? In that case, it's $200 for the ride."

Aria swats at his thigh, and Griffin feels electricity run through him.

"I bet you'd waive the fee for a friend."

He gulps, willing away the fireworks that are ricocheting through his middle. Willing away the rising attraction. "For you? Of course."

Griffin turns to look out the window, and inside he's telling himself off. It's not that he shouldn't be enjoying his time with Aria; it's the obvious swelling of what was once a crush becoming a genuine attraction. She's now a real-life woman—one who is even more interesting than the public version he'd already grown a soft spot for.

Stay in the friend zone. Friend zone only.

Griffin was sure that Aria did not sign up for this arrangement looking for a date.

Chapter 8

Aria

Aria meant it when she said Griffin was being generous for offering the ride. After one too many strange rideshare experiences, her security team made her promise never to use one again, and if she were to have done it tonight and they'd found out, they would take to following her around everywhere again. Nights like tonight where she can pretend to—somewhat—be a regular person are nice. Like shedding the Aria Wilder persona for a little while and just being herself.

Griffin sits beside her, his giant palms planted on his wide knees.

Aria rests her head back onto the leather seat, closes her eyes, and lets out a long, slow breath. When she opens them, Griffin sits grinning at her on the other side of the seat.

"Tough life, huh?"

A lazy smile crosses Aria's face, then she shrugs. "There are perks. But . . ."

Again, Aria is overcome by the impulse to keep her professionalism before her like a shield, to be grateful for the fans, delighted by her success. But for a moment she wonders whether Griffin is someone she could be honest with.

"It's not all fun and games."

Aria nods. "What's the hardest part for you?"

Griffin reaches an arm across his chest to massage his shoulder. "Aside from getting beat up every weekend during the season, it's how it takes over your whole life."

Aria, too, feels like she's been consumed by the public-facing version of herself. There's so much more to her, but all of her people—her agent, Kelsey, the record label—don't seem interested in including the other parts of her in her professional work.

"It's like getting boxed in."

Griffin turns and looks out the window, even though beyond the glass is only the dark of night. "You have to show up and be that same person every day."

"Did you always know you wanted to be a football player?"

"Well, it wasn't exactly family tradition. Everyone else is a doctor, nurse, or some sort of tech in the field. But I was always a big kid. I grew fast, and football came easy to me." His cheeks turn slightly pink. "Sorry, I'm not trying to brag—"

"You're safe with me," Aria cuts in. She really does mean it. It's surprisingly interesting hearing more about Griffin. Despite his success, he seems so down-to-earth. So genuinely kind. "And I know what it feels like to always watch your words. To worry about saying the wrong thing or being misunderstood and being canceled or shamed online," Aria says.

Griffin casts his hands across the front of him as if he's presenting the hypothetical headline: "Griffin Hayes, star tight end, also an arrogant devil?"

Aria laughs. "You know they would."

It's the truth about being famous. Every word can be pulled out of context and circulated online with no regard for the meaning or intent behind the words. It further reinforces the pressure to be one person with canned talking points, to never stray too far from the script.

"I guess to be entirely honest, football is really the only thing I've ever been good at," Griffin says.

"I'm sure you've got plenty of hidden talents in there."

Griffin's face drops momentarily before he pulls in a breath and speaks. "What about you? What's the hardest part?"

"There's plenty of hard." Aria considers telling him about her real struggle—the new album. Even though she feels remarkably comfortable with him and they have become fast friends, she just met him. They barely know each other. "Definitely the same stuff you mentioned, but also the restrictions. There are so many times I'd love to just spontaneously head out for coffee with Bailey or go shopping. But again, security has to be notified. Sometimes I manage to get out on my own, but there's so much freedom and independence lost."

"I got it easy in that department. I'm just too big for most people to kidnap."

Aria's cheeks crease into a smile so deep it starts to hurt. "A perk, for sure."

Aria wasn't sure what to expect from Griffin Hayes when

the two first became intertwined. Maybe she had no expectations at all. But she can definitively say she's happily surprised by what she's come to know of him so far. She's no football expert, but she saw him in action with the Wardens before she met him. His physical power on the field becomes obvious within a play or two on game day. He's aggressive and explosive.

The side of Griffin that Aria's gotten to know in person thus far is so difficult to marry with the tough athlete that hits the field on Sundays. His genuine kindness, humility, and generosity are just as much a part of him as his muscular build and his intensity on the field. It seems like something that should be a contradiction, but with Griffin Hayes living and breathing as such in front of her, there's proof that it's possible.

Aria of all people knows how much more there is to public figures than what's broadcast to the world. Of course she knew it'd be the same for Griffin. She just never expected to *like* so much of who he is off the field.

Griffin pulls out his phone now that the conversation has slowed, and the screen lights his face in a way that accentuates his cheekbones and his wide jaw. His mouth curves gently upward—not a smile so much as a mouth poised in waiting for a smile. Like perhaps he's wired for optimism.

Griffin's been objectively attractive from the start, but only now in this moment inside the dark car, with him carrying her home to safety, does her heart do a tiny, barely there flutter.

Is Aria attracted to Griffin Hayes, her fake friend for PR purposes only?

She pushes the thought away. It's nothing more than a side effect of their arrangement. Her team has already pulled him into this scheme, one that serves his football career far less than it serves her pop star engine, and the last thing she wants is to complicate it. He's not here to woo her.

He's here for the job.

But at least he's easy on the eyes—as well as a good guy, funny even—while he sticks around.

Chapter 9

Griffin

Griffin flew down to Florida the day after the gala to play the Stingrays that Sunday. He got to see one of his college teammates who is now the quarterback for the Stingrays, and to make it even sweeter, the Wardens took the win. Their record so far is strong, and Griffin and his teammates are hopeful they'll make the playoffs.

It might be unlikely for this year, but that doesn't mean they'll take their sights off the goal.

On Tuesday the following week, Griffin attends practice, which includes weight training, mapping out plays, and reviewing film once more from the previous Sunday. Griffin practically lives in the weight room, so that part of the day comes easy. He eventually makes it to the film room where the lights are dimmed and the screen is lit up with clips of the game.

"What's up, guys?" Griffin calls out in greeting to the other offensive players already seated, and a sea of greetings are murmured in reply.

All of the players sip their drinks as the play coach kicks off the meeting by reviewing the tasks at hand.

"We saw some great work from y'all last week against the Stingrays. They have a strong defense, but it didn't stop you. There were also spots we can improve on for next week."

Coach begins reviewing plays one at a time, and the first few don't include Griffin. His mind wanders.

In all honesty, his mind has wandered on several occasions since last week, and every time, it wanders to Aria. Every time he sees the scarf she accidentally left behind in his car now sitting on his coffee table at home. He replays their evening at that glitzy old Chicago hotel, Aria being the glitziest thing in attendance. She was stunning, as always, but he can't shake the feeling of her pulling him out of his comfort zone again, helping him through the fundraiser, and her utter confidence in his ability to navigate it. Despite all that, the car ride was even better.

Should he feel bad that he was sort of glad her driver got sick? The sparks he'd felt sitting beside her were almost embarrassing. A big, tough guy like him letting his little crush take the wheel like he was an awkward teenager. He wondered for a moment whether Aria had felt the same thing pass between them, but as quickly as he considered it, he dismissed the thought.

Aria is busy with far more important things than entertaining his crush.

Still, his heart jumped a little when he got Mike's email yesterday about an appearance on a late-night talk show for the pair of them next week. His first instinct was to feel excited at the prospect of teaming up with Aria again, but then he realized he would be filming an actual segment for a talk show. Whatever happened to this being easy like Mike promised?

"Griff, you with us?" Coach said.

"Yes, sir."

Griffin's eyes dart around the screen, and eventually he orients himself to the film. It was a moment he made a catch but was pushed out-of-bounds before he could plant his feet from the jump. Griffin takes feedback from the coach and remains focused for the rest of the session.

Once he's back on the road heading toward his condo, he dials Mike on the hands-free system in his car. Mike picks up on the second ring.

"My favorite client. How you doing?"

"Good, good. Just leaving practice now, and I wanted to follow up on *The Late Night Show* invite."

"It's great, isn't it?"

Griffin reaches up and squeezes his chin. "In some ways. It's definitely not my forte, all this being onstage in front of people. Weren't we going more for photo ops?"

"The two of you were incredible at the gala. Another viral moment. Well, almost viral. The fans loved it. You've been dubbed 'best friends' just like we wanted."

"She's fun, that's for sure. And I didn't call to try to get out of the gig."

"Okay, well, how can I help?"

"So, both times we've gone onstage together, she's led the way, totally guided me through it so I don't look like a clown—"

"The fans love that part too. Some of them say you're her protégé. Did you see that clip from the *Hot Girls* podcast where they were speculating about whether you're trying to get into the music industry?"

Griffin squeezes his temples with his free hand. "I didn't, and it's probably for the best. None of them want to hear me sing. I can promise that."

Mike laughs. "Don't worry. I wouldn't let you stray down that path. You might be built for direct hits, but you're not built for that."

Griffin pulls in a breath. "I wanted to see if you could connect me with Aria. Either get her phone number or give her mine? She left a scarf behind after the gala, and I'd like to get it back to her."

"I'm sure that'd be fine. And probably a good plan. I'll also make sure you get the talking points ASAP."

"Plus, she can help me prep for the show. I don't want to be thinking about it all week." Griffin's statement is true, but it's not his only motivation for getting her phone number. He'd genuinely like to talk to her before next week.

"You're right. We both agreed this would not get in the way of the game or your training. The last thing we want is for you to fumble a catch because you're worried about doing a bit on *The Late Night Show*."

"Precisely."

"All right, man. I'll talk to her people and get back to you."

"Thanks. Take care."

Griffin hits the button to disconnect, and he can't help but notice the lightness that's filled his chest. Maybe it's the release of tension over the talk show appearance, knowing that he'll be able to talk it through with Aria before. They can practice before they go on. Do guests typically do that? His guess is most likely not.

When he thinks about flopping on national television, a wave of nerves hit him again. He reminds himself that he does a version of this every weekend during the season. With football, he gets lost in the game, consumed by it so much that the rest melts away.

Perhaps it's not entirely different from the way it feels to stand beside Aria on a stage, the rest fading into the background as she pulls him into the bright light that surrounds her, the one that emanates from her.

Stop, he tells himself.

He's doing the crush thing again.

Griffin's phone dings with a notification in the cup holder, and at the next light, he lifts it to check.

> **Mike:** Here's Aria's number. She says text her whenever.

Griffin smiles the whole drive home.

Chapter 10

Aria

Aria is happy to see the first text from Griffin come in. He didn't waste much time either, as it was only an hour or so ago that she gave Kelsey permission to share her personal number. Aria sits in the corner of her comfortable sectional sofa that is set before the grand stone fireplace in her living room. The cathedral ceiling peaks into an antique wooden beam, and white shiplap lines the walls.

Bailey drops down onto the sofa beside her in pink sweats—a set from the merch line from Aria's last tour, one that was resold online for absurd prices. It made Aria's blood boil to know some of her fans paid those prices.

"Want to watch a movie?" Bailey asks. She twirls her honey-brown hair into a loose bun and fastens it with a hair tie.

Aria's eyes remain trained on her phone screen—on Griffin's text. "Sure. Anything happy. No slasher or serial killer stuff."

"Anything for you, sis. Though the moratorium will only last so long."

Aria smiles. It's funny how Bailey's serial killer interests are so keen while her own flesh-and-blood sister can't stomach the stuff. "You're too good to me."

Bailey snatches the remote from the coffee table and clicks through the options, humming and hawing along the way.

Griffin: Hey! How's your week going?

Aria: Pretty good. No shows this week, so lots of R&R.

She stows the phone at her side.

Bailey turns to her, holding a hand out toward the TV. "Acceptable?"

Aria glances at the description. A classic rom-com about a single mom who takes a job at a bakery and falls in love with the head baker. "Sold!"

Bailey grabs for the blanket that lays crumpled in a heap at the end of the sofa and pulls it up over her. She leans back and wiggles to get comfortable. "You know, for the amount of romantic movies you watch and love songs you sing, one might be surprised you don't have a lover of your own by now."

Aria pretends to huff, but a grin slips out instead. It's an act they do all the time, but they both know why Aria doesn't date. Where would she find the time? Even during this "rest" week she's currently having, she will hit the gym to keep in performance shape, spend hours in vocal coaching, find opportunities to steal studio time so she can desperately paw around for material for this new album, get fittings for her next series of concerts, approve sets, and go through one hundred tapes for backup dancers. Sure, she's probably more hands-on than other performers, but she never has a spare minute.

Her phone buzzes beside her, and she retrieves it as she tells Bailey, "Maybe one day, honey."

"And for now you have me." It's the same line they always end on.

Sisterly love is just as good as romantic love.

Aria unlocks her phone screen and taps on the new text from Griffin.

> Have any time for your best friend this week? I have a scarf that belongs to you.

Oh, and Aria forgot to add her faux friendship with Griffin to the list of responsibilities. Even friendships have to be part of an effort for her career. Her heart squeezes a little when she considers slotting Griffin into this category. By all practical accounts, he's squarely in this category, but he's also nice and enjoyable to be with, and she feels mean-spirited even mentally begrudging their appointments.

Thus far, he's been plenty more fun than most tasks on her to-do list.

Aria types her response. In the background, while having coffee at the bakery, the female lead in the rom-com is overheard bemoaning the fact that she can't find a job. Bailey is complaining about the fact that the woman also missed the blatantly obvious Help Wanted sign hanging behind her.

Aria pauses her texting, reaches out, and pokes Bailey. "Stop having such an ice-cold heart. Can you imagine how tired she is? She's got three kids and an ex who still lists her as his emergency contact."

Bailey laughs. "Fair enough."

Aria resumes her texting, types, deletes, types, and finally sends:

Aria: Tomorrow afternoon?

The reply comes in almost immediately.

Griffin: Sure thing! I have morning practice, so I can come by afterward to drop off the scarf.

Aria had assumed she'd left the scarf at the venue and hadn't yet been bothered to chase it down.

Her mind wanders back to the gala night. Griffin's chivalry, his generosity, his reluctance to tout his own success. She can't remember the last time she met anyone in the public eye who was that grounded. How on earth does he stay that way with all the glory he's given as the Wardens' golden boy? Surely it says something about the depth of who he is.

But Aria stops herself before she gets lost in thoughts of Griffin Hayes.

Again, her to-do list generates items to be checked much

faster than she can eliminate them, so she can't let herself lose focus. That's where quality slips.

Aria: Looking forward to it, my BFF.

She smiles to herself as she hits Send.

She taps on the emoji page and selects a winky face with the tongue poked out, and before she overthinks it, she hits Send again.

A rush of uncertainty thrums inside her. Is she making herself look like an idiot? Just as she's determined that she is, in fact, making herself look like a total nerd—and the furthest thing from the cool, unshakable Aria Wilder—the phone buzzes in her hand.

Griffin had marked the wacky emoji with a heart.

Aria's shoulders settle, and a smile crosses her face.

He really is such a great guy.

Chapter 11

Griffin

Griffin only stops long enough in the locker room after practice to grab a lightning-fast shower, then hurries toward the exit.

"Where's the fire, man?" Elliott calls out behind him.

"See you guys tomorrow. Great work today!" Griffin says in response to Elliott and the whole team.

Elliott knows about the friendship PR-stunt agreement between Griffin and Aria, so he's finally let up a little on the teasing about Griffin's crush. Now that Elliott knows their continued time together is purely a business deal, any attempts at claiming Griffin has puppy-dog eyes for the woman are easy to deflect.

Even if Elliott is kinda, sorta, mostly correct.

This time Griffin is the one doing the driving to Aria's house, and as he nears, he feels the flutter of excitement. *Get a grip*, he tells himself. *You're just dropping off a scarf.* He pulls up to the gate, reaches out his window, and hits the call button on the keypad, and disappointment flashes when Aria's voice doesn't come over the intercom. Instead, the box emits a harsh buzz, and the gate swings open. Griffin pulls through cautiously, down the long driveway, and finally stops in the round driveway.

One of three garage doors is open, and as his vehicle grinds to a halt, Aria strides out waving widely. Griffin smiles reflexively. She's dressed in leggings, an oversized sweatshirt, and tennis shoes with long socks. Even dressed down, she's a total knockout.

Griffin grabs the scarf from the passenger seat, steps out, and returns the wave with a flourish of the scarf.

Aria walks forward, and Griffin meets her halfway. He holds it out, and a twang of sadness runs through him as she takes it.

"Thank you," Aria says. "I know it was a hassle to drive out here and return it."

Griffin shrugs. "No big deal. I figured you might want to wear it again before *The Late Night Show*, and I didn't want to leave you hanging."

Aria looks up at him, her eyes sparkling with warmth. "That's very thoughtful of you."

Griffin glances past Aria into the garage and notes boxes that've been stacked, some partially unloaded. "A little late for spring cleaning, huh?" he teases.

"Or early, depending on your point of view. I get so many incredible items for PR that I genuinely don't know what to do with them. Hopefully that doesn't make me sound spoiled, but it's just too much for one person. Well, *two*, really, since I share everything with my sister, Bailey."

"We get a ton of clothing from brands too. Probably nothing compared to this." Griffin hesitates for a moment. He wants to offer to help her. More so he wants to stay. "How about I tag in?"

Aria's face leaps, and a chuckle escapes her. "Oh, I couldn't ask that. Not even I want to be doing this, and it's *my stuff*."

Griffin reaches out and sets his hand on her arm. She feels strong but small, inconveniently like someone he could see himself sweeping into his arms. "Well, you didn't ask. I offered."

Aria turns and holds her hands out. "Well, you did come all this way. Might as well make it worthwhile, right?"

Inside the garage, rows upon rows of wire shelving have been arranged, and upon those shelves sit boxes of cosmetics, clothing, decorations, household goods, even nonperishable foods. It's like a small department store more than anything.

Griffin must be standing there with his mouth hanging open, because Aria interrupts his thoughts: "I told you it was over the top."

He begins to walk the shelves, running his hands over the boxes, taking stock of the contents through clear plastic. "It looks pretty organized. I'm not sure what you're cleaning out."

"I get alerts from local nonprofits about what they need, and last night I got a message from the women's shelter asking for winter clothing. I know I have a ton of easy-wear stuff in here that I've received recently—tags still on—so I'm working through."

Griffin stops at the end of a shelf and spots a football. His hands lurch to it as if pulled by a magnetic force. "You been holding out on me?" He peeks out from behind a shelf, and Aria goes to him.

When she spots the item in his hands, she laughs. "Again, these are things sent to me on the off chance I post about them or use-slash-wear them in public. Alas, the football company was disappointed."

Griffin makes eyes at the ball in his hands. "May I?"

"Be my guest." The grin that spreads across Aria's lips is delicious, and Griffin can't pull his eyes from it.

"Oh no, no. This is not a one-person activity. I need you too."

Aria's eyebrows fly high. "Absolutely not. I am many things, but a football player isn't one of them."

"And here I was thinking we were friends. You know, I'm a pretty good teacher." He tuts playfully as he walks out into the cool sunshine and onto the grassy island in the middle of the circular driveway.

Griffin keeps going, hoping that Aria joins him out there on the grass. If his desire alone could orchestrate the events of the world, she would be right beside him. When he reaches the middle of the grass, he turns to look back.

Aria stands on the threshold of the garage, hands propped on her hips, her eyes squinted as if she's taking stock. What Griffin can't help but notice is that she's moved closer.

"Surely you could use a break by now? Plus, we have two sets of hands. I promise I'll stay until we find everything you need to give to the shelter."

When a smirk catches at the side of Aria's mouth, Griffin's heart leaps. It's a crack in her resistance, perhaps even a window to her saying yes.

Chapter 12

Aria

Aria was never a sporty girl—probably to very little surprise. She was always a music girl, a poetry girl, a performer. In fact, she hated team sports in PE so much that she made every excuse possible to sit on the sidelines with her notebook.

Despite the deep-seatedness of her resistance to sports, there's something about Griffin that brings a surprising promise of fun to it. And he's right: She has more than earned a break by now.

Aria drops her hands from her hips and marches toward Griffin. "Well, I guess why not? But if I get injured, you might have to step in and do my next show for me."

Griffin laughs, and he sounds like a giddy youngster. Aria can't help but smile back. "We're just throwing the ball. No tackles."

Aria plants her legs wide, claps, and says, "All right, give it to me."

Griffin tosses the ball her way gently, telescoping it directly into her held-out hands. When the ball lands with a satisfying plop in her hands, a surprising thrill runs through her. She yelps.

"I told you, right?" Griffin says with a playful raised brow. "Now lob it back."

Aria rears back her arm and lobs the ball. She brings her hands to her mouth as she watches it fly far too high, like a rocket bound for the stars, and finally shuttle down to earth about fifteen feet behind Griffin.

Aria parts her hands covering her mouth. "I told you I was a beginner."

Griffin lopes to the ball, then jogs over to Aria. "Here." He starts to hand her the ball but then pauses, assessing. "May I?"

Aria gives a quick nod. Griffin wraps his wide, strong hand around hers and places her fingers gently along the laces, one by one. "This is the placement you want every time. It'll make sure the ball doesn't go wild."

Aria is primally aware of Griffin's closeness, his large figure at her side. The tingle in her skin underneath his fingertips. Everything else falls away, and it's just them in the world.

She nods at his directions. "Got it."

"Now"—Griffin lightly takes her arm and repositions it—"this is how you want to pull back, find your target with your eye, and then release."

His arms are wrapped around Aria like a hug, and her heart beats faster. When Griffin breaks away, then jogs to his receiving position, the glow inside releases then shrinks.

Griffin stands before her, hands out, nodding encouragingly. "You got this!"

Aria follows his directions, and when she releases the ball, it goes almost directly into Griffin's hands. He reaches out and snatches it, then leaps in the air, crying out in celebration. "Touchdown pass from Wilder to win the game!"

Aria laughs, eyes dropping bashfully. "Okay, now, let's not get ahead of ourselves."

"Hey, you have to celebrate the wins when they come."

"I don't disagree."

As the two toss the ball back and forth, Aria focuses on practicing the technique Griffin showed her, but she also thinks about *him*. About having fun with him. So much of Aria's life is scheduled and optimized, a requirement for fitting in all the components her career requires. But now, in this unplanned moment of Griffin sticking around, making fun out of an unglamorous task, it feels like experiencing something brand-new.

Maybe it makes Aria sound boring to admit that she's such a perfectionist workaholic that she never really has fun, but it's also not entirely untrue. To be fair, her difficulty making and keeping friends absolutely plays into that as well.

Still, as Aria watches Griffin's face as he throws and receives the ball, the grin that never truly leaves his face, the eagerness in his eyes, she can't help but feel pulled to him. Despite the odds, it seems this professional-football-player-turned-PR-stunt-partner is someone Aria actually really enjoys being with.

As soon as she begins to break a sweat, Aria calls an end to the activity, citing the fact that she already completed her scheduled time in the gym for today. Griffin doesn't fight it, and after they stop at the garage fridge for a couple of cold drinks, they get back to the boxes.

Aria is surprised at how locked in Griffin gets as they sort through boxes.

"Grab anything comfortable or easily wearable, which should be most stuff out here. The super-glam stuff is usually on loan, or I send it back if I won't wear it—that way someone else can. So, think cute casual."

Griffin works alongside Aria, his brow knitting in concentration as he assesses the items he pulls out. He sorts through a box and refastens the lid. "This is all good to go. It's mostly sweats and workout gear."

"You're the best," Aria says. She'd planned to do this on her own, and although she's grateful for the practical help, it's the company that truly makes the difference.

"Just making good on my promise," Griffin says.

"I'm sure you have a million better things to be doing."

Griffin stops, looks around, and shakes his head. "Nope. This is right where I want to be."

"I guess the golden-boy rumors are true." Aria warms as if his golden effect is the sun radiating upon her.

"Don't ask my mother. She has plenty of evidence otherwise."

Aria shoots Griffin a playful look, then gets back to her sorting. She won't say it out loud, but she doesn't believe him. Aria suspects that Griffin is being modest, that he really and truly is golden.

If he wasn't, he wouldn't have offered to help, he wouldn't have stayed after he handed off the scarf, and he wouldn't have even made the drive out. No, all the evidence points to Griffin Hayes being just as much a gentleman as promised.

Perhaps even better.

Chapter 13

Griffin

Griffin loses track of how much time he spends lugging around boxes in Aria's garage, but after a while, they have amassed a healthy stack of boxes marked for the shelter. Both he and Aria step back and pause, admiring their handiwork.

"Where do these need to be loaded?" Griffin asks.

Aria waves him off. "Oh no. The organization will come by with their truck, but thanks for the offer."

A quiet falls between them as their task ends. Griffin wonders if Aria is feeling the same disappointment that's settled inside him, but he doesn't linger on that thought long. What Griffin wants is more time together.

"We never really got around to talking about *The Late Night Show*, huh?" he says.

"Oh, that's right!" Aria's surprise edges close to excitement.

Aria can do these sorts of interviews in her sleep, so it's

probably up to Griffin to take the lead. The simplest solution would be to chat briefly about it now. But Griffin doesn't want to discuss *The Late Night Show* now because then he wouldn't have a good excuse to see Aria before the taping next Monday.

"Do you have any time tomorrow?" Griffin wonders if he's testing his luck as he says the words, asking a world-class pop star if she has even more time for him.

"Sure!"

The reply is bright, not a hint of bothered, and possibly even enthusiastic. Griffin latches on at once. "Perfect. I'll be done with practice by three. What's your schedule?"

Aria pulls out her phone. "I don't have meetings tomorrow, and it's my day off from writing. Well, the one I give myself."

"Do you need any more help with the garage?"

Aria bursts into laughter, and Griffin squints back in confusion. "What? I'm serious."

"I'm not going to take advantage of your kindness," Aria says warmly, the laughter not yet completely run out.

"I'm a Midwestern guy at heart. We help a neighbor out."

"How about we grab some coffee? There's a place close to the stadium that's amazing—it's an old house, so they have these cozy little rooms where I can usually fly under the radar. I'm rarely ever over there, so this gives me a great excuse to meet you on your turf."

"Great! Text me the details and you're on."

When they say goodbye Griffin pulls Aria into a friendly side hug before climbing into his Bronco. Griffin leaves feeling lighter, buoyed by the down-to-earth fun he and Aria had today. That's the thing about being a public figure: There's always someone willing to do the hard stuff for you, always someone to pay to do the boring stuff. But sometimes that's where the unexpected comes from, or those are the moments when the simple delights in life are highlighted—the satisfaction of a job well done, the afterglow of helping out a friend, laughing with someone new.

As the country roads turn slowly into city streets, Griffin becomes more certain about the fact that Aria is someone special. He can't wait to see her tomorrow.

Chapter 14

Aria

Aria sits in her favorite room at the coffee shop, the one so small and tucked so far in the back that it only has room for one table. Her hat is pulled down low and drinks for both of them are on the table before her. When Aria had texted Griffin to ask his order, she couldn't help but smile at his reply.

> **Griffin:** Green tea, please. Let me know how much, and I'll Venmo you.

Of all the people who claimed to be "friends" of hers over the years, most assumed that she would always pick up their tabs anyplace they went. It wasn't that she minded; she could afford it. It was more the assumption that the friendship came with financial benefits.

Aria hears the creaking of the old wooden floors of the

coffee shop before she sees Griffin. They squeak in a way she can only presume is due to the massive bulk of a professional football player. When Griffin appears, he has to duck slightly to enter through the small opening.

"People back then must've been smaller," he says by way of greeting.

"Nowadays most people are *still* smaller than you." She lifts her cup and sips.

Griffin settles into the chair, and Aria loves that he blocks them from view in the doorway, that passersby will see only his back and his cap-covered head. To anyone else, they're two regular people having coffee. It's a luxury to disappear in public.

Griffin nods to his tea. "Thank you for this."

"Sure thing. Double mocha latte with extra whipped cream, right?"

Griffin falters for a moment, eyes darting between Aria and the lidded cup, when finally she bursts into laughter.

"I'm *kidding*. That's what I got for myself, minus the extra whip."

Griffin lets out a breath. "And there's nothing wrong with that."

"Did you see the *Late Night* talking points that were emailed over?" Aria asks. She pulls a flat brown bag from her purse and takes a jumbo chocolate chip cookie from inside it. She sets it on top of the bag on the table between them.

"I did. And honestly, it seems pretty simple?" Griffin's voice lilts upward as if he suspects he's being deceived.

Aria picks a small bite from the side of the cookie and nods while she chews. "They're very easy, and this show is known for going easy on noncontroversial celebs. So, I think they just want to see us be friends. They'll ask us their questions, and we can answer them however we like."

Griffin taps around on his phone screen. "I'm looking again. Yeah, you're totally right."

"Obviously we just stick to the story," Aria says. "We got connected when you first went viral over 'Glass Heart,' and we hit it off from there. We can make up any answers that sound good to the other questions about our friendship, and we'll just back each other up and work together."

After the time they spent together yesterday, "working together" seems like the easiest thing in the world.

Griffin nods. "You're right. Maybe I was making too big of a deal over this."

Aria pushes the brown paper bag, cookie atop, toward Griffin.

He shakes his head. "No thanks."

She smiles, cocks her head, and in a singsong voice says, "I played *football* for you, and you won't even share a teensy cookie with me?"

Griffin's face cracks into a smile that sends wrinkles across his face. Aria revels in it. As Griffin sighs in defeat, Aria looks on, butterflies of fun flapping in her middle.

"A little." Griffin demonstrates a tiny amount between his thumb and pointer finger.

Aria snatches the cookie from the tabletop, and using both hands, she bends the cookie in half and breaks it apart. She holds out his half.

When Griffin reaches out and takes it, their fingers momentarily touch. Aria's eyes fly to the spot where her hand feels like it's sizzling. Before Griffin pulls his hand away, he rubs his thumb once back and forth over the thin skin of her hand. It's a seemingly unconscious motion, so small she almost misses it.

She hopes he doesn't notice her sharp intake of breath.

Griffin doesn't hesitate before taking a massive bite of the cookie. He chews with his eyes shut, and once he swallows, says, "Please never take no for an answer if you offer me a cookie like that again. Holy cow was I wrong."

Aria looks on in smug delight. "A little bit of cookie won't break the football machine."

Griffin finishes the cookie, takes a sip of his tea, then checks the time on his phone.

"You rushing off?" Aria asks, attempting to mask the desperation threatening to resound in her voice.

She's been looking forward to seeing him, and their planned discussion went far too quickly.

"Not unless you are. I want to get the full experience." Griffin gestures to the coffee shop around them.

A calm settles inside Aria, and she drops her head to one side. "Isn't it great? I feel so at home here."

"Yeah? What about it feels like home?" Griffin holds eye contact even as he tilts his cup to sip.

A familiar twinge cuts across Aria's chest, her body's way of reminding her to keep her walls up, reminding her that most people can't be trusted. It doesn't take much for her to override the warning and barrel right in. Griffin is different. That much is obvious by now.

"I grew up in a small, old house. Nothing as cute or quaint as this, but there's just something about being in a place like this that feels like being welcomed home. Getting to be myself and not the 'official' Aria Wilder. Like I can kick my feet up and breathe for a moment."

Griffin sets down his cup, and his gaze warms Aria. He's almost inspecting her. "I'm glad you said it, because you really are so much more than the persona on all the promotional stuff."

"Yeah? What do you make of it?"

The quiet that passes feels a bit like awaiting a verdict. Does Griffin like what he sees of her like she's terribly intrigued by what she's seeing of him? When a smile teases at the corner of his mouth and he runs a hand through his wavy hair, Aria can't take her eyes off him.

She's already hoping they get another round of drinks. Green tea is healthy, right?

Surely she could convince Griffin to stay, even if the time for him to go hasn't yet come.

Chapter 15

Griffin

Griffin knows he needs to tread lightly when Aria asks him what he sees in her. He makes a deal with himself: Be honest but not sappy or weird.

"There's far more to you," he says. "Don't get me wrong; your branding is amazing. It gets the whole 'powerhouse performer' down to a T. But in real life you have more details. You're a loving big sister; you care about others, like the way you tracked down those clothing items for donation. Honestly, I didn't expect you to be as funny or laid-back—" Griffin stops himself. "Am I rambling?"

"Trust me, I won't ever ask you to stop saying nice things about me."

"You're softer, layered."

"I'm like a quilt?"

Griffin pauses. In some ways, Aria really is like a quilt, even if she's joking. Because every time he's around her, he feels warm and wrapped up in her.

"Not sure that was the direction I was going, but if you want to, say so."

Aria reaches out and squeezes his wrist. "I'm kidding!"

Her skin is soft against his, and Griffin momentarily loses his train of thought. "Thank you," he says. "For helping me through this PR stuff."

"It's only fair since you taught me how to throw a football."

Griffin smiles, then sips his tea. It might seem like a fair exchange, but he is realizing that simply being in her company feels like an added bonus.

"But thank you from me too," Aria says. "Very few people in this world understand what it's like to be in the sort of jobs we are, and it's been really nice to be with someone who I don't have to explain myself to. You just get it, you know?"

Griffin can't help but smile at Aria saying he makes her feel understood. "It's a pleasure," he says.

He sips the remainder of his tea, and when the tea runs dry, he feels a flash of sadness. The cup echoes inside as he sets it down on the table. Aria's eyes join his on the empty cup.

"Can I bribe you to stay with me with another cookie?" Aria's eyebrows pull together in an adorable knot.

A bubbling excitement passes through Griffin's middle, something he can't remember ever experiencing. "You don't need to bribe me. I wasn't planning on leaving."

Aria's shoulders drop so much that Griffin sees it happen.

"I know this is an 'arrangement,' but you're pretty fun to be around," Aria says.

"Fun, huh? I'm definitely not pegged as the fun one on the team." Griffin can't help but think of all the times the other guys gave him a hard time for his meal prepping or his penchant for a quiet night in.

"Oh yeah, no wild nights out for you?"

Griffin scoffs. "Hardly, and if so, under duress."

"I guess it tracks. Midwest golden boy, quiet nights in. But what I mean is that I never would've stopped to play yesterday afternoon without you. Where you saw an opportunity to enjoy ourselves, I saw an opportunity to finish a task faster so I could do more work."

Griffin shrugs. "We can balance each other out some, but I'm not all fun either."

"Whatever you are, it's something good." Aria's cheeks turn pink, and she looks away. "Sorry if that came out weird. You know what I mean."

Griffin reaches over the table and squeezes Aria's hand. The last thing he wants is her to feel uncomfortable, and especially so around him. "Hey now, anything goes between best friends, right?"

Aria looks back over, a reenergized glint in her eye. "It does. And I think we're starting to do a really good job with the whole thing. We're amazing as best friends."

Griffin's shoulders and chest lift as if his good fortune in meeting Aria has precluded him from the effects of gravity. "We really are incredible friends."

"It'll make the rest of this so easy." Aria grins like they've cracked the code.

Griffin returns the look.

Maybe they have. Maybe they have cracked some wild code and found another human who just gets them. A person they can be themselves around.

Whether for PR purposes or just life in general, making a new friend is always a wonderful thing.

Chapter 16

Aria

Aria locks herself in her studio on Monday morning, promising to use the hours leading up to *The Late Night Show* filming to work on her new album. It would be more fitting to call it "the label's album," seeing that they've already sent over a list of concepts they'd like to see reflected in the lyrics. She sits on a stool, a foot on the support beam, and her guitar held across her chest. She'll shower later and get dressed up in one of the dresses her stylist sent over for *The Late Night Show* filming, so for now it's sweatpants, thick socks, and no makeup.

Before she starts any work, Aria pulls on her favorite cozy cardigan, part of her writing ritual.

She strums at the guitar, and bit by bit, she puts a melody together. It's reminiscent of a hit from two albums back, "Love Found." Aria sighs. She knows the record execs will love it, so she forges on, but the song feels hollow. Her heart squeezes at the thought of trying something new, like it's a friend she misses already.

Eventually, she reminds herself. *Eventually*.

Aria gets up and sets the guitar back in the case, and in exchange, she picks up her songwriting notebook. She pages through, and it's disappointingly bare. Didn't she jot down ideas last week? Then she remembers that she'd tried, but her mind had been a blank. In fact, she spent some of that time thinking about the publicity project with Griffin. She smiles. Aria watched his game yesterday, flipping around the channels until she found the familiar gold and red uniforms front and center, a commentator mumbling low.

Bailey had taken the opportunity to poke fun at her. "You're really committed to the part. Watching his game and everything?"

Aria doesn't mind sports, but she's also never been one to pick that over a rom-com.

"They might ask me about it tomorrow on *Late Night*." Aria hadn't taken her eyes from the screen because she knew Bailey would be able to sniff out the rest: Aria was genuinely intrigued by this guy. "I'm committed to selling it."

"And it's working." Bailey grabbed her phone and tapped around. "See? I just opened three different apps, and clips and pics of the two of you are within the first page every time. Obviously the algorithm knows I'm an Aria fangirl, but I never see anything football related. It's like you're bringing worlds together. World peace, here we come?"

Aria scoffed. "Yup. One color-by-numbers song at a time."

Bailey had put a loving palm to Aria's back. "Hey now. Go easy on yourself. Even if it's not what you want to keep doing, they're great songs. Songs that bring lots of people fun and joy in a world that can be harsh."

"You're right." Aria had been trying to remind herself that her loyalty needed to lie with her fans. They made her what she is, and she should give them what they want.

"And when the moment strikes for you to debut your new sound, they will all be there, still screaming for Aria Wilder."

Aria's stomach had dropped. But would they be? Perhaps even more so than writing an uninspired album, Aria worries about letting down her fans. Part of her believes that it's possible to wed the two: making music that feels creatively satisfying while also pleasing the fans. But the more the label pushes for her to keep doing more of the same, the more she wonders if she'd just be letting everyone down by switching gears.

Aria and Bailey watched the game all the way through, and even once the Wardens were handed a loss, Griffin walked with pride from the field, shoulders back and head held high. He waved to the camera and stopped for fans.

Not that it was Aria's business to feel this way, but she was proud of him too. There really was so much more to him than the game.

Aria is pulled back to the present by a sudden thunderbolt of inspiration. A game. Of course.

He holds his head high even when they lose the game,
She stands by with pride and loves him just the same.
Even when the chips are down, he's the one to call,
Because life isn't easy wins and gains after all.

A football player love-interest song would be exactly the fans' speed. Aria did a cheerleader–football player song two albums back, so she'd need to switch it up with the female part. Maybe a theater girl? She is also keenly aware that she'd have to make enough adjustments to erase any possibility for speculation that her song is about Griffin now that the two are connected. Although, who knows? If the two of them keep getting along as well as they had thus far, maybe Griffin would even spill about a past relationship and let her write a song about it. He'd already been so easygoing and surprisingly open.

Bailey's voice echoes in a shout down the stairs to the studio. "I'm feeding you before you start getting ready. Want chicken salad?"

"You are an actual angel fallen to earth." Aria slaps her notebook shut, hops up, and stows it.

"Fallen to earth? Doesn't that mean I got kicked out of heaven?" The half-powered offense lining Bailey's words is a telltale sign that she's smiling through her complaint.

"I'm not sure that's the only situation, but for clarity's sake, let's say you were *sent* to earth. For me."

Aria crosses the room to the foot of the stairs and looks up to meet Bailey's eyes before taking the steps two at a time. "For my sanity. For my health. For keeping my life anything but the sad, sad thing it would be without you."

Bailey props a hand on her hip and raises a brow. "You're sweet-talking me for chicken salad?"

Aria reaches the top of the stairs and shrugs. "Don't I get more credit than that? You remember the label offered a chef service in order to speed up the arrival of the next album, right?"

Bailey tips an invisible hat. "They can just put me on the payroll."

Aria and Bailey melt into laughter, and Aria pulls her little sister under her arm. Together they head for the kitchen and assemble plates à la Chef Bailey. Bailey has put the chicken salad on a slice of baguette with a serving of fruit on the side, and Aria's stomach grumbles. Despite the hunger pangs, she hadn't even thought of lunch. Bless Bailey Wilder. Aria would be lost without her.

Chapter 17

Griffin

The small leather couch creaks beneath Griffin in the green room at *The Late Night Show*. Mike suggested Griffin wear nice pants, a button-down, and a sweater layer over it, and he did as he was told. A second deep groaning from the couch suggests the heft of him might break it, so Griffin pops up. Just as he does, Aria walks in and reflexively his eyes go wide.

She's wearing a gold knee-length dress with thin straps. It's fitted perfectly to her, and her curls cascade down her back. Her lips are shiny with something red and glossy, and his eyes linger there.

"Everything okay?" Aria asks, looking confused at his expression.

Griffin kicks himself on the inside. Could he *be* more obvious that he thinks she's stunning? Granted, most of the world would agree with him, but this is a professional environment.

"Oh. Yeah. Sorry." Griffin points at the fashionable but questionably durable couch. "That thing was making all sorts of sounds with my weight on it, so I got up before I broke it."

Aria narrows her eyes playfully. "Haven't even been here an hour, and you're breaking stuff already?"

Griffin slips his hands into his pants, then looks up sheepishly. "I think it's partially due to the nature of my size. Oh, and the showrunner said they're going to pull us up there soon."

Aria places her bag on the couch and grabs a bottled water from the coffee table in front of it. "You're much more relaxed this time, Mr. Hayes. You're learning."

Griffin smiles, and like clockwork, a redness starts to bloom at the base of his neck. "I have to admit you're right. And your prep helped."

To be fair, his calling their time at the coffee shop "prep" was a bit of a stretch. Perhaps "good company" or "rapport building" might be a better fit. But whatever they called it, there was no doubt about how much Griffin enjoyed it.

Knuckles rap at the greenroom door, and it flies open.

A stern-looking young man wearing sweats appears in the doorway wearing a frown. "We're behind already. You two ready?"

He doesn't wait for a response before turning and marching down the hallway, presumably toward the action.

Aria's eyebrows go sky-high, her eyes wide, and the threat of a laugh pulls at the corner of her mouth. She reaches out and grabs Griffin's arm and whisper-yells, "Come on, slowpoke, this guy's not messing around."

A deep grin cuts across Griffin's face, and he moves with her. He'd never allow her to exert herself enough to actually tug him behind her, especially when she's looking so determined. Aria leads him out the door.

When she looks over her shoulder mischievously, he feels his heart pick up. Is this what having fun feels like? A laugh escapes him.

"Shhh," she warns. "This is no laughing matter."

They screech to a halt behind the showrunner, who has stopped at a hair and makeup chair right by the entrance to the stage. From this position, the host's desk is visible, and staff buzz around it adjusting lights to make sure they will hit the famous Mario Villarreal just right.

"Only a quick one," the showrunner barks to the makeup artists. "They're already late."

Griffin knows that he and Aria weren't late, but apparently in this venue being on time is considered late. He knows better than to argue the fact. A fluffy makeup brush deposits a dusting of powder over both his and Aria's faces, and they're brought onstage.

The live audience goes wild, and together they look out and wave before taking their seats as instructed.

"Ready for the mic check!" the showrunner calls out to the technical staff, then disappears offstage.

A much calmer crew bring tiny microphones to be attached to their clothing, and they're asked to perform a few test words. The crew gives them a thumbs-up. The crowd breaks out into chatter, and Griffin takes the cue that they're all in a holding pattern until the host arrives.

He leans over and whispers to Aria, "We got this, buddy."

She reaches out and pats his back. "You know we do. What's

on the docket after this? A delicious meal-prepped plate reheated in the microwave?" She closes her eyes and groans in mock delight. "I can just taste it now."

"Might treat myself to something else after I get through this gauntlet."

When he looks up, Griffin is met by a few "awww" sounds from the crowd. Lights from several recording smartphones shine back at him from the darkness of the crowd.

"Guess our mics are hot, Griff," Aria announces.

The crowd claps, and a few people cry out, "The two best friends ever!"

Griffin resists the urge to gulp. Good thing he didn't say anything incriminating. Well, anything that might give them away. It's probably for the best that the two of them seem to be finding a version of real friendship within this setup. The time helping Aria in the garage and the coffee shop felt just as natural as hanging out with his teammates. Well, plus an extra spark.

Griffin looks out at the crowd. "If you'd told me two months ago that Aria Wilder and I would become buddies, I'd laugh. We're an odd pair, but we have fun."

"It's true. I mean, what do we have in common, Griff?" She smiles at him like it's part of their act. It *is* part of their act.

If they weren't in public, if they weren't miked, if maybe it was a moment that could be forgotten as quickly as it happened, he would tell her what he really thinks. That maybe it's not about counting surface-level things in common. Maybe it's about how the other person makes you feel. Maybe those differences are things that allow them to stand on their own feet inside a friendship. That salty and sweet is perhaps the best flavor combination in history. That soft and strong are both necessary when it comes to the heart. That she doesn't need to be the female version of him for him to be captivated. In fact, quite the opposite is preferable.

But he bottles all those words up, and instead Griffin gives her a shrug. "We make it work! I'm already a pop music fan—as most of the world has seen footage of by now. We just need to get you on the sports bandwagon."

The set manager comes over as Aria begins to reply and politely mutes their microphones. The crowd groans, and a few "boos" ring out.

"Sorry, sorry!" the manager calls out, squeezing her hands in front of her. "But we need to save all of this for the show. We can't leave our TV audience hanging!"

As the crowd goes back to their chatting and the staff mill around the stage, Aria looks over to Griffin. She winks.

He winks back.

Chapter 18

Aria

Mario Villarreal is wearing so much stage makeup that Aria wonders if it'll melt like hers once did under the Texas sun. Surely he knows what he's doing; he does four episodes a week. And as he opens the show and eventually introduces her, then Griffin (to the studio audience they've already warmed up), her thoughts are pulled away from his makeup.

"So." Mario slaps his palm on the wooden desk. "This friendship between you two is fairly new."

"Yes, sir, it is! Griffin came to one of my concerts, and only after my incredible fans caught him on video belting out the lyrics to 'Glass Heart' was it brought to my attention that he even knew who I was."

"Well, I think most of the world knows who you are by now," Griffin says at the other end of their shared couch.

The one in the greenroom was so rinky-dink that Griffin

couldn't even sit on it, but this one is deep, wide, and sturdy. Fit for guests of any build. Despite the space remaining between them, Aria feels his presence close to her. Griffin is like that, taking up more than just physical space. He has a force to him. When he sat across from her in the coffee shop, he practically eclipsed the rest of the world.

"Did your friends know you were an Aria Wilder fan before the video went viral?" Mario asks.

Griffin nods slowly but deeply. "I've yet to live it down for blasting 'Get Over It' in the locker room after our playoff loss in Minnesota last year. At least it created a little bit of a distraction for the guys."

"Griffin, you're known as a golden-hearted player in the league. What's your say on that?"

Griffin tugs at his collar, and his Adam's apple bobs hard. Of all the potential questions that might spark nerves, why this one? Journalists often throw difficult questions his way before high-stakes games. This question is basically a compliment wrapped up as a question.

"Well, I don't know. I . . ."

Griffin pauses, his eyes briefly flicker to Aria's, and she cuts in.

"May I, Mario?" She gives him a playful look. "Because I have had a front-row seat over the last couple weeks of Griffin Hayes off the field, I can attest to the fact that the rumors are true: He's not only the golden boy, but he has the golden heart."

The crowd erupts into applause, and eventually Aria has to hold up a hand to ask for quiet.

"He is kind and generous. On a whim, he matched donations for homeless animals with me. He helped me out when I found myself stuck without a ride. He's the most down-to-earth guy I've met—and yet, he's also a professional athlete on television every Sunday."

"Note for anyone trying to impress Aria Wilder: It's about character, folks!" Mario announces.

Aria smiles, but she can't help but wonder about his statement. What else *would* it be about for her? Is her image that curated around glam and special-effects shows that people assume there isn't more to her? This is when a personal, deep album drop might come in handy.

"That's all very complimentary. And I'm lucky to have found such a generous friend in Aria, but that's enough about me."

Griffin looks so adorably awkward that Aria can't help herself. "Y'all want to know a secret? Griffin Hayes blushes if you give him too many compliments."

Griffin dives into the couch—presumably to cover his blushing cheeks.

"Perhaps a strategy for rival football teams? Aria, you aren't leaking tactics that'll hurt our beloved Wardens now, are you?"

Aria sucks in a loud gasp and pulls a hand to her chest. "I would never! All I want for Griff is for him to dodge the hits, catch the ball, and get a touchdown every now and then."

The crowd applauds.

"Aria, have you always been a football fan?"

"Probably to little surprise, no. But I just watched the game yesterday, and I was very proud of the Wardens. The guys fought well, but it wasn't their night."

Griffin has emerged from the couch next to her. "Really?"

All of this is for show—both of them know it—but something about the way Griffin says it lets Aria know that he's genuinely asking.

"Of course. I wanted to support my friend. I had heard it was going to be a tough game, and what do friends do if not support each other?"

Admittedly, Aria could've skipped watching the game and caught the highlights this morning, but she wanted to see it herself. She can't help but press herself into this role of friend; it's more fun than she's had in a long time.

"Well, let me know if you want to come to the stadium. I've got excellent friends and family box seats, and the nachos up there are top notch."

"You had me at nachos." Aria smiles over at him, and heat blossoms in her chest. The smile, the fun, it's all thrumming inside her like something very real.

"And don't skip the jalapeños."

"What, are they fancy?"

"They're *Wardens* jalapeños, so, yes?"

"Dang. I definitely don't have my own line of spicy peppers." Aria looks off and cups her chin thoughtfully. "I've got to make a note on my phone to ask my publicist about that."

"So," Griffin starts, then stops, and when Aria turns to look into his eyes, they glint at her. It feels like an invitation. To what? She's not sure. Probably fun and friendly. Still, there's an edge to the way he speaks next that makes her wonder if there's more. A thrill rushes through her like a sizzle of electricity. "Can I count on you at the Wardens' stadium on Sunday?"

Aria's heart takes off beating quicker, and her breath catches in her throat. It's like how she feels at the end of a concert, after going full out on the grand finale, giving it her all. But tonight she's simply sitting here, still and unmoving. The only force encompassing her is Griffin Hayes's indisputable presence.

"Absolutely. All I need is fan wear."

"A number 13 jersey will be on your doorstep tomorrow."

Aria's insides balloon with lightness. A jersey with his number feels like being invited into a special club. Sure, there are thousands of 13 Wardens jerseys out there—Griffin has his own contingent of fans—but one hand-delivered is a special friend perk.

"You're such a good friend, Griff," Aria says, feeling the truth in each word as she says it. "I'm such a lucky lady!"

"The pleasure's all mine." Griffin's voice rumbles deeply in his reply, and their eyes stay locked on each other. He grins. "Hopefully the fans will capture your own viral moment this time. You know, to repay the favor."

Aria bursts into laughter, the belly-deep kind that's usually reserved for Bailey. "I guess it would only be fair."

"Well, thank you both, Aria Wilder and Griffin Hayes, for coming on *The Late Night Show*. We can't wait to continue watching your budding friendship online." Mario looks into the camera, and it slides closer to him. "I'm Mario Villarreal, and this is *The Late Night Show*. Good night, everyone."

"Cut!" the stage manager shouts.

The crowd begins to chatter, phones pulled out to check notifications, and Griffin rests back onto the couch, letting his head fall backward.

Aria just watches him. This interest of hers is growing. Undeniably so. She feels new things around Griffin. Is this what real friendship feels like? Has she never experienced it the right way? Or could this be . . . something else?

Griffin pulls himself upright, and Aria rushes to look away, hiding her lingering eyes. “Hey. Want to grab something to eat after this?” he asks.

“So the ‘treat yourself’ thing was legit?”

He shrugs. “Only on special occasions.”

“You’re on.”

The same young man wearing the sweats arrives back at their side, and the two are escorted offstage. Only this time, both of them hurry behind him without any prodding required.

Chapter 19

Griffin

Vic pulls the car into the service alley behind the studio building, a damp passage squeezed between the brick walls of the city high-rises pressed together. Griffin must've driven past this building countless times over the years, and only today did he discover that up on the ninth floor sits the studio. Before now, it never would've concerned him.

When the black car comes to a stop, Griffin reaches out, swings the door open, and gestures for his guest to go first.

Aria has pulled her coat tightly around her, the oversized hood pulled up. "Thanks," she says quietly and slides into the seat.

Griffin shuts the door behind her and rounds the car. When he slides in on the other side, Aria pulls her hood down. "Where to?"

Vic turns around in the driver's seat. He's gray-haired with a thick mustache, and his deep brown eyes are warm. "I was wondering the same."

Griffin pulls out his phone. "Let me double-check," he mutters to himself. "Yup, he'll be there. Enzo's on Twenty-Seventh."

Vic nods, turns back to face the front, and shifts the car into gear.

Aria looks over. "Is this some fancy spot?"

Griffin shakes his head. "It's one of Chicago's little-known secrets. Well, unless you're on the Wardens. Enzo DiCamaro is brother to Alessio DiCamaro, former defensive lineman to the Wardens. What started as a postgame tradition—wood-fired pizza at Enzo's—grew to the point where the whole team wanted in. Eventually Enzo needed a bigger kitchen and dining area. So a bunch of us pitch in to rent the spot on Twenty-Seventh, one big enough to hold the team."

Aria's eyes shine as she smiles back. "So, like a pizza speakeasy."

"Precisely."

In only a few minutes, Vic stops on a quiet street a little outside of the busiest part of the city. Griffin thanks Vic and climbs out of the car. He starts to round the car to get Aria's door, but she beats him to it, climbing out and calling her thanks to Vic.

She stands on the sidewalk. "So, what happens next? Secret password? We cast a spell?"

Griffin sets his wide palm on Aria's back. He ignores the tingle beneath his fingertips at the touch of her—the gentle curve of her back that's toned yet delicate. He then points across the street at a red wooden door, unmarked, but the wall-mounted gas lamp beside it glows.

"Just follow the red door." He sings the words like they're a nursery rhyme.

Aria squeaks, "This is so fun!" then takes off in bounds—despite her heels—across the vacant road.

Griffin catches up in a few strides, and when they reach the door, he retrieves his keys from his pockets, and after a moment, slots one of them into the lock. He turns the knob and stands off to the side as he lets the door fall open. Griffin wants to see the look on her face when she sees this place.

Aria gasps, and her hands go to her mouth as she steps slowly inside, head turning to take the whole place in.

Like Griffin promised, the place isn't large or fancy, but it's a hidden, cozy gem right in the middle of an industrial city known for bitter-cold weather. The narrow entryway is lined with Victorian woodwork and black-and-white tiles on the floor. The rows of coat hooks in the tiny entryway are empty, all but one this evening when Griffin reaches out to Aria.

"May I take your coat?"

Aria looks over at him with surprise, a quick crinkle of her smooth brow that melts into appreciation. "Sure thing. You're quite the old-school gentleman."

Griffin takes her coat as he laughs at the comment. "Please tell my mother that."

As Griffin hangs Aria's coat, then his own, she wanders a few steps farther, and she gasps at the living room turned dining room.

He falters for a moment. Is this over the top? Griffin

decided to bring Aria to Enzo's because it's private—they can be genuinely "off script," not having to worry about a fan two tables over recording them talking candidly. That's always what he wants at the end of the day—to escape the spotlight, which he achieves so easily at his condo. Inviting her over seemed like a step too far at the time, but as he joins Aria on the threshold of the dining area and spies the table Enzo has arranged for them, the others pushed to the sides, he wonders if this was the right choice. The table—usually bare, aside from a stray grease stain here or there—is covered in white linen. Three taper candles are pressed into empty wine bottles and lit. The silverware looks far sparklier than usual. Griffin swallows his mortification.

"Oh my goodness." Griffin feels his cheeks heating. "I'm sorry. I told Enzo I was bringing a friend, and I'm wondering if maybe he thought that was code for a date."

Aria looks over at him and laughs. "Oh, Griff, you ladies' man. You bring girls here often or what?"

Griffin swallows a groan and takes a moment to massage his temples. "Almost never. Maybe once in all of history. But I also don't typically bring friends here because most of my friends are guys already on the team."

Aria rubs her hands together. "Well, I don't know about you, but I say we enjoy it, right? I'm starving, and it's a very sweet setup." She crosses the room and takes the back of a chair, pulls it out, and begins to sit.

Usually in this situation, Griffin might offer to pull out her chair, as he was taught to do growing up for any female guest, but he abandons that concept swiftly. He needs to move *away* from anything that could be interpreted as him pushing romance on Aria. He swallows hard.

At least she's being a good sport about it.

Griffin slides into a seat across the table. "I'm hungry too. Enzo will be out any minute with the pizzas—a variety. I kid you not, despite the fact that the interior designer made it very cozy in here, it's usually greasy tabletops, slopped drinks, and burly guys shoulder to shoulder. Zero candles, zero fuss."

Aria looks up, and the candlelight illuminates her face, adding to the natural warmth that exudes from her and highlighting the brightest streaks of almost silver in her curls. Her cheeks glow.

His heart picks up.

"I like this version," Aria says.

A voice calls out from the short hallway to the kitchen. "You here, Griff?" Enzo appears right after his greeting, a pizza tray balanced on each hand.

Griffin stands to greet his friend, and after Enzo slides the trays onto the tabletop, they clap hands and pull into a hug, back slaps exchanged.

"You're looking good this season," Enzo says.

He looks like his older brother—just smaller. He has dark eyes and hair, olive skin. He's fit, but with a mostly average build. Running this place has become a version of being a private chef for the team. Enzo feeds them well but focuses on using quality ingredients and packing in protein wherever possible. In exchange, they pitch in to keep him paid at a good rate.

Griffin glances at the pizzas. "Your work this season doesn't look too shabby either."

Enzo laughs. "The rookies came in for the first time the other night. Wide eyes all around, I tell you. *Wide eyes*." Enzo's pride is obvious in his words, and Griffin feels himself swell along with him.

The conversation slows, and both men look to Aria.

She holds out a hand. "Aria. Wide-eyed rookie."

Enzo does a double take. "As in Aria Wilder?" His eyes open as far as humanly possible.

Griffin laughs. "Now it's your turn to be 'wide-eyed rookie,' Enzo. Yes, this is Aria Wilder. She and I are friends."

"My daughter is a massive fan," Enzo says. "I think you're great too. Just, you know, not screaming and crying in the front row like my little Rosie."

"Hey, man, don't knock it till you try it," Griffin says.

Enzo laughs. "Never say never. I'll bring out some water for you, Griff. Aria, anything else to drink? Wine?"

"I don't want to tempt the professional athlete, so I'll stick to water too."

Enzo pours from the carafe into both glasses. "Just holler if you need anything else. I'll be in the back." He turns and leaves the room.

Griffin settles back at the table. "Can I serve you?"

Aria giggles as she reaches for a slice of pepperoni and slides it onto her plate. "I'm not that high maintenance, you know. Even if the media would have you think so."

"I know. It's not that. I just try to take care of the people in my life."

Aria pauses to finish her bite. "I'm not surprised since getting to know the other side of you."

"The other side of me?" Griffin takes a hearty bite and groans.

"You're right—the pizza's incredible. But the other side of you is obvious."

Griffin chews and pulls his eyebrows together. He's always been football, and football has always been him. Griffin Hayes starts and ends with football. Sure, he's a real person in the uniform, the same one who hits the field, but he's never had much to offer beyond that.

"You're thoughtful, kind, relatable, empathetic. Anytime we've done a gig together, you've looked out for me. I saw you on TV stop for every single kid. You were the only player out there still signing when the others hit the locker room."

Griffin shrugs. "It's not that special. But I do like to make sure to never leave a kid disappointed if I can help it. Most of the time it's a signature that takes a few seconds of time, and it means the world to them."

Aria holds out a hand. "That's exactly what I mean. You're a natural with kids. I'm sure the list goes on."

"You mean I haven't lost my soul on the field, is all."

Aria takes a sip from her glass.

"It's a lot of pressure to have all those people banking on me. When I fumble a catch or mess up a play, I always think about those kids I'm letting down. It's not like I'm saving lives like the rest of my family, but I want to make people proud. I want to do my best for the team, and everything is in the public eye. I can't have a tense word with a teammate without it being discussed online."

Aria's eyes are focused on him when he looks up. She listens intently, and he takes it as an invitation to go on.

"And there's the pressure to say the right thing to the reporters, to show up to the right events, even to wear the right thing, if you can believe it. But sometimes it just feels like there's not enough of me to go around. Football and the fans want every little bit of me."

"It'll weigh you down."

"Do you even feel a little of the same? You make it all look so easy the way you pop out hits and sell out arenas, always with a smile on your face."

Aria scoffs. "Griff, I feel every single thing you do. Every time I put together a song, I worry that the fans won't like it. When we plan a concert, there's always the expectation that we outdo the last one. I want to show up for fans too, but I can't ever get to every kid. Then there's the fact that I want to write new songs when my label only wants more of the same. I'm not the same person I was when I started out with eyes for only happily ever afters. I want to infuse more, be more honest about life, about the parts of love that are hard too. Even if it's still beautiful."

"Sounds even harder than football."

Aria shrugs. "Eh. It's not about comparing. Being in the public eye is hard. Especially when you care. You're right that we're not saving lives, but we can make people's lives a little more enjoyable for a while. It matters to us both, it sounds, but carrying the pressure to always perform and always be perfect grows heavy."

"It's why having a place like this is a godsend." Griffin gestures to the room.

He pauses. Being with Aria gives him the same feeling as being at Enzo's.

Aria raises her glass. "Here's to 'just getting it.' And now that you've brought me here, you have to promise to bring me back. Even if Enzo got some mixed signals, I'm glad we came here. A place we can just be ourselves."

They clink glasses and drink.

"We could've easily blown our cover with those live mics," Griff said.

"Guess it's a good thing we're actually starting to become friends of a sort," Aria says.

Griffin feels a warmth spread over him. It's not news to him that he genuinely enjoys Aria's company, but it sparks a new energy in him to hear her confirm that it's mutual. In fact, he's far more interested in their off-script time together than the official appearances.

"It makes these appearances far better than if we had to fake it."

Griffin and Aria fall into a discussion about their PR plan as they finish their food. The taper candles eventually drip wax down their sides, and Enzo comes out to check on them.

When Griffin calls Vic to pull back around and pick them up, he feels a twinge of sadness, knowing the night is coming to an end. Fortunately for him, his next activity with Aria—filming a commercial—isn't far around the corner.

Chapter 20

Aria

As promised, a Griffin Hayes number 13 jersey arrives on Aria's doorstep the next morning. She opens it as soon as she brings it inside and throws it on over the tight long-sleeve T-shirt she has on. Aria twirls in front of the mirror but stops when she notices a card in the package. She pops open the envelope and reads:

Aria,

Thanks for being such a good sport (pun intended) about all of this. Especially when Enzo overdid it last night. I can only hope the quality of the pizza more than makes up for it.

Griff

Aria washes the jersey and even steams it in preparation for the game.

She can't remember the last time she counted down to something so eagerly, but over the next five days, she slowly plans out the rest of her outfit as she marks off the time. She also texts with Griffin every one of those five days. He sends goofy locker room selfies and funny memes about old cartoon shows she's never seen. She sends cute cat pictures and eventually divulges that she's been yearning to adopt a pair of kittens ever since the gala event.

Just go for it! I'll cat-sit when you go on tour, Griffin offered.

I refuse to be an absentee cat mom, she replied.

After two days of texting that only ramped up in frequency—so much so that even phone-obsessed Bailey was giving her a hard time—they decided to meet up. Griffin rented out a movie theater outside of town, and it touched Aria so deeply, she threw her arms around him and hugged him tight.

They sat in the theater, lights on, the entire time, never getting to the part where they clicked on the movie. Griffin told her all about his history in football, and although football wasn't usually her thing, Aria sat rapt. Her mind painted pictures of little Griffin, front teeth missing and tanned from hours in the sun, pulling on an oversized jersey. He told her about his *actual* favorite foods—anything with a carb in it—and admitted his secret love for karaoke.

Aria snatched each tidbit of information and stored it in her mind like the precious treasure it was.

She didn't hesitate before matching his candor. Aria told him all about the awkward middle school years when her schoolmates teased her about her musical aspirations. She told him about her secret love of British cozy murder mysteries, a fact even the scrappiest tabloids had yet to uncover. Aria even told

Griffin about how she'd paid to put Bailey through college—back before she really could afford to—because her parents could afford to even less.

It was as if in the dim light of the movie theater on the outskirts of town, one so infrequently visited that the owner permitted a last-minute full rental, all of the pretense fell away. Even once the manager came through and told them he was locking up for the day, Aria didn't want to leave.

She wasn't done hearing about Griffin.

Nevertheless, they reluctantly packed up. The next two days, they continued to message, then video call, frequently in stints between football practice and Aria's meetings with set designers and wardrobe consultants.

On game day, Aria thrums with excitement. She pulls on the gifted jersey that's sat at the ready in her closet, relaxed-fit jeans, and tennis shoes with gold sparkles—to represent the Wardens even further. She keeps her makeup and jewelry simple, pulls a Wardens ball cap down low in an attempt to stay under the radar, and heads for the stadium with her sister at her side.

They find the box easily with the help of security Griffin set up to meet them at the entrance. Inside it's like a small restaurant outfitted with various food stations and buffets, as well as a well-stocked bar. "Didn't Griffin say something about nachos?" Bailey swivels her head, sporting her own Wardens fan wear, freshly purchased.

"That's right!"

Before they can make it to the bar, a server greets them. "Miss Wilder, am I right?"

Part of Aria deflates, and she removes the cap, her golden

curls spilling out and onto her shoulders. "Guess this wasn't as good a disguise as I thought?"

The server smiles. "No, the hat worked well. It's just that when you checked in, they notified me. Mr. Hayes asked that we take extra special care of you. I can show you to your seats, and then I hear nachos have been promised."

"Wonderful, thank you." Aria follows the server out of the enclosed box area and to the rows of seats in the open air.

He brings them to the front row of the section and points them in the direction of their seats. "What else can I bring you?"

Aria and Bailey order drinks. In only moments, a different staff member delivers them, and on the heels of that, the nachos are at their side. A pep band is blasting music at the end of the field, and Aria feels herself getting into the spirit of the game.

She thinks about Griffin. Does he get nervous before games like she does before shows? His husky figure alone might suggest not, but Aria, knowing the rest of him—the tender, down-to-earth parts—might guess otherwise. She hopes they win. She hopes it's a good game. Either way, she knows Griff will play his heart out.

Aria is bopping her head and munching on nachos—which are just as good as promised—when her phone rings. Kelsey's name and photo appear on the screen. It's probably about the commercial filming next week, so Aria picks up.

"Hey, Kels."

"Aria! You're at the game!"

Aria looks around. "Are *you*?"

"No, but there are photos of you online. Are we going off script? We didn't coordinate this."

"Well, we sort of accidentally promised it on *The Late Night Show*. We just got carried away with the act." Aria's chest hitches. Something about calling it an "act" no longer sits right, but she forges on. "It wouldn't look right if I didn't come through. Plus, Bailey and I are just having fun and hanging out. There's not much to it."

"Well, that's fabulous! If the two of you keep this up, we might not even have to schedule things moving forward." Kelsey's delight oozes in every word.

"Ha! Let's not get ahead of ourselves."

"All right, I'll let you go. Enjoy the game, and I'll be in touch with more soon on day-of details for the commercial shoot."

"Thanks!"

Aria says goodbye and disconnects. She turns to Bailey. "Do you think it's weird that Griffin and I just sort of did this on our own?"

Bailey is in the middle of inserting an overly stacked chip into her mouth when Aria finishes the question, so in the natural pause, she considers it.

Bailey wipes her mouth. "No. It's understandable that you're actually getting to know each other, and offering these tickets to you is just a nice gesture. It's not like he bought them for you or went out of his way. I'm sure it's no more than telling the right person at practice the name to put on the list."

Of course Bailey assumed that Aria wanted confirmation that their attending the game was just a regular part of this publicity setup, and usually this is what Aria would want. Aria even phrased it to suggest that nothing about this scenario would be abnormal. So why does her heart drop a little at the thought that Griffin inviting her here was an offhand, no-big-deal whim?

"You're right," Aria says. "He's just doing his part to play along."

Bailey slurps her soda. "Exactly. Just like you are. And you're both so convincing! He's a great actor for a football player."

"Shhh," Aria says. "You never know who's listening in public."

Bailey pulls back. "Sorry."

Aria reaches out and squeezes her arm.

Aria knows it's unwise to continue discussing this in public, but it only takes one glance around the box to see that all the other guests are still inside where the food is set up. The stadium is so loud, even without the game in action, that quiet conversation is hard to hear.

Maybe part of Aria didn't want the conversation to continue. Maybe she wanted to swim a little in the idea that the rapport being built between the two of them could be—at least in part—built on genuine feelings. The pizza didn't *make up for* the table setting at Enzo's because Aria loved the table setting. It made her bubble in a particular way that didn't happen often. For a woman who is constantly being wooed by brands, invited to the most desirable locations, and given access to the best of the best, something as simple as extra thought, extra care being put into considering what she might *like* for the evening, meant a lot.

This whole arrangement might be a publicity stunt, but Aria cannot deny the fact that Griffin Hayes is golden, through and through. And whoever he might take to Enzo's—on a real date—will be a lucky woman.

Aria waits in the box until the stadium is cleared, and Bailey takes off to meet up with some friends for a dinner close by. The last to leave the box, Aria stops at the security post and asks for directions to the locker room.

The guard gives her a weary look, massaging his chin. "We're really not supposed to give out that information. Security, you know. Plus, Coach runs a tight ship, which means no friends and family in the locker room."

Aria puts on her most dazzling look. "I know. Trust me, I get it. I promise I won't go in. I just want to see him before he leaves."

The security guard's face falls into a smile. "For you? Take the freight elevator to P2, turn left, then fourth door on the right. But don't tell them it was me who sent you."

Aria yelps in delight, then reaches into her bag for a business card that she hands off. "This is my manager. Email her, and she'll set you up with free tickets to my next local show."

She doesn't wait for a reply before waving as she darts off, reciting the directions in whispers under her breath. Aria follows every step, and the rumble of voices that flows out of the locker room door is confirmation that she has arrived in the correct spot.

A few moments later, Griffin strides out, shoulder to shoulder and deep in conversation with another player who Aria can only guess is Elliott. Griffin stops in his tracks when he looks up and meets her eyes. Elliott observes the interaction and hurries a goodbye before continuing on.

She dashes up to him and wraps her hands around his arms. "That touchdown in the fourth quarter? You are Superman in real life!"

Griffin's face cracks into a deep grin. "I'm so glad you came. I was thinking about you while I was on the field. I even tried to spot you in the box."

Aria wiggles her shoulders to show off the jersey. "You couldn't see number 13?"

Griffin's cheeks flush pink. "I'm honored that you wore it, but no, I couldn't see from the field. No eagle-eye vision here."

"Do you have to rush off?" Hope hums inside Aria as the voice in her mind says, *Please say no, please say no.*

"It depends. I'm definitely not hanging around for extra PT, but if you're saying you're free . . . ?" His brows raise as he poses the question.

"For you? I'll clear my schedule."

"Perfect. A lot of the guys will be at Enzo's, so let's do something else."

Aria smiles to herself as she and Griffin navigate the inner tunnels of the stadium, working out their plans, transportation logistics, and timing. She played it like she had a schedule to clear, but the truth is that she left it wide open. Wide open in hopes that a moment like this might come together.

Chapter 21

Griffin

Tuesdays are Griffin's days off—the whole team's—and even though some players still come in to work out, the stadium is quiet when he pulls into the lot. He and Aria are scheduled to shoot a Level Up sports beverage commercial today. He's set to get dressed in game day attire, and Aria is coming with her glam squad so she can put on a concert look.

It's the most involved of their publicity events so far, but it's also the only one for which they are getting paid.

Griffin stops by the locker room, and the automatic lights are all off. No voices echo, no undesirable smells linger. Not a single shower runs. He changes into compression pants and a shirt and makes for the field, where he was told the production crew would be waiting for them.

He exits the tunnel onto the field, and Aria is perched in a director's chair in the end zone with several professionals buzzing around her with makeup and hair tools. Aria hums to herself, eyes closed, and Griffin can't help but smile. Despite what the world sees—the powerful woman who can't quit winning—these parts of her, the quiet singing, her ease in pivoting when their table got set for romance, her quickness to throw money at the animal charity, are what Griffin likes best.

Griffin starts to feel like he's watched her from the shadows too long and calls out, "How do I get a line in 'Glass Heart'?"

Aria keeps her eyes closed, the makeup artist gluing fake lashes to her lids, but a laugh escapes her lips. "Thought you'd had enough of that song by now."

Griffin draws closer. "My viral moment may be over, but my love for the song endures."

"Said like a true fan."

"Now, now. Don't forget this all started because I am, in fact, the true number one Aria Wilder fan."

The makeup artist finishes up with the eyelashes and pats Aria on the arm to let her know she's good to go. Aria opens her eyes and looks over at Griffin with sparkle-lined lids. Griffin cocks his head. "You look so different in stage makeup."

"Isn't it fierce?" Aria asks.

Griffin nods his head because saying yes is the right thing to do, but he's not fully convinced. In his opinion, the best Aria has ever looked was at the game on Sunday—and it was not only because she was wearing his jersey. He loved seeing her in his number, but it was also the fact that she just looked like all of her at once. The glamorous pop star, but also the woman who is sometimes afraid, the woman who craves creative authenticity, the woman who wants to show up with all of herself. The woman who eats pizza, who forgives his friendship fumbles, who is a devoted sister. The woman who inspired him to think more about who he is.

After their conversation at Enzo's, Griffin really did start to think about what else there could be to him beyond football. If someone like Aria Wilder can see value in him outside of the sport, it seems reasonable that he should look a little harder himself.

Kelsey, from Aria's team, strides up wearing knee-high boots with jeans tucked in and a flowy blouse. She claps a few times. "Chop, chop, hair and makeup! We need to start."

Across the field a film crew assembles and begins to unload the equipment.

"We've only been granted a certain amount of time on the field, and after that"—Kelsey mimes a throat-slitting motion—"we're cut off. These Wardens staff don't play."

"I think we're just about done," Aria says, her team nodding back at her. "So hopefully all throats will stay intact."

Kelsey turns on her heel in the direction of the crew, and Griffin hangs back. Once Aria is on her feet, dolled up to the heavens, he offers an arm.

Aria stops in her tracks, glances at his arm held out, and a slow smile creeps over her face.

Griffin feels his face start to heat. "Too much?"

Aria pauses as if to consider it, then swiftly links her arm in his and gives it a gentle tug. "You're so good, like down to the bone, that it might just be the league's best-kept secret."

Griffin starts walking, arm in arm, with Aria. "Don't tell anyone, but the real league secret might actually be how good Elliott's chili is. It's divine."

Aria pulls in a rapid breath. "Share some of it with me, and I think I can keep your secret."

"Deal."

As soon as Griffin and Aria reach the production team, they're cornered by the man in charge and taken to different parts of the field. Griffin is handed a pressed game day jersey that he throws on. He is coached to act like he's running a play, stop, then turn and catch a bottle of Level Up, an icy-blue drink. Griffin leans into the act—now having more experience under his belt—and begins enjoying himself. He hits his line every time after he catches the bottle tossed by an off-camera team member: "Time to level up!"

"You're a natural," the producer calls out.

They only need a few takes, and by the end, Griffin is wondering if Aria was right, if maybe he has other talents hidden under the surface. Not that he has aspirations to become an actor, but if he can pick up these skills, what else could he learn?

"Nice work, Griff!" Aria calls over.

She stands on a stage with a large green screen behind it. Griffin can only guess they're going to enhance the footage to make it look like she's performing on an arena stage.

"We'll let Aria wrap her solo shot—which, let's be honest, probably won't take but a single shot with her track record—and then we'll shoot you throwing her the drink at the end."

"Sounds like a water break to me," Griffin says, and at his announcement, the filming crew breaks up. They chatter among themselves, some check their phones, and the lead producer heads over to the other leadership to discuss time checks and load out.

Griffin stands and watches Aria. She radiates so much energy when she stands on a stage, there might as well be a spotlight behind her powered only by her presence. It's the same magnetism that inspired him to belt out "Glass Heart" that very first night, but today, in Griffin's eyes, she shines even brighter.

It's as if knowing the rest of her makes the image she puts out into the world stronger. Deeper. There's no way that bringing that into her music would turn off the fans. The whole package of Aria Wilder is just like what they've already grown to love—it's just better.

Chapter 22

Aria

Griffin thinks Aria doesn't see him watching her while she lip-syncs along to "The Very Top," her song the crew picked for the shoot. It's a song about a woman being at the top of her game and all of her exes coming out of the woodwork. It's an excellent pick for the product.

Aria basks in Griffin's attention, feeling more energy in each step, actually pressing into the vocals, even though a recorded track will play in the final commercial. Aria suspects Griffin's actually come to categorize her as a friend; hopefully it's not just her projecting her own feelings on him. He's not *that* good of an actor, even if he's come miles since that very first time she pulled him onstage and he almost melted into an embarrassed puddle.

"All right, we got the shot!" the producer calls out with a slap on her clipboard. "Five-minute break, then we go to the final shot with Griffin."

Aria steps down off the collapsible stage, and Griffin meets her, a bottle of Level Up held out.

"Wanna get a sip and really get into it?" he asks.

Aria looks left then right. "Don't tell anyone, but I hate the stuff. It's got a weird aftertaste."

"All for the cause, I guess," Griffin says.

Aria shrinks a little. She doesn't want Griffin to think she's a sellout. "Well, I don't mean it that way. I'm sure other people love it, and of course we've got this setup between us."

Griffin looks away. "You know, I was starting to have so much fun with it, I forgot it's all a setup for a bit." There's a wistfulness to his voice Aria can't help but notice.

Aria reaches out and grasps his bicep, taken aback by the firmness of it. "I don't see any issue with leaning into the fun. I'm enjoying our time together. I mean, you're way better than I expected."

Griffin laughs. "And what did you expect?"

Aria won't say it. Griffin is already sorely misunderstood about the depth of what he has to offer the world. She won't pile on by admitting that she expected the professional athlete stereotypes.

"Come on. You can tell me."

Aria sighs. She'd rather not, but at Griffin's request she elaborates. "You're not like the typical pro player. Trust me, I've come across many—and from all different leagues—and most of them want money, women, parties, fame, and nothing else. Let me just say, none of them would have gone out of their way to offer me a ride when my driver ghosted."

"Not even basic decency, huh?" Griffin says.

If only he understood. It's more than basic decency. It's being considerate of others, seeing beyond oneself. Kindness. It's a groundedness that requires resistance to all the forces of fame, the ones that promise the famous person that they are the be-all and end-all—that they are of utmost importance, unlike some.

"I think it's easy in the whirlwind of it all, the admiration from their fans, to lose sight of what really matters."

"All right! Break's over!" Kelsey marches back up. "You're doing great, but we need to stay on schedule. Directors?" She marches toward the crew, who snap to attention, and soon the final segment is underway.

Aria is directed back onto the small stage in front of the mic. Griffin is set up in front of the stage where he will act like he's attending Aria's performance before tossing the bottle of Level Up to Aria.

"Aria, you leave the mic in the stand, but pretend like you're singing into it, then when Griffin throws the bottle, you catch it. Crack the lid, take a sip, then say, 'Time to level up!'"

Aria nods.

"Do we really think she should take a sip?" Griffin asks. "It seems like it would interrupt the flow."

The producer throws Griffin an offended look at his questioning, and just when Aria assumes Griffin would back down, he holds the man's eye. Is Griffin Hayes going toe-to-toe with this producer? Is this the on-the-field version of him?

"Well. I guess—"

"I'll take a drink. Probably would sell more to see a pro tight end happily drinking it."

The producer's face lights up. "That's actually a really good point. Yes, we'll have Griffin dance, take a drink, then throw it to Aria, who says the tagline."

Aria bites back the smile that teases at her lips. Did Griffin really just go out of his way to help her avoid sipping the drink she hates? He's giving every action hero a run for their money right now. Aria will need to get him a gift before this arrangement is over.

A sudden ache passes through her chest as the thought lands; inevitably this PR deal between the two of them will come to an end. She pushes it away. At this rate, maybe the two of them could stay friends. But what are the chances that Griffin would continue to find time for her in his busy schedule?

The music cuts on, and Griffin dances in front of the stage, swaying and bobbing his head along to the beat. He mouths the lyrics like any true fan and takes a healthy slug of the drink. Aria is so mesmerized she almost misses the catch when he tosses the drink her way, perfectly aimed at her hands.

She snags the bottle, beams at it, then turns back to the mic and announces, "It's time to level up!"

The producer turns to the camera operator. "We get it?"

He smiles at the playback screen. "Oh yeah! You guys are naturals."

"All right then," the producer announces. "Aria, Griffin, thank you. You're free to go! Crew, let's break down and load up ASAP. We're pushing up on the end of our time."

Aria and Griffin wander off to the side of the field, and almost instantaneously the small stage is broken into pieces and wheeled out, the cameras and sound booms packed into their travel cases, the crew scurrying quickly until they all disappear like a parade of ants carrying their spoils.

Even Kelsey disappears without a goodbye.

Aria walks out into the middle of the field, stretches out her arms, and looks up to the domed ceiling. "Wild to think you play out here every weekend—or many—you know what I mean."

Griffin joins her on the field. "I could say the same for you and all of your venues."

Aria sits and lies down on the turf. Griffin does the same.

"Usually this is never the view I'm going for on the field, but I have to say, taking a load off right now feels great."

Aria, lying beside him, laughs. "For today, it's a great view."

Griffin turns his head to look at her. "Hey. I know this might be overstepping. I'm definitely not an expert, but I was thinking about your music."

"I know I said you have more talents than just football, but I can't bring you on my songwriting team."

"Ha ha. Very funny. No, I was thinking about the pickle you're in. About how you want to dig deeper, be more vulnerable in your music . . . I think you should do it."

Aria keeps her eyes trained on the domed ceiling high above. If only he knew how impossible that is—at least at this juncture.

"Unfortunately, I have a contract for the other stuff."

"But you could blend it. The other parts of you are not separate from that music; they're just a deeper level of it. You're powerful and badass, but you also have feelings and all of the other tender parts that make us human."

Aria has considered this herself, and she doesn't necessarily disagree. But it's a risk trying to push this. There's a chance she might be able to take some of the risks she's been yearning for and still meet the brief of the album the studio requires, but what if the fans hate it? What if she lets people down?

Not to mention the fact that the record label will hold her to her contract, and if she doesn't meet their requirements, there will be delays until she creates another album. There is nothing sadder than an artist fading into irrelevance because she isn't making music.

"I don't hate the idea. I've thought about it."

"Aria, if anyone can make this work, it's you. You deserve to do the work you love."

Aria feels a flutter in her middle, and she spreads her hands out, palms down on the turf, reminding herself to keep her feet on the ground. Under this sprawling dome, row upon row of seats soaring to the heights surrounding her, Aria feels small. Especially so when she admits, "I'm afraid too."

"Yeah?"

The single syllable from Griffin floods Aria with comfort.

"What if I try it and it doesn't work? What will everyone say? I'll be a failure. Everything I worked for forgotten."

"And what if you don't try?"

Griffin doesn't know that he is asking the very question that keeps her wrestling with the possibility of the endeavor. She hasn't admitted it to anyone. Not even Bailey. But something about lying here on this massive field, two small people, makes the truth feel easy to admit.

"I'm afraid if I don't try, what I keep holding on to won't matter anymore either."

"I don't think you need advice. You already know what you need to do." Griffin says it gently, like it's a natural conclusion as opposed to a command.

Aria drops her head to the side to get a look at Griffin. Beside her he doesn't look like the professional football player the public knows and loves; he looks like her dear friend. One who deserves all the same good he wishes upon her.

"And as for you, maybe you can spread your wings too. Get involved in some things outside of football. Foster a snake from the animal shelter."

"Can't say I'm a reptile guy, but I agree. Like they say, football isn't forever, so at some point, I need to figure myself out. Let's just hope I'm not disappointed by what I find."

For a guy so capable and genuine, Griffin is a bit of a dummy when it comes to understanding himself. Surely it's as obvious to everyone else in his life as it is to Aria.

"I know I joke a lot, Griff, but I mean it. As soon as you open yourself up to new things, life will meet you there with a whole menu of options. The only thing limiting who you are is your tunnel vision."

Griffin sighs. "It's hard to become something new when you've worked your whole life to become another thing."

"Like a wise person once told me, 'If there's anyone that can do it, it's you.'"

Griffin looks over, grinning. "Using my own words against me? Sneaky but effective. I promise I'll give it some work."

"I'm always here to brainstorm. It's basically part of my job in the scope of songwriting."

Both of them look back to the dome above them.

"It must be a lot of work behind the scenes, writing the songs, getting the music right, and then having all the producers weigh in to get it ready for release. I've always wondered what goes into making a song from start to finish."

A rush of energy that feels very much like electricity runs through Aria. She can't remember the last time a friend or acquaintance had any interest in the less glamorous parts of her job. Usually the friends—the few she actually kept for any amount of time—fell away when it came to hours in the studio, reappearing when it was time for the parties or the celebrity-studded red carpets.

"I'm sure somewhere between these appearances I can give you a rundown." Aria tries hard to sound unaffected and cool.

"Lucky me."

Aria turns her head toward Griffin, and he's already looking at her. Their eyes lock, and her heart picks up. She won't look away, not when his gaze is so intense that it lights her up. The world in that moment seems to slow, to zoom in on just the two of them, and in the middle of it, the brush of his hand against hers on the turf breaks their eye contact.

Griffin tangles his fingers into hers. "I believe in you, Aria." He squeezes, then takes his hand away.

Her breath is so shallow and rapid that it's almost gone entirely, so much so that it feels like time is warping, but eventually she finds her wherewithal.

"I believe in you too, Griff. Seriously, give yourself a chance, and you'll be amazed by *you* outside of football."

And with a loud metallic *clang* like a lever being thrown, the lights around the field go out, and they're cast into darkness.

“Time to load out!” The producer’s voice calls from somewhere over in the hidden corridors of the tunnel.

Finally, with grinning faces, Aria and Griffin get to their feet to leave the field.

Never before has she wanted to stay longer on any sporting field, but here at Griffin’s side in the darkness, speaking truths to one another, she might just be able to stay forever.

Chapter 23

Griffin

Griffin is typically as strict about his phone-free practice policy as he is his diet, but when Aria texts the day after the commercial while he's in the locker room before he hits the field, he can't help but break it. He's been replaying their moment on the field over and over in his mind, and despite going back and forth, he's decided he's glad he reached out and took Aria's hand. It wasn't overtly romantic—well, at least that's what he's telling himself—but he feels less like he's about to combust now that he's made a small gesture of his feelings for her.

Admittedly, Griffin knows it's unrealistic that the genuine care he feels for her would amount to anything between them. But he also wants her to know that at this point, it's far more than just PR between them from where he stands.

Aria: I had a dream last night that I was performing, and someone in the crowd threw a bottle of Level Up at me. Hit me in the head, and I had to be airlifted out. I just HAD to tell you!

Griffin smiles to himself.

Griffin: Hopefully it wasn't me lobbing it at you in the dream. I can't promise I won't sing along, but I'd never throw things at you—concert or not.

Aria: Ha! I know.

Griffin holds the phone before him and drops onto the bench that runs behind the lockers. Teammates mill around him, some slapping his shoulder in greeting as they pass, others laughing together as they pull on their compression shirts.

On the screen, three dots scroll, and Griffin holds his breath in anticipation for Aria's message.

The phone buzzes in his palm as the message arrives.

Aria: I also realized I forgot to thank you. For getting me out of drinking it.

Griffin: I was happy to. I don't mind the stuff, and I know you have to do plenty of stuff you'd rather not.

He thinks about the album situation. It's surprising that Aria's team isn't pushing back harder on the studio's demands, but maybe they all want the same thing: for Aria to continue pumping out chart-topping hits. Every one of them benefits from it.

Not that it's his place to push, but the more he gets to know Aria, her ability to pivot, her quick-wittedness, he becomes more certain that she could meld the more introspective lyrics she wants to write with the popular beats and melodies the fans love. In fact, her fans would likely lap up a new twist.

Aria: I know. But you didn't have to, and you went out of your way.

Griffin: It was nothing. Writing any songs today?

Three dots scroll.

Aria: Ugh. Yes. And no. I have one song that's coming together.

Griffin: Just let me know if my backup vocals could come in handy.

Aria: Such a helpful guy. Speaking of which, did you see that someone leaked a clip of us on the field after the shoot yesterday?

Griffin: Huh? Looking now.

Griffin types their names into the browser, and sure enough, there they are, lying on their backs on the Wardens playing field, arms flung out to the sides. His chest tightens slightly. That was a private moment, a special one, a moment he was really hoping to keep as something only between him and Aria.

He navigates back to their text thread and types.

Griffin: Can't do anything without paparazzi, am I right?

Aria: No truer words. I guess it's another good image for the campaign, though.

Griffin stops. When they started this arrangement, it *was* a setup. He was an Aria Wilder fan with a surface-level crush; she reached even wider audiences when tied to professional sports. But now? It doesn't feel right to call it a campaign or a setup. They're texting like actual friends.

He types out a response:

Griffin: For sure. We're such great actors since we hate each other so much.

Aria: Ha ha. Fair point. This whole thing is a cakewalk now that you turned out to be not half bad.

Griffin: I'll take that as a compliment.

Aria: One of the highest regards coming from me.

Griffin smiles as he types his reply.

Griffin: And the same to you: You're not half bad either.

The three dots begin to scroll when Elliott's voice pulls Griffin from the exchange on the screen. "Hey! Griff! You in la-la land, man? We're due on the field in sixty seconds."

Griffin leaps to his feet, suddenly panicked—and surprised—at how he lost track of time. He's normally so regimented, it never crossed his mind that he wouldn't be five minutes early on the field like his high school coach instilled in him. Like he is at every practice.

Before Aria can reply, he rapid fires a text, hits Send, and tosses the phone into the locker.

Griffin: Shoot! Late to practice! Gotta go.

As he sprints toward the field, helmet in hand, Griffin wonders if she'll reply. If she'll send the message she was typing when the dots scrolled or if she'll delete that and respond only to his message about having to run. Maybe she won't respond at all.

Griffin drops into line and joins in the stretching routine.

Elliott looks over from beside him, his arm pulled across his chest and held in place. "You all right? It's not like you to be late."

"I wasn't late. I was just later than usual." Griffin can't help but smile. He did technically make it on time, and he also got to chat with Aria before practice.

It's the best of both worlds.

Elliott laughs. "Alrighty. Just don't let whatever this is throw you off your game."

Griffin nods, but before he can reply, the coach takes the field and greets the team. Griffin has never allowed anything in his life to interfere with football, always fiercely focused on his goal of making it and succeeding in the league. At some point he *became* the sport. But now, with Aria's arrival into his life, his view is undoubtedly being opened up. The time they spend together pulls him out of his rigidity and inspires him to see the broadness of life.

If ever there was a time when something—or someone—might ever-so-briefly distract him from the game, it's now, and it's Aria Wilder.

Chapter 24

Aria

When Griffin's hurried text about running off to practice comes through, Aria is in the process of typing out a message to invite him over to see the studio. Only once she hit Send on that text about their "arrangement" did she realize her misstep—that might suggest there was nothing between the two of them beyond the scheduled events. Even if she's been pushing away a heart flutter here or there around him—okay, *more* than here or there—it's undeniable that they're actual friends at this point. Even if the formal appearances are orchestrated by the publicity teams, the fun that happens between them is genuine.

Aria truly and wholeheartedly likes Griffin.

She replies first to his hasty message.

Aria: Oops! Sorry to keep you.

Aria takes her time with the next message, knowing he won't get it until he's back at his locker. She types and edits, and eventually she hits Send.

> **Aria:** Would you want to come see the studio this week? When we were chatting on the field—a moment now so rudely broadcast online—you mentioned you'd like to see more about the process. Honestly, it can really help to have fresh, positive energy in the space, so perhaps you'll even lend some inspiration. Let me know.

Aria slips into some exercise wear and bundles a coat over the top. She pulls on long socks before donning her tennis shoes and pressing her earbuds into her ears. She pushes out of her front door to take a walk around the property.

The leaves are ablaze in a fall mix of reds, oranges, yellows, and browns, and the cold air feels good against her face. Like it's waking her up to the world. She puts on a podcast about mindfulness and meditation and heads for the short trail that loops the wooded part of her land. She's always looking for respite from the bright lights, the sequins, the heavy makeup—a place or a moment where she can simply be. Sometimes these walks even bring moments of musical inspiration as well.

When Aria returns to the house an hour later, she warms up with a shower and gets dressed in her most comfortable jeans and a sweater.

Bailey is in the kitchen blending a smoothie when Aria enters the room.

"I invited Griffin over," Aria says, pulling open the fridge. "He's at practice, so he won't reply until later."

Bailey keeps her hands planted firmly on the blender but looks over her shoulder at her sister. "Yeah? What's it for this time?"

It's not that Aria has been hiding things from Bailey. The depth of her friendship with Griffin is all over the internet for anyone with a Wi-Fi signal to see. But she also hasn't yet divulged the rest.

"Just . . . because."

"What? Like, you're actually friends? I get that he's a good guy under the football pads, but you're not a friendship person like that."

Aria emerges from the fridge with a juice in hand and swats playfully at Bailey. "Hey, now! Remember all the weirdness I endured over the years at the hands of 'friends'? Maybe you could be happy that I actually found a friend I can trust."

Bailey sighs. "Fair."

Many of the friends Aria had before she hit it big fell away when she started to edge truly into the public eye. Maybe it was jealousy or difficulty in relating to her new lifestyle, but not one of those relationships endured. There were also the new friends Aria made around the same time, and all of those turned out to be people less interested in her and more interested in the doors her fame could open for them. Once Aria was in the public eye—and from such a young age—it became difficult to trust others. She was friends with some other Hollywood types—a few actresses, another singer, and a model—but all of them eventually moved to LA. Generally they saw each other at award shows or fashion events—when Aria summoned the energy to make it to them.

"There's something about Griffin that's different." Aria leans onto the counter, the bottle pressed between her palms. "He knows the fame game, so he's obviously not a grifter. But he's also a regular person. There's none of the fake bravado or the one-upping or the 'too cool' attitude. He's kind, and we laugh together. Besides you, he's the only person I've been able to let my guard down around."

Bailey gasps in mock horror. "Aria Wilder took off her armor with a stranger?" She puts the back of her hand to her forehead as if she's a Victorian woman on the verge of fainting.

Aria grins. Bailey might be joking, but she's not off the mark. What's worked for Aria so far in life has been keeping her walls up, her circle close, and her heart off-limits to anyone but Bailey—and her parents, who have floated to the edges of her life.

"He's trustworthy."

"If you say it, I believe it." Bailey flips the switch on the blender, and it churns loudly for a moment before she shuts it off and removes the pitcher. She turns her back to Aria and reaches for a glass inside the cabinet. "Can I ask you something else?"

"Shoot." Aria senses what this question will be, and frankly, at this point she wants to discuss it too.

"Are there *feelings* feelings in the mix here? Half the internet is already talking about how it's a budding romance, even though the PR spin is 'best friends this, best friends that.' Everyone knows that friendship is the basis for great romance."

Aria pulls a smile, then releases it. "Realistically? No. How would it even work?"

Bailey shrugs. "Your schedules are lining up pretty okay for these publicity deals."

"You know I hate all this stuff."

"Refusing to be vulnerable might take away the chance of being hurt, but it also takes away the possibility that you might eventually get what your heart desires."

Aria has been burned in love just as she was burned in friendship. One ex turned out to be using her in an attempt to launch his own country music career. Another was a fellow celebrity who got prickly as soon as her fame began to outpace his. So far all life had taught Aria Wilder about love is that it wasn't made for people like her.

Even if her love ballads made claims otherwise.

Aria closes her eyes to make saying it easier. "At the shoot the other day, he went to bat so I didn't have to drink the ghastly sports drink. He grabbed my hand on the field, and it was like my insides lit up like a Christmas tree." Aria's chest swells as she puts herself mentally back in his presence, that comforting force, strong and gentle at once. "Obviously, he's a hunk."

"*People*'s sexiest guy, right?"

"Runner-up, I think."

Bailey barks a laugh. "Right. That changes *everything*."

"I'm not sure he feels the same. I think he's just genuinely kind and attentive to everyone. He does all these sweet gentlemanly things like he's from another century. You can tell he was raised to keep others in mind. Honestly, I think I've just been so starved of genuinely good people—aside from you—for so long that my brain is making it into something it's not."

"So he's perfect, is what you're saying?"

Aria bites her lip. In many ways, Griffin Hayes is perfect. In many ways, Griffin is the type of person Aria wasn't sure she'd ever be able to have in her life. Someone who might be a beast on the football field, massive in physical stature, but in person, one-on-one, entirely nonthreatening. Someone interested in knowing the details of who she is beyond the stage.

Then again, this whole connection started through their publicists, so Aria won't get ahead of herself.

"He might be, Bails. But for now, he's become a good friend, and I know better than to let that slip away."

"You'd better let me get in on the hang then—if it's friends only."

Aria feels a prickle of possessiveness. "*If* he says yes, then you can join us for a couple minutes."

Her phone that's tucked into her jeans back pocket buzzes, and Aria slips it into her hand. Her heart picks up at the sight of Griffin's name, and she rushes to read the message.

> **Griffin:** A backstage look at your recording studio? Heck yes. Sign me up for the audio tour if there's one as well. I promise I'll be on my best behavior.

Bailey peeks over Aria's shoulder and eyes the text. "Oh my gosh." She grabs Aria's shoulders and shakes. "You're holding out on me! He's so into you."

Aria turns the phone over, face down onto the counter. "He's into learning more about music. Let's not get carried away."

Bailey pours the thick smoothie into the glass, then shoots her sister a look. "Whatever you say."

As she glides out of the room, Aria is wondering the same, though. Is it possible the sparks she's feeling are happening on Griffin's end too? Surely that would be too good to be true.

Chapter 25

Griffin

His phone is the first thing Griffin checks after practice, bursting to see if Aria sent him a text reply. His heart leaps when he sees her name on the screen, along with a photo of her he snapped at her concert as the image icon. His pulse races, despite completing the solid twenty minutes of team cooldown required after every practice.

He drops his helmet at his feet, forgotten, at the sight of not one, but two messages.

It feels like winning the Super Bowl. (Not that he'd tell the guys.)

Aria: Oops! Sorry to keep you.

Aria: Would you want to come see the studio this week? When we were chatting on the field—a moment now so rudely broadcast online—you mentioned you'd like to see more about the process. Honestly it can really help to have fresh, positive energy in the space, so perhaps you'll even lend some inspiration. Let me know.

He doesn't stop long enough to think before he hammers out a message to accept.

Griffin: A backstage look at your recording studio? Heck yes. Sign me up for the audio tour if there's one as well. I promise I'll be on my best behavior.

The lazy smile plastered on Griffin's face as he tucks the phone away in his locker lingers as he pulls off his practice jersey, then drops onto the bench to pull off his cleats.

Elliott stops at his locker, squirting his water bottle into his mouth, then turns to Griffin on the bench beside him. "Dude, you look like you're out to lunch again." He laughs. "That smile. You got a girl or what?"

Griffin looks up at his friend. His eyebrows creep upward as he wonders about the best way to answer the question. Obviously he doesn't "have" Aria, but he has feelings for her. There's no denying that. "Well. It's . . . you know . . ."

"Wow." Elliott throws out a hand as if he's blocking something. "This is Aria stuff, isn't it? You caught feelings, even though it's supposed to be business only."

Griffin internally grinds to a halt at the mention of "*supposed to be business only.*" Could he be reading too much into this? He and Aria have a good rapport, they have fun together, but without this PR scaffolding around them, would she even want to be friends with him? He reminds himself of her latest message.

"She invited me to her studio—out of the public eye—so I think it's safe to say I'm in the *real* friend zone."

Elliott pulls off his jersey and uses it to wipe some sweat from his hairline. "But is the friend zone where you want to be?"

Griffin looks left and right to make sure the players around them aren't eavesdropping. It's Professional League 101 that you don't bring your personal business to the locker room. You check it at the stadium gates, to be picked up on close of practice or game play. He and Elliott have been tight for years now, so between them it's different. Probably his teammates wouldn't mind him dissecting his romantic prospects—or lack thereof—but at minimum, they'd never let him live it down. Several of them are still calling him Aria Wilder's number one fan. Little do they know he sort of enjoys that.

Griffin leans in. "Honestly?" He takes a long, slow breath. "I want out of the friend zone and into the boyfriend zone."

Elliott grins and slaps him on the arm. "You are such a softie, Griff. All 250 pounds of you."

Griffin throws back his head. "It was you who got me into this. If you hadn't left for those snacks, the fans would've been way more focused on you and Cassandra, The Beautiful Couple."

Elliott laughs. "We *both* know that's garbage. And you didn't have to take the PR deal. I think you knew what you were doing, signing on the dotted line to spend extracurricular time with the woman you were already crushing on."

Elliott isn't wrong, but Griffin also didn't anticipate liking Aria as much as he does. He couldn't have known that in addition to being talented and charming, she would be smart and insightful and kind. For all he knew, Aria could've been a monster offstage. Many celebrities have reputations for being demanding and entitled when they're not under the bright lights. Fame gets to some people, and professional athletes are not immune. There aren't whispers about Aria, and now Griffin knows firsthand why that is.

"For now, I'm just going to accept this invitation and have a grand old time at her studio."

"I guess it's a good sign she invited you. If she hated you, she'd keep it business only."

Griffin's face heats. "We have fun together."

"Dang it, man, you're going to have to keep that under wraps in here." Elliott looks around the room. "But now you gotta keep me updated because I was there from the start, and I'm invested now. You got me?"

Griffin laughs, then gets up and starts gathering his items for the shower. "I promise. There may not end up being anything to share, but if there is, you're my first stop."

Elliott slaps his back. "I'm going to go get a massage. It's Wednesday, so Katerina's here."

Katerina is a gruff, fiftysomething woman from the former Soviet Union who has a reputation for her no-nonsense approach to releasing the toughest muscle knots, even on players more than twice her size.

"She worked wonders on my thigh last week, so I'll let someone else get a turn."

"Your loss," Elliott calls over his shoulder as he heads toward the physical therapy area where the massage tables are set up on Wednesdays.

The first thing Griffin does in his absence is pull his phone back out. He smiles as he reads Aria's reply.

Aria: Fab! Tomorrow?

Griffin: Sure! I have early practice, so I'll be done by lunchtime.

Aria: Cool. Just text me when you're heading over. I'll be working down there off and on all day. Hit the star button at the gate, and we'll buzz you in.

Griffin types "Awesome" and goes back and forth on whether to add an exclamation mark. Some of his teammates would say no to the exclamation—the enthusiasm it evokes is incompatible with "having swag"—but Griffin hasn't ever been interested in swag.

He is interested in Aria.

So he adds the exclamation mark, hits Send, then heads for the showers.

He's ready to wrap up this day so he can get on to the next.

Chapter 26

Aria

Aria and Bailey pick up the main level of the house on Thursday morning, Aria running the vacuum over the rugs after Bailey wipes down the counters. Fortunately, Aria's biweekly cleaning service came only two days earlier, so the house is in good shape to begin with. Still, she wants to put her best foot forward for Griffin.

Her mother would always shine up their small-town abode for guests, and Aria, who rarely hosts guests, figures she might as well follow her mother's example.

"I went ahead and ordered stuff for lunch," Bailey says as Aria returns the vacuum to the laundry room. "I got a variety of salads, sandwiches, and a few pastries from the deli."

"Perfect. And the drinks are already well stocked." Aria glances at her phone, noting the time. "He'll be here in a couple hours or so, and I'm going to get a head start on writing." Aria waves, then stops briefly at a console table to fluff the flower arrangement.

"Holler if you need anything," Bailey says.

Aria takes off down the stairs and opens the studio for the day. She pulls back the curtains that cover the walk-out sliding doors, flips on the lights, and turns on the recording equipment. She lights a scented candle on a side table and ignites the electric fireplace at the end of the room.

Hopefully Griffin likes it. And fortunately, since he's already part of the fame game, he won't think she's showing off by inviting him into this place. When Aria first got the house and brought her "friends" over, one of them took offense, claiming that Aria knew she was going after her own singing career, and that showing off the home studio was only rubbing salt in her very raw wounds. Naturally, that friendship soon expired, leaving Aria bruised and weary.

Of course she would never intentionally hurt someone like that. She'd innocently thought the friend would want to see it—that she'd be happy for her.

Today Aria has no such worries. A few nervous flutters rise in her middle when she thinks about tinkering in the studio with Griffin alongside her, but only because she hopes she doesn't sound incompetent in front of him. Songs undergo a tremendous amount of work to get from idea to concert-ready, and although Aria expects Griffin will be as easygoing about this as he has been thus far, there's also simply not the same luster to a first-draft song.

Aria does her best to focus for the morning, but despite her best efforts, she finds herself checking the time frequently and getting pulled off track by thoughts of Griffin. She manages to draft the first version of the football player song from notes into a song about the quarterback and the theater girl getting a happily ever after. It's a song squarely in the Aria Wilder safe zone.

When Aria finishes, she's happy with it. She's not enchanted. She's not excited. She doesn't love it. But she knows it'll go over well with the others, and for today that's the assignment.

Before long, she migrates upstairs and picks at lunch. Bailey asks her why she's not eating, and Aria says she's just not that hungry. Honestly, it's because she's suddenly extremely nervous for Griffin Hayes to be in her house.

She's become an expert at keeping her walls up, and even though Griffin has shown himself to be worthy of slipping behind them, it feels like a great risk to bring anyone new into her home.

Bailey reaches over the table and squeezes her arm. "It's okay, sis. He's not going to break your world with one visit to the studio."

Aria lets out a breath that'd been crowding her chest. Her shoulders drop. "You're right. It's my buddy, Griff."

Just hearing the words come out of her mouth sends a smile across her lips, and in perfect timing, the landline connected to the gate call box begins to ring.

"Speak of the devil," Bailey says before loading a forkful of salad into her mouth.

The gate camera broadcasts to a screen built into the kitchen cabinetry, and it shows a new Bronco, window rolled down, and Griffin sitting in the driver's seat. Aria's body warms at the sight of him. Even on the grainy, low-quality screen, he looks like a Greek god.

She hits the button to open the gate and pulls the cover over the screen.

Bailey grabs the plastic container holding her salad and takes off. "I'm letting you have your privacy—see how good I'm being here?"

Aria laughs. "We'll see you later."

Moments later, a firm but friendly knock comes at the door, and Aria skips over and yanks it open. There Griffin stands with his hands folded in front of him grasping a bouquet of flowers. He wears jeans, a knit quarter-zip sweater, and leather boots.

Aria waves him inside as she ignores her racing pulse. "You clean up nice."

Griffin smiles as he pats the front of his sweater. "I wasn't sure how to play it, honestly. I figured I didn't need to show up in sweats, but I also wasn't going to pull out the suit again."

"The woes of dressing a professional athlete."

As Aria stands before him in the entryway, they both glance at the bouquet in his hands.

"I'm realizing now maybe I shouldn't have brought these," Griffin says.

"No!" Aria reaches out for the flowers and gently takes them. "They're lovely."

Griffin scratches his head like he's regretting the choice. "I didn't want to show up empty-handed, but you said you already had food covered."

Aria turns and leads the way through the grand entrance into the open living area with the vaulted ceiling, and onward into the kitchen. She fills a vase with some water and deposits the flowers. "I'll trim them later on, but they'll make a great addition to the kitchen. Hungry?" Aria gestures to the food Bailey arranged.

"I'm a professional football player. I'm always hungry." Griffin leans against the counter and looks around the house. "Is it always this tidy?"

"Pretty much, but I might have picked up a little this morning. Wouldn't want you to have to dodge piles of laundry."

"I honestly wouldn't mind seeing a pile or two of laundry around here. Just shows that you're human," Griffin says.

Aria smiles as she hands him a plate, and after he's loaded it, she leads him down the stairs and into the recording studio. Now that Griffin is here, the worries that kept bubbling up earlier have abated, and Aria feels a peacefulness settle inside her.

At the base of the stairs she points out the beverage fridge over by her writing corner. "Anything you want to drink is in there, so help yourself." She grabs her favorite cardigan from the mixing table and pulls it on.

Griffin sets down his plate on the table and turns around, almost in wonder, examining the place. "This is where it all happens, huh?"

Aria props her hands on her hips. "For the most part. The new stuff always comes out of here first. We'll record final tracks elsewhere, but this is pretty much where every song is born."

Griffin smiles and waggles his brow. "Can't believe I'm here. So, tell me about it. What's the process? Where do the ideas come from? How do you keep variety in the actual melody?" He grabs a sandwich from the plate and takes a bite.

Aria laughs. "Well, that's a lot to answer at once, but we've got time." She wanders over to the writing corner, bends to her guitar case, and uncovers the instrument. "This here is Old Faithful, the guitar I've had since I started out. She never goes onstage, but I work out all my new melodies on her before I take it to the piano."

"That's so cool. And it's almost like you get to keep a special piece of it to yourself."

Aria looks again at the guitar. In all this time, she hadn't ever considered that, but alas, Griffin is showing her what it is to see with fresh eyes. "You know, you're right. I cherish it, even though it's only an old beginner model."

"But one that was *your* beginning."

Aria sets the instrument back into the case and leaves it open. She picks up the writing notebook. "This very high-tech notebook is where I work out lyrics—for better or worse. I always write in pencil." She glances over at the electronic equipment, a walled-off microphone and a few table boards. "I won't bore you with the details of the mixing equipment, but I can record vocals in here with pretty good quality."

"Not to mention there's a great fireplace."

A laugh spills out of Aria. "You don't miss a thing."

"So do I get to see you at work?" Griffin looks away for a moment. "There's no pressure."

Aria takes in a breath, then lets it out as she crosses the room to him. "In theory, yes. It's just that this new album isn't coming easy. I have one song—with a football theme, thanks to our time together—but that's it."

"You're trying your best but your heart's not in it?"

"Bingo. Everything's coming out flat and boring because that's how I feel about it."

"We can get you over the hump." Griffin sets down the sandwich and dusts off his hands. "The lyrics are the problem?"

Aria nods. "To steal a slogan from some of our friends, I just want to 'level up.' Just because everyone else is all right with me doing the same thing over and over again doesn't mean that I am too."

"Grab your lyrics book, Aria. We're going to brainstorm."

Aria can't help the smile that cracks across her face. And it's hard not to feel confident when the mighty Griffin Hayes is so certain and enthusiastic that she can get to the place she wants to be.

Aria drops onto the writing sofa and picks up the notebook.

Griffin paces in front of the coffee table. "All right, so go-to categories for the Aria Wilder brand. First I can think of is love, heartbreak, and crushes."

Aria nods. "And I can't get away from that entirely."

"Of course not, but what if you just dig deeper into each? What's the problem with the current songs?"

"They're too bubblegum and young. It's what I wrote as a twentysomething who thought love looked like being swept off her feet or the popular guy picking her."

"So, what is it now?"

Griffin's eyes land on Aria like they have a weight behind them, and she can't look away. She gulps hard, pulls in a breath, and yanks her gaze from his. "It's showing up for someone else, it's sticking around, faults and all. It's the simple stuff of noticing when she might need a hand up or remembering the work issue that's been bothering her."

"Why can't you write that? What if you blended the two? You're a storyteller, so you can weave them together."

Aria thinks about the rest of the experiences she herself is wading through right now: the terrifying feeling of falling for someone, the uncertainty of letting feelings grow, the temptation to shut down and deny, the ease of a life with high walls around it.

"It's worth a shot," Aria says.

She flips open the notebook and scribbles down some ideas, feeling a lightness in her chest, a freshness in her mind, a feeling deliciously like inspiration. She glances over at Griffin.

"I might regret telling you this, but trying something different—even if I'm spinning it to look like the same—is terrifying."

He wanders over and takes a seat at the far end of the couch. "The best things lie outside of your comfort zone—that's what my peewee coach told me, and apparently I took it to heart."

Aria tilts her head sideways. "Isn't football 100 percent your safe zone?"

Griffin massages his chin, his brow dropping seriously. "Yes and no. I told you that my family is traditionally all medical professionals, but they're also all overachievers. If someone is a nurse, they're the best nurse on the unit, or if they're a doctor, they're practicing and doing research. They're always unit leads. All of them graduated with advanced degrees, top of their classes. I guess I latched onto football because it was something I could do. School was all right for me, but I wasn't a science wiz like the rest of them. Mostly I got accolades for athletics. My parents were proud—even if they stood out like a sore thumb at the games. Being excellent at something—that for me turned out to be football—was the only way I could prove that I belonged."

Aria's heart squeezes for him. It would be easy to assume that this big, burly football player is a person so physically powerful that he could never suffer like regular people, but Griffin makes it quite clear otherwise. Aria feels a pull to go to him and take him in her arms.

Instead, she reaches out and runs the tips of her fingers down his back. Maybe she's imagining it, but it feels like he leans in.

"Oh, Griff. I'm sorry. You know there's no way anyone wouldn't want you in their family. You're just as golden as the newscasters promise. Even more when someone gets to know the full you."

Griffin nods. "I'm still trying to work out *who* that is—the full me. But I did promise to get working on it."

Aria smiles at him. "And while we're trading war stories, I'll admit that I started writing music and performing to escape feeling invisible in my small-town life. I loved my family and my town, but everyone there was fine with staying small and quiet. It felt suffocating to me, and I just had to bust out. Sometimes I worry that my parents will think I'm not grateful for them raising me or that I don't respect their way of life, but I do everything to make sure they know that's not true. I was just born to feel the bright lights of a stage. Whether it's a dive bar or a sold-out arena, it's simply something I cannot live without."

"You were born for this stuff," Griffin says. "It's obvious."

It's a concept that's been part of the narrative of her life for so long that Aria had almost forgotten the truth in it. She really is born for this work, and she owes it to herself and her fans to put her all into it.

"I think you're right about the music. I have to try to do it my way."

Griffin remains quiet. Aria clicks into her focused mode, and it's almost as if he melts into the background. She scribbles lyrics, then strums on the guitar. Over at the piano, Aria moves along the keys, knitting together chords that sound like her—but new. With every inch of progress, Aria's optimism lifts. She loses herself in the music, forgetting all inhibition.

When she glances over at Griffin, he's mesmerized just like he was at that very first concert. It's the first time Aria's ever allowed someone so close to her work before. Well, aside from Bailey.

Griffin doesn't say a word and only rests back into the sofa like he's planning to stick around.

After an hour or so, Aria's shoulders begin to ache, and her throat grows dry. She gets up from behind the mixing tables and bends to look through the mini fridge.

"I think I have the basis for three or four songs. I like the way they're sort of connected by the chord progression similarity but totally distinct with the beats I played around with."

Aria pops upright, cracks the can of sparkling water, and drinks. In the pause, she falters. "Sorry! Did you want something? I have a tendency to just get lost in my own world when I really get into it. Hence why I don't usually have visitors."

"I count myself lucky to have the front-row seat. And I'm good on drinks."

Aria drinks again, then props a hand on her hip. "What did you think of what you heard?"

"I thought it was cool. It's definitely recognizable as your style, but it's got a fresh twist. I think your people will love it."

"Thanks." For the first time in weeks, Aria feels sincerely confident about the future, about the prospect of making this next album something she's proud to stand beside. "It means a lot coming from my 'number one fan.'"

"Hey! No need for the air quotes. I wear the title as a badge of honor."

Aria feels her cheeks heat, then the warmth spreads across her, and suddenly she's desperate for fresh air. "I'm going to get a breather."

She points toward the slider door and walks over to pull it open and step out onto the small patio outside. Griffin follows behind her into the cool fall air.

When Aria turns back to look at him, despite the crispness in the air, the warmth he inspired still lingers, like the outside elements have no effect.

Chapter 27

Griffin

Griffin isn't sure there are words to describe what he just witnessed from Aria in her studio. There are people who are put on earth with very specific talents, and there isn't a single doubt that Aria is made to create music. The media focuses on what she's wearing, which events she attends, how much fans are willing to fork over for tickets to her most desirable shows. She is made into social media memes weekly, and her fashion choices are constantly making lists. When there's distance, it's easy to make it all about the superficial. But what Griffin just witnessed blows all of that out of the water.

Aria makes her own music like a baker makes their goods from scratch.

Despite rumors—ones Griffin never believed, mind you—Aria isn't propped up by a team of behind-the-scenes writers and musicians who carry the real talent. She is a powerhouse from front to back.

When she turns to look at him, the wooded landscape past the patio frames her, and leaves fall in the trees as if announcing her presence. Aria is always beautiful, but today, up close and with her truest self on display—talents, fears, passion—she is gorgeous. The sunshine filters through the leaves and highlights her as if giving her a full-body halo.

Aria pulls in a deep breath. "The fresh air always feels good on a day like this."

She rubs her arms, as if feeling the chill, despite her eagerness to get outside, and wanders the small patio. Griffin thinks about going to her and wrapping an arm around her. He isn't wearing a jacket, or he'd offer it.

Aria stops at the edge of the patio and looks out into the thicket of trees. "Thanks for coming today."

"Thanks for . . ." Aria has brought so much good to his life in the past weeks, it's hard to know what Griffin should thank her for, but undoubtedly there's a list. "Honestly, thank you for reminding me that there's more to life than just football."

Aria whips around, her eyes bright with surprise. "Yeah? I thought I was just pointing out the obvious."

Griffin's face breaks into a smile. "Sometimes my hyper focus helps with the game, but all of us guys have that ticking time clock, knowing that eventually our time on the field will end. You've shown me just how much there is out there. You've made me consider that I might have more to offer too."

Aria closes the gap between them, gives his arm a friendly squeeze, and says, "Well, without your belief in me, what just happened in there *wouldn't* have been a thing. Guess we're a pretty good team after all."

"Don't tell Kelsey, or she'll have a camera crew start following us behind the scenes."

Aria throws back her head and laughs, and an ache to hold her runs through him.

Griffin can't help himself. He reaches out and places his arms around her. "You were incredible in there, Aria. It blows my mind."

Aria drops her gaze bashfully, and Griffin detects a pinkness rising in her cheeks. "It's nice to share it with someone. There aren't that many people I can trust."

Griffin thinks of his own experiences with fame, the opportunists that've come his way. At least he can easily find friendship and shared experiences with teammates to whom he has little to offer besides friendship. But Aria is solo. What an extraordinary stroke of luck it's been for him not only to have gotten to be close to Aria off script but also to get to know her, get to know the parts that stay hidden. He's not one of a sea of friends as he'd assumed; he's one of a few in a small circle.

"I know the whole 'number one fan' thing is a joke, but know that I do genuinely admire what you're doing. Thank you for trusting me."

Aria's hands run from Griffin's arms to his back, and she draws closer. Every inch of her that touches him is a sensation more intense than being tackled by a defensive player, like his nerves go haywire only for her. As if he's programmed to desire her. Griffin's breath deepens, and he can't pull his eyes away from hers.

He desperately wants to kiss this woman.

Not only because of how she mesmerizes him, but more so

because of the fact that she's let him in, behind her walls, and who she is behind them eclipses even her brightest concert act. Being next to her might be the best Griffin has felt in years.

She is absolute magic.

Aria looks up at him, and she floats closer. "You are easy to trust, Griff."

In her blue eyes is an intensity Griffin hasn't seen before, a vibrance that comes from within.

"The things about me—growing up and the unknowns of the future—aren't things I talk to people about either. My friends are my teammates, and we talk workouts, nutrition, and sometimes grab the occasional game of laser tag."

Aria's mouth lifts into a smile at the corners.

"I guess that's my way of saying I trust you too."

Their faces are held mere inches away from one another, and Griffin's heart is pounding so hard he can hear the blood rushing through him.

He lowers his face, and as Aria's lips part, he reaches a hand up, places a single finger under her chin, and brings her face to his.

The rest of the world falls away, and Griffin's every fiber is focused on Aria's warm mouth wrapped in his.

He can't be sure, but this just might be what falling for someone feels like in real time.

Chapter 28

Aria

When Griffin props his finger under her chin, Aria melts. Griffin sits closer to Aria's heart than anyone has in a long time. Never once when the arrangement kicked off did she think that she and Griffin would talk about meaningful things; never once did she think she'd discover he was so remarkable. Most of the athletes she's come in contact with haven't been the deepest of beings.

Everything about Griffin so far has been one happy surprise.

His face lowers before hers, and her eyes are trained on his. Aria can tell by the way he looks at her, the desire flickering, that he wants the same as she does. She trusts him.

So she closes her eyes and lets herself fall.

Aria weaves her arms around his neck and lets his hulking figure hold the weight of her. It feels like being caught midair when their lips meet, her breath knocked from her at the very moment she's held by someone big and strong and bound to keep her safe.

Aria stays in the kiss for as long as she can before breaking it for a hungry breath.

As she pulls back, her eyes popping open, she meets his gaze. Something like surprise passes between the two. As if both of them—despite the force driving them together—realize that this kiss is way off script. That despite their talks, never have they broached this.

Aria's hand goes to her mouth and tentatively touches her delicate lips. Her breath is still light and quick, and beneath her, her legs are wobbly.

Aria steps back, and reflexively, Griffin pushes his hands into his pockets, hanging his head ever so slightly.

Aria mentally fumbles around for the next thing to do. This kiss itself was electric—as evidenced by the full-body shiver still running through her. Despite this fact, plus the fact that Griffin might be the highest-quality guy she's ever come to know, letting things between them slip into romance is a big step. A scary one.

"Well, that was unexpected." Griffin looks up from under his brow sheepishly.

Aria realizes the silence has sat between them a beat too long, and this is surely Griffin's attempt to smooth things over.

"Yes! Sorry. Gosh. *Should* I say sorry? I don't even know."

Griffin reaches up and massages the back of his neck like he, too, is stumped by the situation they've found themselves in.

He looks adorable when he does so, and part of Aria wishes

their whole PR commitment had never existed. That they were just two regular people free to kiss as much as they wanted without anyone trying to take their picture, free of the harsh spotlights of fame, free of the public's demands.

"You don't have to say anything, Aria." Griffin's words are comforting and heartbreaking at once.

It's him acknowledging the fact that it's not a clear-cut situation. That he, too, sees the intricacy here.

"I don't want to upset you." Aria squeezes her hands together as if she could wring the discomfort out.

"You're not. I'm not sure you ever could." Griffin looks at his wristwatch. "But I should probably get going. Another morning practice tomorrow, and we have a team breakfast before."

Something in Aria's chest hitches. Maybe it's guilt. Maybe it's disappointment in this day ending this way. Maybe it's a longing for clarity in the middle of this muddy situation. But most likely it's at the prospect of distance growing between them.

"Of course. Totally. I hope I didn't keep you." Aria resists the urge to roll her eyes at her clumsy comment.

"I hope I didn't keep you."

Yes, by kissing him, then only realizing after the fact that maybe just following the whims of her feelings isn't a great plan. That in fact there was *no* plan.

Griffin pulls the sliding door open, then stands back and holds out a hand to indicate she go first. Faithful Griff, always a gentleman, even—apparently—in the face of a surprise kiss.

"Thank you," Aria says quietly as she passes through.

She walks slowly enough for Griffin to close the door and

keep up behind her, but Aria keeps the momentum going through the studio, up the stairs, through the kitchen, then into the entryway to the door.

She pulls it open, and Griffin pauses before he steps out, standing there face-to-face with Aria.

The same position they were in just moments earlier locking lips.

"Regardless of"—Griffin gestures widely with a single hand—"any of that, everything I said stands. You're killing it, and staying true to yourself is the way to your next album being your best yet."

"Thanks." Gone is Aria's ease, gone is the bubbly banter that's become their routine. She speaks plainly.

Griffin cracks a smile. "And that's coming from your number one fan."

He reaches out and squeezes the top of her arm before turning quickly for the door. He steps out onto the wraparound porch and digs into his pocket. Once he has retrieved the keys, he unlocks the car with a click of the remote and turns back—very briefly—to throw her a single wave.

Aria returns the gesture, pulls a tight smile, then shuts the door. Only then does she let herself fall back against it and let her head loll back. She closes her eyes, and inside her eyelids, the kiss replays over and over again.

What on earth is she supposed to do about that? Surely marrying their PR arrangements with real feelings is only a recipe for disaster.

Aria's heart is still hammering, and there is no question it's out of fear. She's already let her walls down enough with Griffin, and now this happens. Opening the gates to feelings and dating would only make her more vulnerable, only make the ultimate letdown hurt more. Even if it's Griffin, even if most of her brain agrees that he won't hurt her like people did in the past, it's a terrifying concept to consider.

Griffin would probably give great advice on the situation if he weren't already wound up in it.

When she's ready, Aria will have to talk it over with Bailey. She always knows what to do.

Chapter 29

Griffin

Griffin makes plans with Elliott to stop at Enzo's for dinner after practice on Friday. The Wardens have a bye this week. Usually, Griffin gets antsy on those weeks, wishing for a game even when his body demands rest. He's always better when he stays in his routines and focused on his goals.

But usually he wouldn't be fresh off a kiss with Aria Wilder.

"So, did *you* kiss *her*?" Elliott sits across from Griffin at a sticky-top table.

Griffin bobs his head from side to side. "Yes. But also I think there was a lean in from her side. It wasn't as if I swooped in fast and surprised her. We were both in the moment. Like a mutual thing."

Elliott sips on the foamy top of his beer, a treat he only affords himself on a bye week during season. "Huh."

"It's weird, isn't it?"

Griffin has already filled Elliott in on Aria's reaction to the kiss and his hasty departure following it. Memories of it have bounced in his mind, ricocheting around without any resolution for the past twenty-four hours. He even dreamed about it last night.

Aria looked so shocked by it that surely her feelings don't mirror Griffin's. Even if there's a special fondness between them, her feelings were obviously mixed about the kiss. She wasn't jumping for joy, throwing her arms around his neck, or going in for another. More than anything, Aria seemed confused.

Of course Griffin wishes the only response from Aria was continued affection, but he understands. Rationally, he, too, sees all of the ways something between them would be set up to fail. Their established PR deal, their becoming coworkers in some sense, the media storm that would come following a relationship coming to light, and the impacts it could have on their careers. The potential for distraction as they go for their goals.

There's a reason coaches love the married or single players—there's less chance for relationship drama.

"I don't know. Other players have stranger entrances into relationships. Remember Andre Block and the physical therapist?" Elliott says.

"Do I *remember*? It was perfect until he broke up with her, and no one knew she still had the code to the locker room door."

The locker room was only the beginning, and the personal drama turned work drama tanked his season. The following year, Block couldn't find his footing again, and he never quite got back to his previous performance level.

"Yeah. I was just thinking about the beginning where they got that spread in *Sports Life Magazine*."

"It's all fun and games until it falls apart."

Griffin might be trying to make friends with the notion that football isn't forever and that there has to be more to him than the game. But he also doesn't want to bring about a premature ending to the season. Griffin—forever responsible and levelheaded—should know better than to start a high-profile relationship mid-season.

One of Enzo's staff delivers steaming hot pizza to the table, along with plates and rolls of silverware, and the men thank him before he turns to go.

Elliott slides a slice of sausage pizza onto his plate. "Fair enough. Cassandra's no pushover, and she respects the need for peace during the season. It may not always work out, but it's also not impossible."

Griffin fills his plate. "True."

The pair eat in silence, a ritual they and the rest of the team are used to, especially on the tail of a hard practice. Griffin takes in the place and how different it looks from when he was here with Aria. Enzo had really pulled out the stops to dial up the atmosphere that night. Tonight, without candlelight, the interior is warm but doesn't capture the same sparkle. The tables are pushed together into strange arrangements—a hangover of whatever constellation of players stopped by earlier. The fireplace isn't lit. In some way it makes that evening between him and Aria feel like something that happened somewhere else, to someone else. On a planet in an alternate universe.

After both of the guys have downed two slices, their rapid

pace of eating slows, and the conversation resumes between them.

"So, what's your plan?" Elliott asks. "I know you have one."

Griffin would usually have a plan, but since Aria came into his life, she's recast a lot of the way he sees his world. He wants to have a plan, but he hasn't quite arrived at it yet.

"I'll see her at the humane society tomorrow. There's a pet adoption event they asked us to make an appearance at, so we're doing the friend thing."

Truth be told, Griffin's nerves are piqued over this engagement. Fortunately, they'll be surrounded by adoptable puppies and kittens, but he knows there's only so long they can serve as a distraction before they have to talk about what happened.

He already has a sense of what Aria will say: that they shouldn't mess up what they've got—the arrangement, maybe even the friendship—and he agrees. Griffin worries that he would be crossing a line, taking advantage of the professional relationship that's been established in an agreement set forth by PR. He never would want to be that guy.

Both Aria's feelings—her personal ones, but also her desire to be respected professionally—and his reputation are of the utmost importance to him.

Griffin would be beside himself if Aria ever felt like he was being opportunistic. Of course the kiss and the feelings smoldering behind it were genuine, but the barriers still remain. Aria has already been burned by enough people she's let in; Griffin can't accidentally become one of those too.

"Honestly, I'm going to try to get back in the friend zone. Even though I can't believe I'm saying that," Griffin says, then takes a bite of his crust.

"Dang, man." Elliott draws out each syllable in commiseration. "Can you believe your celebrity crush came so close to being more?"

Even if he's also a celebrity himself, it truly feels wild. But when Griffin stops and thoughtfully considers Aria, he's also struck by how grateful he is to simply know her. To hopefully still call her a friend. She doesn't need to be romantically connected to him to be all of the wonderful things she is, and if friends is the closest they'll ever get, Griffin will be satisfied with it.

"What is it that Coach says? '*Build me a bridge and get over it.*'" Griffin even impersonates the head coach's style of speech.

The men burst into laughter, and with it, some of Griffin's trepidation leaves him.

Being able to laugh about it is a good first step.

Chapter 30

Aria

Aria made laps around the house, calling out for Bailey as soon as Griffin left yesterday, but when she'd gathered the wherewithal to check her phone, she discovered a text from Bailey.

> **Bailey:** Going out for some shopping and errands with Sidney, maybe dinner too.

Sidney is Bailey's best friend, and Aria never worries about her sister when the two are together. Aria forced herself back down into the studio and, with an aggressive dose of self-talk, willed herself back into the zone and created some more material for the album. Whether it will sound decent in the morning is still to be determined.

After dinner, Aria texted to check in.

Aria: You girls behaving?

Bailey texted back quickly.

Bailey: Ha ha, very funny, MOM. There's a wait at the tapas spot, so we're window shopping for now.

When Aria called it an early night, Bailey was still out, so Aria lay wide awake in her bed replaying the kiss.

By all objective standards, the kiss was incredible. Griffin is charming yet chivalrous, strong yet gentle; he is irresistible, according to every fiber of her body. Nevertheless, Aria can't let herself forget the fact that magical moments like the one that occurred between them are a result of music making—at least according to her personal theory. She's always suspected it's one of the reasons musicians are notorious for having chaotic lives or getting carried off by the party scene.

Aria and Griffin have a PR deal, for goodness' sake, and although they have a real friendship, neither of them needs the complication of a romance heaped on top. Every time they appear, the photos are shared thousands—sometimes hundreds of thousands—of times. They are under more public scrutiny than perhaps Aria has ever been because now her fans *and* his are watching.

The idea of living out a real relationship under the same magnifying glass would be enough to send Aria into heart palpitations. She might put herself on a stage near weekly, and she might take the comments about her body and fashion on the chin. But the *real* her? The one that Griffin has teased out? That one stays hidden from the stage, from the public—even from her music.

Aria is working on pouring more of herself into her music, something she counts as growth. But having the public dissect and criticize her for falling for someone, dating, being part of a couple? No way. Absolutely no way. That is entirely too far.

Eventually Aria fell asleep, but when she wakes early the next morning she doesn't feel particularly rested.

She is already posted up at the kitchen island on a barstool when Bailey rolls out of bed, into the kitchen, and toward the coffee maker in a straight shot. As soon as a sip of coffee hits Bailey's lips, she does a double take of her sister.

"You don't look right," she says.

"Thanks," Aria replies.

"What's up?" Bailey stands across the island from her, sipping her coffee as she slowly becomes more alert.

Aria pulls in a breath and explains in great detail the afternoon in the music studio with Griffin and their eventual, glorious kiss. "You always know what to do, so I figured you could help me navigate this."

"How am I supposed to know what to do?" Bailey says. "This is *way* out of my wheelhouse. Yours too. You're not exactly the queen of dating—no offense."

It is a true statement. After only a couple of burns from grifters and fake friends, Aria walled herself off from romantic prospects. Why wouldn't she when all of her experience showed her that no one was chasing her for genuine reasons? She has Bailey, her family who she doesn't see as much as she should, her professional team, and a few friends who, come to think of it, she hasn't seen in quite a while. Aria is busy, however. Having an army of friends simply isn't realistic for her. None of it ever felt realistic.

Until Griffin.

"We have to backpedal." Aria announces it with certainty despite her lingering daydreams over repeating the kiss. "Keeping it professional is for the best. Plus, Griffin has actually become my friend."

"Your first one ever." Bailey winks.

Aria casts slitted eyes her way with a playful glare. "You're not wrong in some ways. We just *mesh*, you know?"

"So it could be more."

"I'm Aria Wilder. I don't get to have a boyfriend that I don't share with the entire internet. Griff is obviously an internet darling at this juncture, but I don't think he quite understands what us canoodling would be like to endure. Right now everyone loves us because we're 'the two best friends.'"

Bailey wraps both hands around the mug. "There's definitely romance speculation too."

"Where I'm sure most of the ugly comments lie." Aria swats at the air. "Still, it's all a moot point. Griffin wasn't exactly pouring his heart out, so I suspect he knows keeping it professional is the safest route. I do too. We'll have to talk it over at the event tomorrow."

Aria swallows, and she feels a hardening in her chest, one that feels like taking care of necessary business.

"And what will you say?"

Aria clears her throat. "That I care for Griffin as real friends, but that we can't be more. That we need to forget the kiss and keep it professional."

Aria's shoulders pull back reflexively, her chest popping out like it does when she channels her most powerful self before a concert. The way she does when she puts on her armor before stepping out into a barrage of press on the red carpet.

"That's what you want?"

Curiosity rings out in Bailey's words, her warm eyes leaving room for Aria to change her mind, and it makes Aria fumble. Aria wishes that Bailey understood that there's not actually room for her to make that choice, not without making a mess. That Aria is "Aria Wilder, Pop Superstar and America's Darling," and that means her world, despite its reach across the globe, has also shrunk her personal life. A necessary hardship to protect herself—the real, smaller version that is the only thing she gets to keep.

The only part of her that's out of the public's reach.

"It's the right choice." Aria hops up, signaling an end to the conversation. "I'm going to get a couple hours of work in this morning, but do you want to do yoga this afternoon? I have an instructor coming. We could do takeout after."

"Music to my ears," Bailey says.

Aria smiles and turns to head upstairs. She needs a shower. That always helps her reset her mind—and this time, hopefully her body too.

A quick hot shower will wash all of it away.

She'll emerge fresh and focused, kisses and butterflies permanently in the rearview.

Chapter 31

Griffin

Small fences are arranged on the park lawn into multiple pens that house puppies, kittens, and even a handful of bunnies. The animal adoption event this weekend is a follow-up to the gala where Griffin and Aria served as surprise celebrity guests. He didn't know having a bunny as a pet was a real thing, but when he kneels down to pet one, he is astounded by how soft its fur is. The animal is sweet and quickly he understands the appeal. He stays there, his tall figure casting the tiny bunny in shade, and uses two fingers to gently pet the space behind the bunny's ears.

Without warning, a little girl appears at his side, and without introduction asks, "Are you going to get that bunny? I would get that bunny if I was a grown-up."

Griffin looks over. She stares at him intently with deep brown eyes, her face framed in a bevy of tight chocolate curls.

She wears a pink dress with sparkly leggings and tennis shoes he suspects probably light up in some manner.

Griffin sighs. "Unfortunately, I don't have a backyard, so bunnies are out of the cards for me."

The girl frowns. "You poor thing. I have a swing set and everything. Maybe you could come over sometime."

As darling as this little girl is, Griffin knows better than to entertain invitations to her home, so he gets to his feet and scans the crowd. "That's very nice of you to offer. Do you have a grown-up here with you?"

The girl points to a man wrangling a little boy who looks just like her and is scanning the busy park in a panic. "That's my dad. My brother is a runner, and sometimes my mom puts him on a leash just like those puppies. Another reason we can't have a bunny."

"How about I walk you over there? I think your dad is looking for you."

Griffin walks at the little girl's side, pointing the way to her family, and as soon as the dad sets eyes on her, his entire disposition relaxes. He rushes, the little boy under his arm, to close the space.

"Giselle! I couldn't find you!"

"I think she was lured over by the bunnies," Griffin jokes. "They even got a massive guy like me."

The dad sighs. "Thanks, man." He looks at Griffin, turns away, then back again. "Hey, I know you!"

Griffin shrugs. In all honesty he hates these moments when he's transformed from anonymous stranger to football celebrity. When he was a rookie, he loved the attention, but nowadays, there's a big part of him that simply wants to be known for being himself. No football.

He holds out a hand to shake. "Griffin Hayes of the Chicago Wardens." He nods his head toward the pavilion where some sound equipment is being hooked up. "I'm here for an appearance but stopped to check out the bunnies."

"He doesn't have a backyard," Giselle says.

Her father shakes Griffin's hand heartily. "Well, I can't thank you enough, Mr. Hayes. I'm a big fan too. You're a pro with kids as well as football, apparently."

The small boy under his other arm begins to wriggle, and the dad and his children bid Griffin farewell. He holds his head a little higher as he walks back over to the pavilion, considering the man's comment about his talent with kids. Aria also mentioned his attentiveness to the children when signing autographs, and Griffin wonders if there's something there—room to develop his non-football talents.

As soon as his eyes lock with Aria's—who is visible from behind the pavilion only because she's leaning out—he forgets everything that was on his mind. The day in the studio, the kiss, and his departure all flood back to him. He was already walking in her direction, and as Griffin makes his way across the grass, dodging the occasional Frisbee or running child, he reminds himself of the talking points he's prepared.

He's almost to her, and she doesn't betray a hint of inner whirling like he has going on inside him. Of course she's calm about this. Aria is a professional. Not to mention, the kiss probably didn't mean as much to her as it did to him, even if she felt sparks.

Griffin reaches her, and Aria stops before him. She wears

jeans, sparkly Nikes that Giselle would approve of, and a sweater with a peacoat layered on top.

"Nice kicks," he says.

Aria kicks out a foot. "Thanks."

Without thinking too hard about it, Griffin pulls her into a side hug, then releases her quickly. "Be warned: If you go visit the bunnies, you might just bring one home."

"Aww." Aria almost sings the sound. "Unfortunately, we have coyotes that come through the woods, so we can't."

Griffin shudders playfully. "There are also puppies and kittens."

"Did you hear I'm doing a world tour next year? When the new album comes out?"

Griffin thinks about next year, and it hits him that, by that time, he might not be seeing Aria much. Perhaps even not at all. He deflates. "You'll have to hook me up with a US show."

She looks up and smiles. "You know it."

A quiet passes between them, and Griffin knows it's now or never to broach the topic. Once they get going with the photo op, the fans will clue in to their presence, and there won't be a private moment to talk before they're loaded up into their separate rides home.

"About the other day—"

"It's okay." Aria is firm.

"I hope you know that upsetting you was the furthest thing from what I intended."

Aria pulls her brow together. "You didn't upset me, Griff. I mean, I think we need to discuss the kiss because it's just not—"

"I shouldn't have overstepped. I know you signed up for a

professional relationship, and I always make it my goal to meet or exceed every professional ask." It's what Griffin's known for in the league—his reliability.

"I'm not sure I'd call it an overstep. If you overstepped, then so did I." Griffin's inner turmoil cools at Aria's mention of her willing participation. "I agree that we need to keep things professional. I, too, shoot for professional excellence, and I let you down too. We both have a lot going on in our careers, which also means a lot to lose."

"I would never want to put you at risk of losing anything," Griffin says. He means it, despite the feelings that he must deny himself in the process.

All of this talk of professionalism and deals and careers feels so icy against the warmth he holds inside for her. Romance or not, Griffin adores Aria in a way that should transcend all of that. Nevertheless, they're both right. Contracts are in place. Even if he has allowed himself to become entangled with Aria like he never planned, none of that is part of this deal.

Aria turns slowly and meets his eyes. "We're having a great time being friends, and the media, the internet, love it. I love it too."

Griffin nods. "And I want to be clear that I love having you as a friend too. Even though we have this agreement and we're both set on keeping it professional, I'm not faking it. You—especially the side not everyone gets to see—have lit up my life since you walked into it, opened my eyes to so much of the world I kept myself blind to. I appreciate you on so many levels."

If he had his way, *appreciate* isn't the word he'd choose, but for today it seems like the right one.

Aria's face lights up, and for the first time today, it's like all of her has shown up. "You're incredible too, Griff. Without you, I might just be forever friendless. Which sounds like the title of a very sad movie."

Griffin pulls her into a chaste side hug, but this time he holds her deeper and longer, like he's holding on to the remains of something that's escaping him. In the next breath they fall into their regular back-and-forth.

"So the bunny was a no, huh?"

"Regrettably. The condo board would have a fit."

"*If* they found out."

"Here you go again, testing the boundaries, Wilder."

"Isn't that what friends are for?"

When Griffin meets her eyes, Aria's twinkle back at him. It sends a thrill through him to see her eyes sparkle after all of the mental gymnastics he'd completed as he considered whether she'd request a hard break following the kiss. Then again, as the delight runs through him, it leaves a nagging pain in its wake.

A pain that sounds like "if only."

If only the kiss had been the start of more.

Chapter 32

Aria

In the week that's passed since the animal adoption event at the park, Aria has kept her head down. Although the musical inspiration is coming only in fits and spurts, she's started her new workout regimen with her trainer in preparation for the album tour. It may seem early, but Worldwide Records has already made their intent to drop the next album "as soon as humanly possible" once it's ready, so Aria needs to be in top shape. The workouts are kicking her butt currently, another sign it was probably best to start now, so she's also spending a decent amount of time in a warm bath.

A couple days earlier, she'd bemoaned her suffering to Griffin when they took some shelter dogs out for a walk in the park—cosplaying pet owners for an afternoon.

"How do you endure this for a living? I feel like my muscles are breaking after every workout." Aria hobbled for the first quarter mile before she got warmed up.

"Technically they are because muscle fibers have to break and reattach to grow muscle," Griffin said, sounding terribly like a professional athlete know-it-all.

Aria threw him a look through slitted eyes. "Not the support I was looking for."

"Stop in for a cookie on the way out after we bring the dogs back?" Griffin's face turned sheepish. "Admittedly I've stopped in once or twice after practice since you clued me in to them."

Aria took great pleasure in converting Griffin to a cookie regular, knowing full well the one from her special coffee shop was the best in town. An hour later, the pair emerged from the coffee shop, this time each with their own sweet treat.

"How's Sunday's game looking?" Aria asked between bites as they walked back toward their cars.

"Eh. The Panthers are formidable. Especially the defense. So we offense players need to really look out." Griffin bit into his cookie, taking down almost a quarter of it at a time.

"You've got this. I can't wait to see you guys win."

"I'd offer you the box tickets, but I let Elliott take mine for this week. He has a whole crew of family flying in from Atlanta."

"No worries. I'll be able to see each of your long eyelashes in HD on my big screen."

Aria wished she had reworded that last one. It sounded a bit too loving and adoring and a little bit outside of the friend zone they had agreed to play within.

Griffin had pulled her under his arm in the friendliest of bear hugs and said, "Your faith in me will take me the extra mile, no doubt. That and the promise of another one of these ASAP postgame."

This evening, as promised, Aria sets herself up on her comfortable couch under the cathedral ceiling and turns on her massive TV. She has her favorite soda, popcorn, and a minibar of her favorite candy as treats for her viewing.

Much like Griffin, she's on a "performance enhancing" diet as part of her physical preparation, but she's far less happy to follow it than he is.

The game kicks off at 2:00 p.m., and by 2:15 p.m., Bailey is posted up beside Aria, hand in the popcorn bowl, asking which one on the field is Griffin. Aria points him out, instructing Bailey to look for the jersey with the number 13 on it.

"So things are good between you?" Bailey asks between bites.

"They're great. There's zero funny business, but we're having a ton of fun in the friend zone."

Bailey presses her lips tight and pops her eyebrows knowingly.

Aria catches her doing this and slaps at her playfully. "Cut it out. That's not helpful."

Bailey raises her hands as she backs away. "Sorry!"

"We're being adults about the whole thing."

"My mistake," Bailey says.

The first half of the game isn't pretty for the Wardens. They're down 14–0, and the offense can't seem to hit their stride. Aria mutters under her breath, cursing the Panthers.

"The QB really needs to step up," Aria says. "He's getting intimidated by the defensive linemen."

Aria won't say it out loud because it would make it all too real, but they're a big crew who look grisly and angry. She wouldn't want to be put up against them.

"Since when do you know any of these things?" Bailey asks, bewildered.

"Since Griff and I became friends. I want to support him like he supports me, so obviously I'm going to watch."

"You're a good friend."

"I finally have a real one, and I'm all in on it. Not to mention I know what it's like to go on under the lights, under the pressure."

"You two really are a match made in heaven."

Aria can tell Bailey is biting her tongue, and she appreciates it. She grabs another handful of popcorn just as the clock starts to run down to the end of the first half. The Wardens have possession, and she knows that if they can get the ball into Griffin's hands, he might be able to get points on the board. He's great under pressure.

As if her mind's been read, the ball snaps to the quarterback, and he telescopes it directly into Griffin's hands. Griffin presses the ball into his chest and turns, but before he can thrust himself into a forward step, he's hit hard in his blind spot by a massive linebacker. Griffin falls to the ground like his knees were cut out from below him.

Aria gasps as she shoots to her feet, both hands flying to her mouth. "Holy sh—"

"Is that Griff?" Bailey says.

In the pause that follows, the camera zooms onto Griffin's

body, which remains flat out on the green turf. Aria begins to whisper, "Get up, Griff. Get up."

Her heart races, terror coursing through her. She sucks in a rapid breath at the sight of him moving. He rolls around a little, and the athletic trainers swarm him.

The commentators speculate:

"He took that hit pretty hard."

"Looks like he's awake, but he's in no rush to get back up."

"We all remember five years ago when he had a similar hit and a knee injury ended his season."

"Hayes is a strong player, but when anyone gets hit like that, it's going to take you out."

Aria is glued to the screen, and when he sits up with his helmet removed, she feels like she might cry. Relief that he's awake and upright. Pain that he's injured. Fear that there's more to this. Aria, just like anyone else, knows the risks of playing professional football, the impact of many tackles over time, the finicky nature of the human brain. She wants to run onto the field and hug him.

Foolishly, she grabs for her phone to call him, but she looks back to the screen, her reminder that his phone is stored far away in the locker room.

"He's getting up," Bailey says.

The trainers help him off the field, and the crowd erupts into cheers.

"Looks like that same knee that gave him trouble years ago is hurt, and he's putting no weight on that foot," one commentator states.

Aria's heart rate slows as the camera zooms in on Griffin in the back of the truck that's driving him out of the stadium. He waves at his adoring fans, even attempting a smile, but she knows he's not all right. The camera betrays worry etched into his face, keenly obvious to those who know him, as it follows him.

The commentators chirp their accolades to Hayes, their well-wishes for his speedy recovery as he departs.

Aria keeps her eyes on him all the way until the truck cuts out of the shot.

And she could see his long eyelashes the whole way.

She reaches for her phone and texts anyway.

> **Aria:** I'm watching, Griff. I know you won't get this until later, but call me as soon as you can. I'm thinking about you. xoxo.

Probably she shouldn't have added the "xoxo" part, but this is an emergency situation, and she'll allow herself some leeway.

Chapter 33

Griffin

The moment Griffin hits the ground after the tackle, he knows what's happened. The searing sensation in his knee, the one he spent a year rehabbing, feels like it explodes under his skin. Professional athletes know these stories, familiar as campfire ghost tales traded among them, but no one wants to be the subject of one.

Griffin lays on the ground, the pain in his knee pulsing. Nausea wells in him, which signals something far more serious happening in his body than getting the wind knocked out of him. The whistle sounds, and Elliott's voice is at his side.

"You okay, man? Here comes sports med."

"Hey, Griff, what's giving you problems?" Brandon, the responding trainer, has been on staff for several years and knows Griffin well.

Between the bars across his helmet, Griffin meets Brandon's eyes. Brandon is worried, despite his efforts to mask it.

"I'll give you three guesses, but I bet you only need one," Griffin says.

Brandon frowns. "The knee?"

Griffin gives a single, silent nod.

"Can you sit up?" Brandon asks.

"Yeah." Griffin accepts the help to sit up, then plucks off his helmet. He wishes he could delete all of the cameras, the crowd even, and suffer in private.

"All right, man, we're going to pull you up and get you to the truck." Brandon and a couple of his colleagues are at Griffin's side, and despite their numbers, they groan under the effort of lifting him.

Once Griffin is up on his good foot, he presses on the two guys at his sides and hobbles for the truck. The crowd applauds for him, and he pulls a tight smile, seeing the sideline camera zoom in. He mouths the words, *"Thank you."*

The fans have always been good to him.

The trainers help load Griffin in the bed of the truck, and the vehicle starts its exit to great applause. Once the truck pulls all the way out of the stadium and out of camera sight, Griffin lets his shoulders drop and his head sag.

He could choose to be optimistic right now. All his teammates would tell him not to count himself out until he sees the doc. *"No sense digging your own grave if you've still got time on the clock,"* Elliott told him last year when he got a concussion that took him out for a game. And Griffin subscribes to the same approach himself most of the time, but nothing about this injury is business as usual.

Griffin knows this injury because it feels exactly the way it did last time, five years ago. Only this time he's already had the talks with the doctors, and they warned him that he needed to protect this knee. That it was hurt so badly last time that another bad hit could be even worse news.

Griffin should probably make his peace with the fact that his season is over.

If not more.

The truck stops in front of the medical suite, and a staff member waits at the door with a wheelchair. He pushes it to the back of the truck, releases the tailgate, and once Griffin has slid himself to sitting on the edge, the staff member helps him into the wheelchair.

The medical suite is brightly lit, and the team doctor stands waiting in the room. He is friendly and far too jovial for the occasion, but that's always been his way. The doctor starts with an ultrasound of the area, and he squints with focus at the screen as he moves the wand around.

Griffin's knee has already swollen to double its normal size, and the doctor only confirms the fact when he says, "The swelling makes it hard to see the actual extent of the injury, so we'll have to wait for a full prognosis."

"Surely I'm out for the season."

The doctor pulls back the ultrasound wand and looks at Griffin through wire-rimmed glasses. He doesn't wear a white coat and instead is outfitted in the same gear as the athletic trainers.

"It's likely." He throws his hands up. "I don't want to say too much while it's swollen like this, but we're both aware of your history."

Griffin nods solemnly. "I've been having to ice it more

often than usual, and we did a few shots earlier this season for inflammation."

"That's right, I remember. But we addressed the small-grade irritation. A hit like this will of course have the potential for worse impact on a healed injury like yours. But no amount of ice or shots could have prevented it. This was simply a bad hit in a bad spot. Wrong place, wrong time."

Griffin lets out a pressured breath. The doctor is right: None of this was in his control. But it doesn't help at all to make Griffin feel less unmoored. He does the right things, sticks to the schedule, skips the parties, does the recommended recovery exercises, and *still* he's hurt. It's as if all he's put in amounts to nothing.

A darkness wells inside Griffin, a hopelessness that feels a lot like football writhing in his grip, attempting to escape him.

"You know what to do: Ice, keep off it, and I'll see you again in the morning. The crew will make sure you're set up at home. You're welcome to hang here for now."

The doctor gives him a fatherly pat on the shoulder on his way out of the exam room, and Griffin mutters his thanks. As quickly as the doctor is gone, a knock comes at the door and Elliott appears.

"Hey, what'd they say? You okay?" Elliott eyes the knee. "Dang, you're swollen."

Griffin forces himself to make eye contact with his friend, and he tries for a smile.

Elliott narrows his eyes warmly. "You know you don't have to play it like that with me."

Griffin sighs, letting the facade drop. "I think it's bad. Doc can't say much for sure right now with the swelling, but I'll tell you, it felt like an explosion. Exactly like it felt the first time."

Elliott drops back on the wall. "I know it was a hard recovery last time, but if anyone's up for the rehab, it's you."

"Thanks, man."

It's too soon for him to spill it to his friend, but Griffin's worries don't lie in his ability to buckle down and do the painful recovery work. It's the possibility that the recovery work will be only for the purpose of walking again. The possibility that his knee is too busted up to get back to playing shape. He's not a rookie anymore. He's thirty-two years old.

"Well, I gotta run before Coach finds out I left the locker room during halftime." Elliott throws a wave over his shoulder and takes off.

"Thanks for risking your rear to come check on me."

Griffin is lucky to have a friend like Elliott—all of his teammates really. He sits quietly, waiting for staff to come and get him, to eventually help him home. Naturally there's a protocol for this. But in the quiet, alone with his mind, Griffin can't help but wonder how much longer he'll have those teammates.

How much longer his body can hold on to the football life.

It wasn't supposed to happen this quickly.

He doesn't have a post-football plan yet, and his mind goes to Aria. If she were here, she would know what to say. Probably she'd assure him that it would all turn out in the end. If only. Because Griffin can't help but think otherwise.

Chapter 34

Aria

Aria knows Griffin's priority won't be to text back when he exits the field via truck, but by Monday afternoon, she's itching for a reply. This morning she went for a walk, hoping to take her mind off it, and eventually she searched for news online.

"Griffin Hayes Suffers Concerning Injury to Knee."
"Will Griffin Hayes, Golden Boy, Bounce Back Again?"
"Bestie to Aria Wilder Taken Down Unreasonably."

Aria stifles a laugh at the last headline, but it makes sense as soon as she discovers the article links to a fashion blogger's site.

One would think that Aria, in supposed best friend position, would be able to garner some insight, but she's left speculating and pondering just like everyone else. She checks her messages again, confirms *again* that they have been delivered.

Aria heads down to the studio, striking a deal with herself that if she can work for forty-five minutes, she'll call Griffin after. It's playing games like this with herself that allows her to work even when she doesn't feel like it. The public assumes that making music is as glamorous as it's often made out to be, but ultimately it's a business where she owes work on a deadline. Case in point are the calls she's been dodging from Gerald at Worldwide Records, checking in on her album progress. Typically she sends clips of raw tracks as she works, but this time she hasn't. Aria knows that if she wants to sell a slightly new direction, she'll need to polish them up before sharing.

Down in the studio, Aria can't settle. She moves between her guitar and the piano, back to the couch for lyrics. Eventually she dials Griffin, with less than forty-five minutes of unproductive work. The phone rings and rings, and eventually it goes to voicemail. For the first time, Aria starts to worry. Of course she was concerned when Griffin got injured, but seeing him get up and even wave to the crowd assuaged her immediate fears. Now that he is off camera—presumably resting or preparing for treatment—Aria's mind slips back to the moment of terror when he went down and didn't get back up.

She pages back through their texts to look for his address. The two had been texting about Chicago popcorn, and when Griffin admitted that he hadn't tried Aria's favorite flavor, CheeseCorn, she ordered some to be sent to him.

Aria finally finds Griffin's address. There's a chance he'll be startled by Aria showing up on his doorstep, but she's also not willing to sit and wonder about all the horrible fates Griffin might be enduring. As she drives to his building, her maps app leading the way, Aria lists all the reasons it's a good idea for her to show up: Maybe he needs help, probably he needs groceries, meal prep won't be easy with a bum leg. Not to mention he might enjoy the company. Showing up unannounced when you know a friend is in need is decidedly within reason.

Aria may not have the greatest depth of experience, but she's certain this is what Griffin would do for her in a comparable situation.

Aria parallel parks on the street, then walks right through the front door. She waits for the elevator and presses the button for the penthouse when she enters. She breathes a sigh of relief that it doesn't require a special fob or passcode, and when the elevator stops, the doors slide open before a single front door.

Aria walks up and knocks.

She waits. Eventually Aria knocks again, louder this time. Could Griffin be staying elsewhere? Maybe somewhere with support staff? It would surprise Aria if he wasn't already up on crutches after all the stories he shared about his first knee recovery, bragging about the skills he developed getting around on them.

Just as Aria is about to turn and leave, the door clicks open to reveal a tired Griffin, crutches inserted below his arms.

"Hey!" Aria is bright, the happiness at seeing him a natural response despite his situation.

"Hey." Griffin's face sags, not a hint of a smile.

"I'm sorry, is now a bad time? I texted. And called." Aria laughs at herself playfully. "I was worried and wanted to see if I could help in any way."

Griffin casts his eyes downward, and the difference in him since Aria saw him last is striking. The man before her is drawn and serious and completely foreign from the man who bemoaned his inability to take home one of the bunnies at the pet adoption event.

"Sure, come on in, but fair warning that I'm not the best company right now."

"Of course," Aria says quietly.

Griffin bites on his lip for a beat before turning and leading the way. He wrestles with the crutches, navigating the turns of his condo like he's still finding his footing with them.

"You take a seat, and I'll help. What do you need? I can cook, clean, or run errands, but I can't promise the cooking will be particularly tasty." Aria tries on a cheery tone.

Griffin stops at the kitchen, and he slowly lowers himself onto a barstool at the peninsula. He lets out a sigh. "You're all good. The team has already lined up people to help me with all of that stuff."

Aria's hands drop at her sides, and a flash of helplessness catches inside her. "Well, you have to let me help somehow." She wanders over to the open living area that's connected and passes through it to the floor-to-ceiling windows. "Wow. You weren't kidding about the view."

When Aria turns around, Griffin is gazing at the windows, dazed and nodding. "Did you get a concussion from the hit?"

"No, but it sure feels like my brain is misfiring." He glances at his knee, wrapped in bandages. "It's like it's too much to process right now."

Aria walks back over to him, and she grabs one of his hands and holds it with both of hers. "I'm here for you, Griff. I'm so sorry this happened to you. It's okay to feel mixed up, and I know you'll work through this. I know you have a comeback in you."

Aria does her best with the pep talk, hoping she hit the right notes. She smiles at Griffin as she releases his hand and gently rubs his shoulder.

He looks up and pulls a belabored smile. "Thanks. We'll have to see about the 'comeback.' It was a pretty bad hit."

"Yeah?" Aria pulls her brows together in concern.

Griffin waves her off. "I'd rather not rehash it again. I've already talked to the coaches and my agent and the athletic trainers and the doctor, and one more round might just take it out of me."

"Say no more." Aria dashes around the peninsula into the kitchen, locates the pantry, and pulls out the specialty popcorn she sent over. "We have snacks; all we need is a movie."

Griffin smiles the smallest of smiles—the first real one of the day—when Aria prods him to get up. "You're making me move?" he pretends to complain.

"Well, you can't quite sit for a whole movie on that hard stool. I'm here to stay awhile."

During the movie Aria sneaks glances over at Griffin every few minutes—as much as she reasonably can without being noticed. Though their friendship is still new, she's never seen him like this before. Frankly, she never could have imagined him so shaken and down. An impulse to take care of him thrums inside her, and it's why when he eventually dozes off, she looks over more often.

If only she had a magic wand, Aria would wave it over his knee, then double tap it on his heart to revive the real him. Maybe Griffin won't need her for household tasks—and perhaps that's for the best in some categories, considering her skill set—but Aria has decided: She will be at Griffin's side through this thing.

He may be hurting, but she'll make sure he won't be alone.

Chapter 35

Griffin

Before Aria stopped by his condo unannounced, Griffin was already having one of the worst days of his life. To some, it might sound overly dramatic, but earlier that morning, the doctor confirmed that Griffin's knee would require surgery. Despite having the same suspicions himself, it was still a blow to hear the confirmation come from the professional's lips.

"*We'll have to see how much we can do when we go in. There's already scar tissue from last time*," the doctor told him.

Griffin picked at the edge of the exam bench, knowing that this meant his worst fears were in the cards.

"*There's a chance I never play again*," Griffin said.

The doctor paused. "*I'm not ready to tell you to hang up your cleats yet, but there's always the chance. If you were five years younger or this was the first time this knee had gotten blown out, we'd already be talking back-to-practice game plan.*"

"I appreciate the honesty," Griffin said.

Soon after Griffin arrived home, Aria's call came through, but he muted the ringer. He'd catch her up eventually—once he had himself pulled together—but for that moment all Griffin wanted was to be alone. He sat on his sofa, looking out the expansive windows at the overcast sky, and stewed in his thoughts.

Any professional player with an ounce of intelligence—or anyone decent on their team—was thinking about the end of their football career as soon as it started. Being a career athlete is typically a short-burst deal, even for the best. It has never been corporate America where you put in the years or climb the ladder. Athletes have to be explosive and intense for short periods, and everyone knows they need a plan for when it ends.

Some players invest and live in comfort off their earnings, playing video games and taking vacations for the remainder of their lives. Others pivot into coaching roles or become staff. Some invest in businesses, an entrepreneurial second act. Regrettably, some fail to plan and find themselves at the end of their careers with empty bank accounts and beat-up bodies.

Sitting there on his couch, Griffin wasn't worried about finances, his fastidiousness extending to personal finances. Instead, it was the internal panic at the thought of that hit being his last appearance on a professional league field. The idea that football could be stripped away from him too soon when he was supposed to have so many good years ahead of him.

Mike's voice echoed in his head. *"Not that we welcome it, but injuries happen. And to the best of them."*

Griffin always agreed with Mike—well, he thought he agreed. He voiced his mirroring opinion, but only now does Griffin realize that up until this point he hadn't truly considered the reality that it could happen to *him*. That even if he saw the dots of logic connected, he didn't truly assign that fate as a possibility for himself.

A knock came at the door, and Griffin ignored it. The team always sent a gift basket when a player got injured—their favorite snacks, numbing patches, supplements, extra pajamas with the team logo—as a well-wish. Whoever shops for them does a great job, and that's probably who's at his door. He'd hobble over there once he mustered up the energy. That is the other thing about being injured—it takes a mental toll, and before a player knows it, his attitude, persistence, and optimism are as beat up as his body.

When the knock came again, Griffin took it as his sign from the universe not to let himself slide into complacency, and he got up. He didn't rush, careful to avoid hurting his good leg. Before he opened the door, Griffin caught a whiff of a floral perfume, and momentarily it sent a warm relaxation over him.

The same one Aria uses.

If his mind wasn't hobbling along today, he would've guessed it was her at the door, but he stood surprised. At once he was flooded by embarrassment and shame. He probably looked like the polar opposite of the strong, supportive guy she's gotten to know. Griffin has been reduced to a shadow without football, and Aria is the last person he wants that on display for.

Still, as she stood there on his doorstep, he couldn't bring himself to turn her away. Despite feeling on display in many ways he'd prefer not to be—his physical brokenness, his place not prepped for guests—Griffin couldn't deny the way she lit up the place. He didn't realize how much he needed her in that moment, his friend who was all too ready to remind him that this wasn't the end of the road.

Later when he wakes up on his sofa, it's dark outside the windows. Aria is curled up at the opposite end of the sofa asleep, serene as breath fills, then escapes her in deep waves. She looks like an angel.

Griffin checks the time, then texts Enzo's about dinner. The reply comes in almost at once.

> **Enzo:** Anything for our man down. We'll have the driver walk it up.

> **Griffin:** Thanks, man.

Aria said she would stay awhile, so the least he can do is arrange for them to have dinner. It's a simple task, but it leaves Griffin with a sense of purpose. He might not be able to walk, let alone play professional football right now, but one thing he can do is take care of his friend.

A friend he fights the urge to curl up beside. Instead, he pulls himself to his feet, grabs a blanket tucked at the edge of the couch, and gently lays it over her. She stirs as he tucks her in, rolling into the softness of the cover, and Griffin forces himself to look away. He can't be admiring her beauty. It's a friends-only deal.

Chapter 36

Aria

Four days have passed since the heavenly scent of Enzo's pizza woke Aria from her slumber on Griffin's couch, and after a nice dinner, she left for home. She stopped by again two days later, toting an over-the-top care package with health supplements, healthy snacks, and interesting beverages. Aria can't deny that Griffin didn't look great as she presented the basket, and when she asked, he admitted he'd really only left home for his medical appointments with the team. It was obvious how the weight of his situation had set in. His face was unshaven, his sink full of dishes, and his laundry piled at the end of the couch.

"Perfect! You left me some helper jobs," Aria had announced as she rolled up her sleeves.

Griffin had turned beet red and rushed to his feet. "No, no. That's not for you. I'm getting to it, I just needed—"

"It's okay, Griff. Let me help."

Griffin pulled his chest up and spoke with a new terseness. "I don't want you to be my caretaker, Aria. I have people coming for that."

Aria nodded, dropping her gaze. Why on earth wouldn't he let her help? She had been more than clear that she *wanted* to.

Griffin had reached out and cupped her cheek, raising her head so their eyes could meet. Tenderly, he said, "I'm sorry. I didn't mean to snap. Want to hang out in the mess with me and tell me all about your grueling workout today?"

His words paired with his caring touch cast a deep smile across her face. "I come prepared with material."

It was clear that this post-injury time was new territory for the pair, but it seems to Aria that both she and Griffin are committed to finding their way through it as friends. Admittedly, with the way he cupped her cheek and raised her head, she couldn't help but think of a kiss. For a moment she wished he would, but they had both agreed that was behind them, and it was for the best.

In the time since, Aria has continued with her personal trainer and is slowly building stamina as she alternates running on the treadmill with weight training with swimming and even water aerobics. Truth be told, Aria sort of loved getting in on the lesson with the senior women in the pool. They welcomed her as one of their own without the bat of an eye.

Bailey's been managing a lot of Aria's press this week. She has a couple of virtual interviews and an appearance on a talk show in a few weeks to drum up excitement about the nonexistent album that the record label is already teasing. There isn't even a title yet, but they're acting like it's intentionally secretive as opposed to TBD.

Aria simply cannot find her way with her music.

Griffin brought so much enthusiasm and fun to the studio that day, and in full transparency that's what Aria's been craving. Of course, she's Aria Wilder, so she would never rely on any single person for her success, but she also can't deny that life with Griffin sidelined doesn't have the same kick. She thinks about the energy he brought to the studio, his pure belief in her ability to execute the music she's secretly dreamed of. He might just be the first friend who's made Aria more herself, who's dialed up who she is at her core.

Aria pulls into the garage from her Pilates class—part of today's training plan—and Bailey is in the kitchen unloading groceries. Aria tags in, grabs a bag of pantry items, and heads across the kitchen to put them away.

"I have good news and bad news," Bailey announces from inside the fridge. She reappears with old takeout containers that she walks to the trash.

"Hit me with the good news first."

"*Glam Girl* magazine wants you for a cover story! They're asking about March. I know it'll be right before you hit the road, so I wanted to run it by you before I said yes."

"Amazing! Yes, of course!"

Bailey drops the containers into the trash, and they land with a thud. "Bad news: Griffin canceled on your appearance at the Wardens Fan Fest. Kelsey said his team wants him resting." Bailey nods kindly. "I totally get it, but also, it would suck for him. He's benched for the foreseeable future, so hitting the fan zone has to be salt in the wound."

Aria ignores the way her stomach drops with disappointment. "Yes, that's understandable." She dips into the pantry and calls over her shoulder, "When's our next thing?"

"Kelsey said Griffin needs to pause on engagements until his knee is healed up some. He's really only supposed to move around as needed right now." Bailey balls the reusable bags up into one another. "She said something about him getting surgery, so I imagine he'll be holed up after that for a good while."

Aria remains inside the walk-in pantry for a moment longer than strictly necessary. She lets her face drop. Surgery? The news itself isn't surprising. It's the fact that discovering this through her sister, through his publicist, highlights the space that's grown between her and Griffin. Why wouldn't he have mentioned an update like that himself? Why didn't he ask to talk through it with her? Every time she's seen him, she's asked about his knee. And every time he has brushed off the conversation, using the same excuse that discussing it is overkill, salt in the wound.

"I guess he didn't tell you?" Bailey says to Aria as she emerges from the pantry.

Aria shakes her head, pressing her lips into a line. "Nope. Honestly? I sorta hate it."

Bailey pinches her face into a quizzical look. "It doesn't make much sense. The two of you are friends, so why wouldn't he want a shoulder to lean on?"

Aria shrugs. "Can't say I'm not wondering the same. Trust me, I've been over there. I'm trying to support him, asking about his knee. I can't help but wonder if maybe he just doesn't want me to be included in that part of his life."

"He probably just needs some time to work this out. It's a big deal. It can impact his career."

"I get it." Aria takes her phone from her back pocket and types. She might understand that this injury is a big, messy thing for Griffin to work through, but she's also not giving up their friendship.

She taps Send, and the message whooshes out across the network.

Aria: Surgery? How am I hearing about this via your publicist?

The dots scroll, then the reply comes in.

Griffin: Sorry. I'm all over the place, and the pain meds they've got me on have my brain feeling like molasses.

Aria: Need a post-op ride?

Aria bites her lip in anticipation of the reply.

Griffin: That would be great, but I'll have to get back to you on details.

Aria "hearts" the message and tucks the phone away.

After the final groceries are put away, Aria and Bailey make a plan to cook dinner together after Aria finishes up in the studio. Downstairs, everything Aria touches seizes up. The guitar doesn't hum with energy, the piano sounds cold, even the mixing board glitches and powers down just as Aria is putting together some beats that sound decent.

Aria relistens to the raw music she recorded with Griffin, and it's even better than she thought.

She could send it to the label. But then she remembers the unanswered emails in her inbox, the ones that all sound the same:

Hi Aria,

How is the new album coming? Please let us know if you need support. Even though you've always declined, we can always bring in songwriters or other musicians to support creating your vision. We understand you're busy with a myriad of commitments. Please send over some samples soon so we can decide on a title to announce, as well as develop concepts for marketing and packaging.

Respectfully,

Gerald Smith
Worldwide Records

Never before has Aria experienced what feels like inner drought. Like everything she writes is an aspiring musician's very first attempt at music making.

She keeps her head down until dinner, working as diligently as she can despite the underwhelming output.

Aria does her best to dismiss the thoughts that float into her head unannounced, the ones of Griffin, the ones that worry that things are changing too much between them.

Chapter 37

Griffin

Griffin watches the game from the bench on Sunday and does his best to smile for the camera. The fans love to see an injured player showing up to cheer on his team, and Griffin also wasn't about to sit at home and stew on his bad fortune when his teammates could use another loud voice behind them. The Wardens lose 28–7 to the Miami Pelicans.

"What sort of mascot is a pelican anyway?" Elliott spits as he peels off his jersey in the locker room.

Griffin sits on the bench in his Wardens sweats, his crutches balanced against the seat. "A lame one, that's for sure."

Elliott growls. He lowers his voice. "We need you on that field, man. It's like an engine without any oil when you're not out there."

"You guys will find the groove. We always do when we lose someone. And I'm here—in support."

Elliott drops down beside him. "So, what's the update?"

Griffin sighs. "Surgery. Maybe next week if it looks good enough. Then I'll get into PT and recovery. I'll tell you, the pain relief injections are saving my life."

"I got them in my shoulder last year. When will you be back?"

Griffin appreciates Elliott's positivity. It's infectious even if it threatens to be toxic. Injured professional athletes have a habit of assuming one another to "be making a good comeback" whether it's true or not.

"We're sort of operating in the 'if' for now." Griffin hasn't admitted this to anyone else yet. "But it's not public knowledge, so don't spread it. Or mention it to the press."

Elliott lets out a whistle. "They sure are circling like vultures."

"I'm pretty sure they all want to crack a story that doesn't exist. At least not yet. Or dramatically announce that I'm dead or something," Griffin says.

"Mm-hmm. And what about the rest?" Elliott eyes Griffin from the side with a half smile.

"I'm missing something," Griffin says.

"Socials. Not the *media*-media. Where are you and Aria? The people are starting to ask."

Griffin lets out a "hmm."

Elliott recounts the comments he's seen in a high-pitched voice:

"Why isn't Aria at his side?"

"Why aren't they taking advantage of this for more bestie time?"

"Maybe he could come on the new album tour if his season is cut short? Omg, can you imagine?"

A laugh falls out of Griffin. "You're kidding."

"You have a career-threatening injury, and all the world wants is to see you out and about with Aria Wilder, being you and having fun," Elliott says. "Must be the life of a pop star. No wonder everyone stops caring about the music past a certain point." He rushes to add, "Not that Aria's music isn't killer, mind you. I'm talking about others."

"I had them cancel our events for now, what with the injury. It's been rough, and I don't want to show up for the things—for Aria—looking like a miserable loser."

"And you know what the Aria and Griffin—also known as 'GriffAria' in certain circles—fans would say?"

"Lay it on me," Griffin says, smiling in a way that reaches the rest of him for the first time since the injury.

"*That's what besties are for!*"

Elliott hoots in laughter, and Griffin can't help but join.

"I'm not really sure I knew what I was signing myself up for," Griffin says, thinking briefly back on where his connection to Aria started.

"It might be just what you need at this point," Elliott replies, wiping tears of laughter from his eyes.

"I have to see to the injury first. Then we'll get back in the swing of things. Maybe I'll chat with Aria about making a joint post on social media or something. Or we can stage a 'bestie time.' I'll come up with something during my many hours of sitting."

"Fair enough, man. Well, I'm heading to the showers, so I'll see you soon."

"Sure thing."

"Enzo's one night this week?"

"You bet."

Griffin leaves the stadium that night feeling better than he has in a long time. Probably it was the game, but then again, he's been to the stadium since his injury to get his injections, massage, or other stretching he's still able to do. Griffin is determined not to get further behind than he must. But tonight it isn't until he and Elliott laugh about the Aria situation that he feels the lightness move in, the lift in his chest that Aria gives him, the optimism.

It's only been a matter of days since he last saw her, but Griffin misses Aria. He should've told her directly about the surgery, but every time he tried, he just couldn't bring himself to do it. Griffin already feels too much like a loser, not even close to good enough for Aria, so what will he be like after surgery?

Probably they do need to scramble to patch up any gaps in their PR story, and maybe—as Elliott suggested—it would do him some good.

Once Griffin is home and rested, he shoots Aria a text.

Griffin: In other news, it seems like the internet is chattering again . . .

Aria: Gah. Isn't the internet always stirring up some sort of trouble? Are we in it?

Griffin: Ha. I only know because of Elliott, and even though he spun it like it was his knowledge, it was probably Cassandra who let him in on it.

Aria: Pause for a Google break.

Griffin sits back and lets Aria do her online sleuthing.

Aria: Eh. This is child's play. But we can put something together.

Griffin imagines seeing Aria again, and it's as if his heart squeezes in hope. The sound of her laugh, the conversation that bubbles like a freshly cracked soda, the traces of her perfume that linger even once she's departed.

But then he thinks of himself, broken and useless.

He pushes the dreams of seeing her away.

Griffin: Maybe a social media post? I'm in pretty rough shape with the knee, trying to rest and all.

Aria: And I'm sure tonight's loss didn't help.

Griffin: Uhhhh. It was salt in the massive, gaping wound.

Aria: 😭

Griffin is smiling at his phone screen when a searing sensation runs through his knee. He jolts, pulling himself upright. With a glance at the time, it becomes obvious that he's overdue for his pain medication. He leaves the phone on the sofa, and as he hobbles across the condo toward his bathroom for his pills, the phone buzzes on the couch.

He plans to get back to it as soon as he downs the pill.

As soon as he's better, he'll be able to manage all of this.

He'll be able to make things right with Aria.

Chapter 38

Aria

Aria waits until the very last moment to sign on for the virtual meeting on Wednesday afternoon. After letting one too many emails from the label sit unanswered, they called a meeting for "updates on the status of the next album." Aria's agent assured her that all the executives want is confirmation that she's working on something that fits the bill and that it will be delivered quickly.

Apparently they're all spooked by Aria's silence on the matter.

The screen breaks into four quadrants when Aria enters the chat from her laptop in her studio. In the top left sits Gerald from Worldwide Records. Beside him is Kelsey from PR, and Aria's agent, Monroe McHenry, is beside her on the bottom left.

"Aria, hello!" Gerald leans in closer to the screen, giving a zoomed-in effect on his thick mustache, the glare of the screen reflected in his glasses.

Aria waves. "Hi, everyone."

Kelsey waves back professionally. Her hair is pulled back into a bun, black cat-eye glasses in place. Not a kernel of nonsense to be had.

Monroe's face is framed in thick, curly brown hair, and her steely resolve doesn't crack on account of a warm welcome. There's a reason she's known as a master negotiator in the business.

"Thanks so much for making time for us today," Gerald says after a brief pause. "I understand you're busy at work."

Aria looks back into the camera.

"I can assure you that Aria is hard at work—as she always is—but it's kind of her to entertain this distraction," Monroe says. "We'll keep it brief, of course."

Aria and Monroe already had a sidebar in preparation for this conversation, and Aria is prepared to share clips of the music she's been working on—even if the pickings are slim. Monroe had said, "*Just give them enough to satisfy them for now. Once you fulfill the obligation for this album, we can renegotiate for the style you're wanting. That or find another label if Worldwide won't play ball.*"

"I can tell you guys that I've been hard at work, and I have some interesting stuff to show you today. I've taken a few liberties with the melodies, and I'm excited to share it."

Aria clicks play on a sample clip she compiled this past week. The tone is moodier than her usual fare, including an unusual smattering of synthesized church bells, but the lyrics are the love song Gerald and his cohorts want.

Kelsey bobs her head enthusiastically, and Monroe keeps her stonewall of a face still.

The short clip ends.

Gerald's face puckers, and his eyes dart around as if he's searching for words. "I'm not sure this is what we agreed upon. None of this should be experimental. It should be the same thing we've always done."

"None of it's a final track," Monroe says. "We all know how much it can change once it's produced with beats and effects."

Aria nods. "This is very raw. And to be fair, you guys were the ones who wanted the meeting, Gerald. It doesn't sound like what we agreed upon because it's not ready."

"It does create concern over what material will be delivered. If you're having a block of any kind, we're here to support. You know we have the industry's best songwriters on hand—and their lips sealed with an airtight NDA—so there's no need to suffer in silence."

Aria bites her tongue. The majority of the suffering she's doing in the studio right now is at the hand of Worldwide Records, the very people strong-arming her into a record she never planned to create. To most people, it would be obvious: Forcing an artist to paint with strict direction doesn't exactly allow for the work to become their greatest personal expression.

"She doesn't need, nor does she want hired help," Monroe says. "Aria, please let me know if I'm speaking out of line."

Aria nods. "She's right. I appreciate the sentiment, but the best way I can be supported right now is to not be on the receiving end of near-constant follow-ups. I hardly imagine that you'd do your best work either with your boss breathing down your neck."

Gerald sighs. "My primary concern is making sure the music is the genre and style agreed upon in the contract. We've been flexible and understanding, but we won't budge on this piece: We want commercial Aria Wilder that fans love. There's no reason to reinvent the wheel when it's already taking us to the top of all the charts."

Aria smiles, but inside she fumes. "If it ain't broke, don't fix it" doesn't exactly inspire artistic expression. If she'd followed this logic, Aria would've stuck to the bar stage route as soon as she started making decent money. That could've worked for a long while. It afforded her a nice living, a fun lifestyle. But if she'd never pushed to get into a true recording studio, she would have missed out on a great majority of the opportunities she's been afforded.

"Message received. I will do my best to please—as always." Aria tacks on a winning smile.

"All right, well, I think that's everything, right?" Monroe says.

Gerald nods curtly, clearly unsatisfied with the lack of assurance given. "Please keep us updated, Aria." His words almost sigh in the manner they escape him, like they've soaked up his disappointment.

Aria nods. "Yup! Thanks, everyone. Have a great day."

She hits the Exit button rapidly and slams shut the laptop.

How could Gerald not like that clip? He's not a "creative," but he should be able to see the appeal in a fresh take. Even purely from a business perspective, opening a new Aria Wilder thread could mean a whole spool's worth of potential profits.

It's not that Aria even has a problem with her old music. She still loves it and stands proudly by it. But it was her style in her early twenties, and she kept with it for almost a decade. Now, coming up on thirty, it doesn't feel authentic anymore. Aria isn't the same woman she was at twenty-one or twenty-two years old. And she shouldn't be. Not if she's growing and learning and evolving.

If Worldwide keeps her locked within that box she built years ago, Aria fears she'll end up looking like that forty-year-old mom who tries to wear the same fashions as her daughter. Like someone who is still chasing their high school peak.

Aria pushes the laptop aside and sits down at the piano. She plays the basic melodies of her original hits, and it feels like visiting an old friend. Could she find a second life in them? Aria plays around with them, but quickly she hits a wall. She throws her head back and a groan escapes her.

Maybe she simply isn't cut out for this industry anymore. Not if they can't support her growth. Maybe she's just not as talented as people think she is if she can't make this work.

Another album, the same but with some differences should be an easy order.

If her insides didn't scream every time she tried to make it happen.

Aria gets up from the piano and paces the studio. Her walls lined in charts, awards, and accolades feel like prying eyes as they watch her pace in her discomfort. She'll go track down Bailey soon for a heart-to-heart. Even when there's no easy solution, Bailey always makes things feel better. But Aria's mind also goes to Griffin.

The feeling of making music with him here was so energizing, like the studio had been filled to the brim with the possibility he poured in. His belief in her was an engine that hummed inside her as she worked. Aria drops back onto the piano bench and runs through the main melody of the song she started working on with Griffin.

It's like slipping into her own skin, like finally being honest about who she is, the woman she's become over the past eight years of stardom. Aside from Bailey, there's really no one else in Aria's life who makes her feel more like herself. Griffin never makes demands of her like the ones she just got on the video call; he accepts her as is and encourages her to lean into that.

Aria felt like she got another glimpse of Griffin's shine when they were texting on Sunday, but then he just sort of *ghosted* her. It wasn't a big deal, just a clarification message about doing a post together, and maybe there was some question over whether he needed to respond or not. Maybe he assumed it'd go through Mike? But Aria noticed the emptiness that arose, and then stuck around, in the wake of his silence.

Before the injury, he would have replied, even sent extra messages, marked it with a response emoji if nothing else.

Aria stopped by Griffin's place unannounced yesterday, hoping to talk him into going shopping at the home goods store with her, but she was unable to convince him. Even when she mentioned the mobility scooter, he wasn't sold.

He put on a smile for her. "*Thanks, but no thanks.*"

"*Come on. We can even look for some throw pillows for you! No respectable adult has* zero *throw pillows.*"

"*Maybe another time. I have PT in a little while.*"

Aria suspected from the way he said it that Griffin might have been stretching the truth about his schedule conflict, and she couldn't help but wonder if pre-injury Griffin would have done the same.

Surely their partnering on something soon will bring them closer together. Forced fun could be a solution.

In the meantime, it's difficult to ignore the way life feels far less satisfying without Griffin Hayes tucked close by her side.

Chapter 39

Griffin

When Griffin gets to the stadium, the team is already practicing full out after their loss last Sunday. Thursdays are typically a heavy practice day, but they can get especially intense on the heels of a loss. The Wardens will play the DC Generals away on Sunday, and they're practicing as if preparing for war. Griffin pauses at the edge of the field, and if desire alone could make magical things happen, his knee would instantly heal and he'd run out there and tag in.

Despite Griffin being thirty-two years old, not much about his passion for the game has changed since he was a peewee and the smallest-sized jersey swamped his frame.

Griffin can only watch what he's missing out on for so long before he makes his way, atop his crutches, to the medical block. Tomorrow is surgery day to take the first steps in repairing his knee, and he has a consultation with the team doctor to discuss the recovery plan. Griffin hopes they only talk about the immediate future—the part where his job is to get the surgery and wait out the worst of the recovery. Not the part where they discuss the viability of his return to practice or game play.

The conference room is past the therapy rooms and the exam tables, past the specialized treatment machines that he is entirely acquainted with. Inside the meeting room, Griffin finds a spot at the conference table, and soon he's joined by the team doctor, Dr. Young, a physical therapist, someone from sports medicine, and the Wardens' rehab coordinator, Karileigh, who makes sure every player has all the necessary services to recover expeditiously.

Dr. Young doesn't say anything that Griffin hasn't already heard. "The surgeon's going to do his very best to fix you up as good as possible with what he's got in there. Plenty of scar tissue makes the job trickier."

"Yes, sir. I understand," Griffin says.

"He might need to graft in some new tissue, but in terms of you getting back to top shape, we'd really prefer to focus on preserving as much as we can first."

"Is there a chance I'll need a second surgery?"

Dr. Young pulls in a concerted breath, cups his chin, and pauses. "I'm never going to BS you, son. This isn't the ideal scenario for having a knee injury, and the truth of the matter is that we won't know how things will or won't go until we just do the thing."

"That makes sense."

Griffin says these words about the practical components, but none of this really makes sense. Not in the sense that he did everything he was supposed to do to keep himself in the best shape. Not in the sense that he's worked his whole life for this career. Not in the sense that, somewhere along the line, he let the other parts of himself go, and he let this sport consume him.

He's grateful when Karileigh clears her throat and begins discussing the logistics of his recovery. Griffin needs to know the details, and he refocuses intently. Karileigh is of small stature and so blonde that her hair is almost white. Her plan is meticulous, and she details it for the group.

"Postsurgery you will be transported directly to Kensington Suites, a luxury rehabilitation facility that will oversee the correct administration of pain medication and wound care, as well as support services such as food, hygiene, and mobility assistance. Your length of stay will be determined by the physician in residence, who will monitor your recovery. As soon as you're able, physical therapy will begin working with you to regain mobility in the knee and aid the appropriate healing. Please find a packing list in your email inbox. Otherwise the facility is prepared to provide necessary items as requested. We have thought of everything to maximize your potential for the greatest recovery. Only the best for our Wardens players!"

The plan is fabulous, and as promised, it doesn't miss a thing when it comes to surgery and recovery. Griffin itches with an impulse to get to his feet and run to the practice field to join his teammates. He might not have a choice, but he wishes he could will the whole thing away. Go back to football. The thing that makes him Griffin Hayes.

Hospitals, doctors, and rehab aren't supposed to be part of his world the way they are right now.

He wasn't made for *this*.

"Thank you for putting together such a comprehensive plan. I will be following all of the orders to make my recovery as speedy as possible."

"We'd expect nothing less from our golden Warden," Coach says from the doorway where he's barged in. "I snuck out for a minute to come check on my favorite tight end."

Griffin gets to his feet, and the coach pulls him under his arm roughly.

"Don't tell Lopez that or you might be down another tight end on Sunday."

Everyone in the meeting room laughs.

"Anything else before I run?" Dr. Young glances at his watch.

"That's all, I think. Karileigh?" Griffin says, and Karileigh nods in agreement.

"Well, in that case, best of luck tomorrow," Dr. Young says. "We're rooting for you."

"And I'll be rooting for the Wardens in DC," Griffin says.

Karileigh slips out of the meeting room with a quick goodbye. Coach follows closely behind as he rushes back to practice after sharing his well-wishes, and Griffin is left alone in the Wardens' conference room. The walls are lined in memorabilia, framed jerseys of legendary players, posters of past Super Bowl appearances, top season awards. Griffin has never questioned his belonging in this organization. He always knew that between his work ethic and his talent, he could live up to the demands of a team of the Wardens' stature.

The throbbing in his knee reminds him how much has changed.

Will he ever get back here? If he does, will he become a drain on the team? The old-timer no one wants to let go despite his glory days being in the rearview? There are no guarantees either way. The only thing of which Griffin can be certain is that his recovery will be difficult and long, and he has to take it one step at a time.

The only other option is to quit. And a quitter—injured or not—is one thing he'll never let himself be.

The ringing phone in his pocket pulls his mind from its musing, and Griffin hits the screen to accept Mike's call on speaker.

"Hey, man, what's up?" Griffin says.

"How you holding up?" Mike asks in response.

Griffin appreciates the consideration, but in equal measure, he wishes everyone—himself included—could forget about his injury for more than a few seconds at a time.

"Ask me tomorrow post-op." Griffin laughs. "No, I'm tired of talking about that. To what do I owe the pleasure of a call?"

"You've got a lot going on, so you probably haven't seen the state of the internet."

"Sounds like I definitely haven't."

"Well, there were rumblings last week about why Aria and you haven't been spotted hanging out now that you're *temporarily* out of commission."

"Ah, I see."

"People are saying it was all a publicity stunt and that all of it is 'too convenient' the way it worked out."

A searing guilt pierces his middle. A better friend would've already done some social media together or something. Heck, if he'd just gone and picked out some throw pillows and snapped a few pictures, that would've more than sufficed. Instead, he's let his own issues eclipse everything.

"Aria's cool as a cucumber as per usual, but she definitely wants to do damage control," Mike says.

Griffin's chest grows tight, and when he pulls in a breath, it feels trapped inside him. His face flushes. How could he be so selfish? Maybe it's further proof that he shouldn't be in Aria's life right now. If he can't even stop to consider her feelings amid all his self-pity.

"I'll do whatever. You know, considering the bum knee. Ballroom dancing might be out."

Mike laughs. "Thanks. We're thinking socials for right now. Kelsey from Aria's team is going to get some mock-up stuff put together, and then I'll shoot it over with directions."

"Easy."

"Yup! Do you have any personal pictures the two of you snapped together? I guess maybe not, but—"

"I do actually."

At the pet adoption, he and Aria took selfies with the adoptable pets as part of the appearance. The event organizer suggested they do it so fans could get pictures of them being friends, but nothing about it was an act.

In fact, Griffin has looked at the pictures more often than he thought he would since he got hurt.

"Nice! Send them over? We could doctor some stuff up, but you know fans are smarter than that. They can sniff out a fake image in a heartbeat, and then I fear we'd be in worse shape than where we're starting."

"Sure thing."

They end the call, and Griffin doesn't linger, instead lugging himself on crutches back to his vehicle. The only silver lining to his injury is that it's his left knee, so he can still drive.

He pauses in the driver's seat and does a quick internet search for himself with Aria Wilder. There's an abundance of posts, hot takes, and talking-head videos to choose from, but all suggest the same thing: Aria Wilder and Griffin Hayes are fakes who played up their relationship as something it wasn't to take advantage of the fans.

Griffin runs a hand through his hair.

He's just like the rest of the people who claimed to be Aria's friends if he's landing her in hot water online like this.

He cranks the engine, puts the car in gear, and backs out of his spot. He weaves through the underground parking garage, and when he comes out into the light he's certain: Aria is better off without him.

She deserves better than the broken, self-obsessed wannabe he's become.

Knowing what he's about to tell her pains him as he drives to the coffee shop where she waits for him. But in the long run, it will be for the best. Griffin has not a sliver of doubt about the fact that he needs to fix himself before he does any more damage to Aria.

Chapter 40

Aria

The moment Griffin hesitates to sit at "their" table at "their" coffee shop is the first hint that something is off. He stands before Aria, grips his hands, and rolls his lips as if he's on the verge of an announcement.

"Something come up?" Aria slides the tea toward him, hoping he'll see it as an invitation to sit. The bag of cookies sits waiting, untouched on the tabletop.

"I'm sorry, Aria, but I can't do this right now."

All of the breath escapes her in one fell swoop. "*What?*"

"I need to focus on rehab, on getting back to myself, and I can't do that with you hanging around."

Aria feels her insides deflate, and her face must show it, because Griffin hurries to explain.

"I'm sorry, that didn't come out right. I just need time alone. I'm sorry."

Aria can't say she's entirely shocked based on his behavior

since the injury, but it doesn't take away the ache his words cast over her. As she gets to her feet, she feels like an irksome little child distracting the adults from the real work. She chides herself.

You should've known better.

This is what happens when the walls come down.

Just like the others.

"No problem." Aria hates the way her voice wavers.

Griffin reaches out for her arm as she passes. "I'm sorry. I just—"

"You don't need to explain, Griff."

She slides to the side to escape his grip. Aria can bear to hold his eye only for a moment, so she looks aside to say the rest. "Have Mike chat with Kelsey about plans, yeah? I'll give you your space."

"Aria, you know I don't—"

"Stop. Let's not." Aria flashes him a smile and raises a hand goodbye. It takes every ounce of her effort to strike a nonchalant tone as she calls over her shoulder, "I'll see ya when I see ya," and slips out of the coffee shop.

Chapter 41

Griffin

The ease in Aria's voice as she floats out of the coffee shop unbothered is only confirmation of Griffin's suspicions that she's far too confident to be bothered by his ask for space. In fact, it's also confirmation that she deserves him at his best and nothing else. Sure, he saw the way her expression fell when he stumbled over his words, but it didn't take hold.

As he looks around, now alone in a shop he's only ever inhabited alongside her, Griffin hates the way the place feels. Cold and lonely despite the murmur of happy voices and the welcome scent of freshly brewed coffee. He dips out of the shop and directly into his car at the curb.

He wishes he was a stronger man, someone who could've not only avoided this injury, but someone who could stand to lose football and still be worthwhile. It's in Aria's best interest to be far, far away from him for now.

In his pocket, Griffin's phone buzzes with calls from media contacts. He has at least one hundred emails unanswered in his box, again from more people looking to break an article about his future. If any one of those reporters could give *him* some idea as to what comes next for him, Griffin would take it gladly.

Griffin drops his head back onto the headrest, closes his eyes, and remembers all the pieces of his life that built his career. The little boy he was scrambling onto the field for the first time, the college hopeful, the football camp summers from the moment school let out to the moment classes resumed. Then the Wardens. Those are all the pieces of him, and he's clueless as to what to do when they end.

Even if it hurt to turn her away, even if he could really use a friend like her to get through post-op and recovery, Griffin would rather suffer than let Aria see him defeated and weak. He needs to figure out how to make this work before he lets Aria back in. She deserves the best version of him, and he's far from it.

Chapter 42

Aria

The Chart Topper Music Awards party begins with a red carpet walk, segues into a seated dinner, and rounds out in the awards presentations—which are also broadcast on television. It's a welcome break from the studio where Aria has been camped out ever since Gerald cornered her on the video chat.

Aria brings Bailey as her guest, and when their limo pulls up to the guest drop-off, they step out to an explosion of camera flashes from the crowd of photographers waiting behind the metal barricades that flank the red carpet.

Aria smiles and waves, temporarily blinded by the lights, and Bailey hangs behind her. It's a comfort to know she's there, like backup in case things get dicey.

Aria is well-trained by now, and she stops and poses, turning so each photographer can get their shot. After a minute, she waves before passing the fenced-in media section toward the true red carpet.

She pauses and slips her phone out of the heavy beaded clutch, thoughts of Griffin floating through her mind.

Griffin had his surgery yesterday, and despite his coffee shop declaration, Aria reached out. She didn't expect a quick response—if at all—knowing he would be groggy. And even if he didn't want to hear from her, it was important to Aria that she send well-wishes at the least.

Aria: How're you healing up? I hear you're in the fanciest of digs.

His reply came surprisingly quickly on Friday evening.

Griffin: It's luxury in a hospital way. Not sure if I'd recommend it to a friend unless surgery is explicitly required.

Aria smiled. She'd been toying with the idea of inviting him as her guest this evening until she learned of the surgery date. It seemed like an easy grab to keep up appearances, and Bailey couldn't care less for black-tie events.

Aria: So there won't be a five-star review in their future?

Griffin: There's no pool, and room service ends at eight. How do they expect me to live like this? 😉

Aria: It's basically prison.

He hadn't replied right away, and Aria assumed he'd nodded off. Or maybe a doctor had come into his room, or support staff asking if he needed help to the restroom.

When Aria glances at her phone moments before stepping onto the red carpet, reporters spread out in dots along the walk, prepared to pepper the musician guests with questions. There's still no reply from Griffin.

It grates at her more than she would like.

Aria closes her eyes, stretches her head gently from side to side, then pulls in a slow, self-soothing breath. She's got this. Walking a red carpet and taking questions is where her superpower—putting on her armor and getting stuff done—shines brightest.

"You ready?" Bailey asks gently at her side.

"I was born ready," Aria says, shoving every thought of Griffin from her mind.

She steps onto the ruby carpet as if it's a catwalk, stretching her legs in large strides, eyeing the cameras with a playful smirk. A few hoots ring out, and Aria knows she's hit her mark. The media loves her when she plays along. In times past, when she's been tired—probably on the verge of burnout—she's phoned it in, walking primly, smiling brightly, and waving like a member of the royal family. Every time it fell flat. What they love is when she puts on the same act as her shows.

"Aria! Aria!" All of the interviewers call out for her to stop and talk with them. It's customary for her to stop once or twice, and admittedly she has her favorites. Aria loves Ken Gossling from *Culture News* because he asks interesting questions and is never looking to trip her up.

Aria spots him and goes to him.

Ken winks as he pushes the microphone out in front of her. "Aria, we're all so thrilled to see you here tonight. There's so much excitement about your new tour, but maybe most of all, fans are desperate for details on your personal life. How is Griffin Hayes healing up?"

Aria's smile falters. She should've known Ken would be keen enough to detect that the friendship between Aria and Griffin was sincere. He wouldn't be asking about it if he thought it was a sham. She rights herself.

"He has been put up in the most comfortable manner with many professionals at his side, helping him get back into tip-top shape, so I guess we can say, as well as possible considering the situation."

Aria smiles and nods, leaning in as the crowd noise around her kicks up.

Ken continues, "And of course, his crew would include you, his best friend? What's it been like to see your good friend endure an injury of this extent? Certainly it's been a challenge?"

Aria lets her gaze drop, and she curls her lips into one another. She likes Ken because he asks questions that reflect her as a whole person, but for this very reason, perhaps she should've skipped him today. The truth is that Aria's been having *many* feelings about Griffin since the injury. She's been concerned for him. She's been confused about his pulling away. She's been yearning for the special shimmer he brings to her life, the way he makes her feel like she's floating away from all the hard parts, as if he's her personal hot-air balloon.

It's been necessary to buckle down in the studio. Gerald didn't mince words about that. But also maybe, just maybe,

Aria has been using that, along with the tour preparation, to avoid having to think too hard about these things. About why her feelings for Griffin are so intense and why she can't simply allow him to pull away like he wants to.

Sure, she's no expert at friendship, but she's practically an expert in the *ends* of friendships. If nothing else, her past friendships have taught her how to let go.

But this time she can't make it work the same.

Aria looks up at Ken. "It's been really hard, to be honest. I can't be as close to Griff as I'd like to be right now. It's the time for his professional staff to be front and center, but it's devastating to know my friend is dealing with such a serious injury."

"I guess that's the thing about friendships—they endure even in the hard parts."

Aria nods. "I'm doing my best. And I'm also working on a new album!"

An urge to go to Griffin to show him that she cares washes over her again. If she could rewind time to when he was in her studio and replay that section in a loop, the album would probably be done by now.

"Oh, don't tease us with new music! Details?"

Aria winks. "You know I can't right now."

"So, what about Griffin? When will we get our next dose of friend content? We're dying out here." Ken grins.

"If I had my way, he'd be my plus-one tonight, but he needs to recover. As soon as we get some content-worthy hang time, I promise you all will be the first to know."

Aria steps back, raising a hand to Ken in farewell, and heads down the carpet. She stops in the middle, where a staff member wearing all black and a headset instructs her to pose. A sea of flashing lights greets her, along with calls for "This way, Aria! This way!"

She plays up the poses, channeling her inner powerhouse, but inside she's a mess of jumbled feelings.

Aria can't stop thinking about Griffin.

At dinner she makes polite conversation with the others at her table, and when she's announced as an award winner, she takes the stage and accepts delightedly. Aria leans over the podium and makes a brief but heartfelt speech, thanking her team and fans.

Still, her mind floats back to Griffin.

Is this just the result of Ken posing good questions? Or is this something real?

Aria gets home that night, and she goes right to bed.

In her dreams, he's there again. Griffin.

Chapter 43

Griffin

Griffin has been at the rehab facility for three days, and it's wearing on him. When it comes to the practical elements—the support, the staff, the cleanliness, even the food—everything has been top notch, but he's looking forward to getting home today. He wouldn't have been able to attend the game in person, but watching it on television from his hospital-style bed felt worse than the hit that blew out his knee. It couldn't be made clearer how far off the field he's fallen. So far that he can't even make it to the bench.

Griffin's knee is painful, and now the incisions from surgery throb as soon as the medication wears off. The surgeon was happy with how the procedure went, but only once he's healed and rehabbed will Griffin know how well his knee functions. Perhaps worse is the fact that Griffin has done little aside from use the restroom, attempt a partial shower, and lie in this dang bed. Physical therapy has been painful, but at least it feels like actually *doing something*. His mind is growing irritable and restless.

He clicks around the various sports networks on the television for an hour or so until the tech comes in with a wheelchair.

"I'm here to bust you out!" The tech is bubbly and cheery, and Griffin can't help but smile back.

"Then you're just the person I want to see."

The tech wheels the chair bedside and instructs Griffin on the best way to slide into it. "Your car service is already waiting outside."

Griffin slides onto the wheelchair, feeling a pinch of optimism at the promise of getting home. "Perfect."

"Here"—the tech grabs a tote branded with the facility's name and wiggles it before returning it to the back of the wheelchair—"is all of your paperwork. Copies have been sent to the team doc and staff as requested, so this is for your personal records."

"And the rest of my personal items?"

A second staff person appears. "I'm here to pack them up."

Griffin wouldn't typically be comfortable with so many people doing so much for him. He wasn't exactly raised as someone who expected to be doted on, but in this scenario he has no choice but to rely on them. "I appreciate it all."

"We're happy to assist," the tech says. "I'm a mega Wardens fan, so it only feels like helping the cause."

The wheelchair glides smoothly down the tiled floor, and

the tech pops open a side door that opens onto a ramp. Griffin shields his eyes as he adjusts to the bright afternoon sun, but he still catches sight of a familiar vehicle.

The driver's side door pops open, and Elliott climbs out.

"How are you here?" Griffin asks, his face creased into a deep smile at the sight of his friend.

"I got an early ride back from the game. I figured we could recap the game on the drive back."

"That would be incredible, man. I've been going crazy sitting there all alone."

The tech helps Griffin into the car, and a staff person brings out the rest of his items and loads them in the trunk. Once they're alone in the car, Griffin pulls in a deep breath as Elliott drives away.

"It feels so good to be out."

Elliott eyes Griffin's knee briefly before looking back to the road. "The recovery is always brutal. The guys who go straight home don't really have it easier."

Griffin nods. "It's the mental part really. We know how to get hurt. We know how to stick with it through discomfort."

Elliott nods. "You going to keep coming to practice?"

Griffin has thought about it, and he can't decide what's the best thing to do. Coach leaves it up to injured players to do what they need to do to recover, and for some players, trekking to and from the facility only to watch is torture. For others, it keeps them connected to the team and feeling encouraged. Griffin doesn't know which bucket he'll fall into. "I might for a bit. See how it goes."

"You can't rot in that condo alone."

"Agreed." Griffin lets out a grunt. "Ugh. I feel like I can't do anything. Like why do I even exist if I can't play the game? I'm totally lost, man."

"You're going to come back," Elliott says. "I know it's rough."

"Maybe. Or maybe not."

Griffin feels the heat rise in him. He's usually good at keeping his anger under control. On the field he channels it into play. But what's he supposed to do with it now?

"Come on, man. You know that attitude will kill you."

Griffin sighs as the quickening of his pulse aggravates the throb in his knee. "You're right. It's just easier said than done."

"You just need a distraction—a project—for the time being." Elliott signals and turns onto the road where Griffin's building sits.

"I'm not sure there's much I can work on outside of football," Griffin mumbles.

"What about Aria? Now you actually have time to run around and do stuff together."

Griffin looks away, out of the window. "I don't want her to see me like this. I don't want *anyone* to see me like this."

"I think Aria genuinely likes you, so I'm not sure why you feel that way."

"Just let me have this *one thing*. I know it's the right thing."

Griffin knows it's a cheap shot, that Elliott's right that spending time with a friend could actually improve his mood. Especially one who reminds him of the world outside of football and has even pointed to the way he belongs in it.

"Fine." Elliott pulls into the circular driveway in front, the one used for deliveries and drop-offs. "But then humor me on my next suggestion."

"I'm all ears."

"South Shore High asked me if I'd mentor some of the athletes, the ones who are dedicated and show promise. I can only give so much time, and there are tons of players who could use guidance. Someone to believe in them."

Griffin perks up. He was expecting something much more up Elliott's alley, like parties with supermodels or attending fashion events, partnering with nightclub managers to host parties featuring the players.

Griffin has always liked kids and enjoyed the times he's worked with them at the Wardens' summer camp. Never before has Griffin gotten a chance to dedicate any real time to it, not with the demands of practice and games, and then the off-season training required to keep him in shape.

"Sure thing," Griffin says.

"Yeah?" Elliott brightens. "It's not a massive time commitment, but these kids will go nuts over time with a Wardens player."

Griffin feels the corners of his mouth twitch. "I'm happy to do it. Now let's just hope they're okay with getting a gimpy one." He glances quickly at his wrapped knee, then away.

"You're not a 'gimpy' Wardens player. You're *Griffin Hayes*. Don't ever forget that."

Griffin accepts the compliment, and Elliott begins the process of helping him up to his place. Griffin puts himself on crutches for the first time in a while, and the small independence feels good. He's always hated having to rely on someone to push him around, and his surgeon didn't want him using crutches in the first couple of days of recovery.

Elliott grabs Griffin's belongings, and as they head inside

and take the elevator up to the top floor, Griffin can't help but linger on Elliott's last comment: "*You're Griffin Hayes.*"

Elliott meant that he's an accomplished football player, but Griffin wonders what else Griffin Hayes could be. Because now more than ever, the reality of the "football isn't forever" mantra is knocking on his front door. It might be now, or it might be years from now, but Griffin desperately needs to find a purpose, a passion, beyond football.

Maybe this volunteering gig will be a decent start.

Chapter 44

Aria

Aria has a team meeting on Monday morning to discuss the schedule for her upcoming tour. Since her team emailed over the details in advance, it was mostly a review for her. Nevertheless, it served as a productive note on which to start the week. After a nutritious lunch of salmon, rice, and vegetables—thanks to Chef Bailey—Aria locks herself up in her studio, determined to make some progress.

Aria still hasn't heard anything else from Griffin. He must be focusing on recovery as he'd so clearly stated. It sends a sharp pain through her chest every time the realization hits that he's pushed her away, and every time she mentally walks down memory lane.

The first viral video of Griffin singing passionately to "Glass Heart" still makes her smile. When she first saw it, Aria dismissed it as cute but inconsequential. Even when they started spending PR time together, Aria kept it categorized as "cute but inconsequential." Maybe she changed—maybe Griffin helped her change—but back then she didn't really consider the prospect of a real connection.

She'd been too scared, her walls too firmly planted, to consider it.

Then there was the chivalry at the animal gala, but really it was more than that. It was consideration. Griffin knew as well as Aria did that she could've easily called someone from her team. She wasn't without options. But Griffin offered a ride, inconvenienced himself, and in the process they had some great conversation. Aria thinks of all of the small moments they shared, swapping thoughts and stories, sharing coffee and snacks, laughing over tiny things, learning each other. In fact, aside from Bailey, Griffin might be the person who knows her best.

Aria remembers them together in this space, and her heart flutters. She wills herself not to go there, but she can't help it. She lets her mind go to the kiss. Her gaze wanders to the sliding doors. In some ways it's hard to fathom that it occurred on that little patio outside, the one that now sits bare and lonely, cluttered with long-fallen leaves.

Aria squeezes her eyes shut tight. How could she let it slip through her fingers? Inside she simmers with frustration that she didn't clue in to what she had before her sooner.

Like she's done reliably for years, Aria goes to the one place she can spill all of her thoughts when it feels too much: her writing. She settles into her writing spot, tucking the notebook in her lap, grabs her pen, and moves her hand feverishly across the page.

It doesn't come all at once, but in words, concepts, then eventually lyrics. She writes, crosses out, draws arrows for inserts and rearrangements. Aria pours all of her feelings, her self-doubt, her hopes into the words. She tells herself no one has to see it if it's awful. For now it's only her and the page. And in that blessed space, it comes together.

Until you came along,
I was living in slow motion.
Playing pop star like they wanted,
For them and their devotion.

But in the dark of night,
I tossed and turned, all wrong.
It started to make sense,
Only as you came along.

In trying to be perfect,
All I did was make me small.
You told me, more than once,
Go ahead and give your all.

Things started to go right,
Me letting go and staying true.
But then you left me in the dark,
And now I know something new.

It wasn't just the music,
Not the hope you sparked in me.

It was everything about you,
I'm like a lock, and you the key.

You're a flame lit inside me,
And I ask you please come home.
Everything is brighter by your side,
Together, not alone.

I don't care about the music
Or about the final score.
All I know is that without you,
I will always be wanting more.

Aria drops back into the pillowy couch and lets her notebook slide to her lap. That's just it: She wants more.

But *the song*. She looks back over the words just to be certain she didn't imagine it. That she has, in fact, crafted exactly the sort of song her heart's been yearning for. A song that's honest and raw. A song that's also romantic. Aria knows her fans will love it.

But her own thoughts trip her up: *Romantic.*

If Aria's being honest in her music, it's probably also about time she's honest with herself: She has undeniable feelings for Griffin, and she doesn't mean friendship.

Even if it "makes sense," no part of Aria's heart wants Griffin in the friend zone. She wants all of him. His company, his laughter. Dress-up events, dress-down events. Simple at-home hangouts. She wants him close. His arms around her.

Kisses on the patio.

She's even willing to endure the online chatter, the criticism and speculation. The fact that the tabloids will blast them both just for clicks. Griffin, of all the people she's ever known, is someone who could endure it, someone who would know to slap on the blinders and ignore it. She can trust him.

This whole time, Griffin has been a safe, reliable place for her, a place she blossoms.

Aria racks her brain trying to think about her past relationships. None of them compare even in the slightest. Her feelings for Griffin are the strongest she's ever felt for someone else.

She pulls in a shaky breath when the realization hits.

Aria is in love with Griffin Hayes.

Immediately, Aria is flooded by doubts. He's already pulled away, so how could he want more? Is she setting herself up for heartbreak like she's already endured time and time again? What if he rejects her? What if she loses what remains of their friendship in the process?

Stop, Aria commands herself. Never before has she felt this way, and she'll be damned if she leaves it up to fate. For better or worse, she's going to tell Griffin.

It's true that he might not feel the same.

But Aria's also not the type to stay in the wings and let something she wants pass her by. Aria gets up and looks around the room until she finds her phone nestled between the mixing boards. As she pulls up Griffin's contact information, she begs the universe to align whatever stars are required for the very best outcome.

She hits the button to dial.

The ring sounds exceptionally loud and clunky in her ear as

Aria waits. Her heart picks up, blood pumping faster through her in anticipation. It rings and rings.

"Come on, Griff, pick up," Aria whispers to herself—or any celestial power willing to lend a hand.

Finally, her call goes to voicemail. Aria hadn't considered the possibility of voicemail, and she's usually much more of a texter than a message leaver, but in the name of giving this a real, true effort, after the beep, she speaks.

"Hey, Griff. Just calling to check in. Well, that, but also there's something I wanted to talk to you about. Give me a call when you have a minute, okay? It'll be good to hear from you."

Aria's palms are sweaty when she taps the icon to disconnect and sets the phone in her palm. She sits still for a moment, wondering if he'll call right back. It's difficult to know. As she sits in the silence and watches the phone screen go dark, Aria can't help but wonder. Could it be too late to fix what they had? Have they drifted too far apart from each other and away from their kiss?

Aria is pulled from her thoughts when Bailey calls down the stairs. "You still alive down there or what?"

Aria's shocked to see that it's past five o'clock already. "I'm probably overdue for a break."

"Good, because I'm getting hungry."

Aria grins as she starts to climb the stairs. "You're always thinking about food in some way, shape, or form."

Bailey, cast in the warm light of the kitchen behind her, shrugs. "Well, one of us needs to make sure you're not wasting away down there."

At the top of the stairs, Aria pulls Bailey into her arms and squeezes. Griffin or no Griffin, she is so lucky to have her sister. She's probably partially right about the meal-skipping part, especially when Aria gets in the zone.

But also, and even more so, without Bailey she wouldn't even know what love is. Not even when it walks into her life by way of a sing-along gone viral.

Chapter 45

Griffin

It's game day, and the first Wardens home game Griffin won't attend since he signed with the team. He considered dragging himself out of the condo and watching from the bench—Elliott even encouraged him to do so—but he simply couldn't bring himself to do it.

In general, he hasn't been able to drag himself to do much since he got home earlier this week. If he's honest, it scares him a little how unlike himself he is at this point. He's abandoned his routine, eats off schedule—even his small home gym seems to be mocking him.

Is this who he is without football?

Griffin knew things might get tough, but this is beyond what he prepared for.

He flips on the television, hopeful for a distraction, and the game is already underway. The Wardens are up 14–7, and a pang of guilt runs through him. He really *should* be there. Not only is he a broken mess without football; he's also a bad friend to his teammates, his friends. Griffin shuts off the television when the first quarter ends; he just can't take the reminder that football, the Wardens, everything that's been his world, is moving on without him.

Griffin wonders how long it'll take for the team to forget him, how long it will take for the fans to forget him. He seems to already have forgotten himself.

When his phone starts to ring across the room, Griffin considers letting it go to voicemail like he does often nowadays, but something inside him whispers to him, *Go get it.* Griffin begrudgingly gets up and slings his crutches under his arms. Despite his worsening mood, physical therapy has been going well, and Griffin's mobility is improving day by day. It doesn't hold any great implications for what he will—or won't—be able to do on the field or in the future of his career, but it does allow him to better manage his everyday activities.

On the phone screen scrolls the name "Coach Pete."

Coach Pete is the head coach over at South Shore High, and stopping by their practice earlier this week was the one thing that's kept Griffin afloat. The players were thrilled to meet him, and he was able to sit down and talk to them after practice. It wasn't the same as being back on the field, but afterward, Griffin felt like he'd made some difference, been purposeful for the first time in a while. And the proximity to the game didn't hurt either.

"Griffin, hey! How's the knee?"

"Old news by now, I'd say," Griffin says, desperate to talk about *anything* but his injury. "How's the team?"

"I'll tell you what, they're holding themselves differently

after your visit. Not a one of them showed up late to practice, and every player came focused, dressed, and gave it their best."

"That's wonderful. I have to say it was a blast for me too. Really brought me back to my high school days. Some really fun times."

"Well, I'm glad to hear that because I'm calling with another ask."

"Shoot." Griffin drops down onto the closest part of his sectional couch, then settles the crutches on the ground.

"We're wanting to put on a nice little senior luncheon—doesn't even have to be a luncheon, a reception is great—for our end of season. These guys work so hard, and for a lot of them, this will be their last season ever. The problem is that the department doesn't have the budget to do it. We had no choice but to fork over a hefty sum to condition the field this year; it was so bad the guys were getting hurt, their feet catching in holes in the ground. I understand if it's too much to ask, but—"

"Yes. Of course. I'm happy to help."

Coach Pete lets out a sigh of relief. "You're a godsend. And we're not asking for anything flashy—just some help making the guys feel celebrated for their hard work and dedication to the program, an occasion to borrow their dad's tie and put on a button-down shirt. A little cake and punch."

"Maybe I can recruit some of the other guys?"

"We're grateful for anything. You bring more Wardens, and the guys might not even care about cake."

Griffin laughs—the first time he's done so since he was at the high school earlier this week. "I'm not about to show up without cake, even if the entire team was behind me. Let me get to work, and I'll get back to you with some plans."

"Thank you," Coach Pete says. "This will be a memory that stays with the players for their entire lives, I just know it."

After the call ends, Griffin settles back on the couch. Eventually he flips the television back on to the Wardens game. The commentators are chattering after Elliott just caught a touchdown pass.

"The team is really stepping up in the absence of tight end Griffin Hayes."

"Has there been any news on his recovery?"

"Ah well, you know that knee was blown out several years ago, and the rate of success in a second comeback is slim. Of course, we're all hopeful to see Griffin Hayes back out on the field, but will he ever be back to pro-league condition? I'm not convinced."

"Griffin's been a powerhouse for a long time; maybe it's a natural end to a vibrant career."

"Don't let him hear you say that! All the messaging from the team and his personal channels is that he's focused on making a comeback and resuming his position with the Wardens."

Griffin's heart hammers in his chest, a sickness swelling inside him, as if he'd just overheard someone gossiping about him. The commentators are there for the fans at home, but of course they're aware that everything they say gets back to the players, team, and staff. It's a business, not a social club.

It's also not like Griffin hasn't been aware of this reality—that this injury could mean the end of his career.

But hearing it broadcast for the entire world over the film of his team killing it on the field without him feels like the sun of his world being eclipsed.

He cuts the television off, curls up on the couch, and pulls the blanket over his head. In the darkness, he brings his phone screen to life and deletes his sports networks apps, the ones that push scores and professional league news. The relief that follows lets him pull in a deep breath, so he takes it a step further and deletes the social media apps where career-end speculation will undoubtedly be circulated too.

Griffin promises himself that all he'll focus on is the event for the South Shore football players. If he thinks about pro football or the Wardens for much longer, he might not ever come back.

And when he does open social media again, it'll probably be to check in on Aria, to see what magic she's been up to.

Despite everything he's dealing with, he misses her terribly.

Chapter 46

Aria

A call from Aria's agent first thing Monday morning is never a good sign. Aria knows that means people have been talking over the weekend, which also means that it's about a topic whose importance has been elevated to critical. She only needs to watch the call come in on her phone to know this is about the new record.

"Lay it on me," Aria says.

Aria is out walking the trails at a park, Bailey at her side and her ball cap pulled low over her face. Occasionally she'll get recognized, but more often than not, the power walkers with whom she shares the trails have their earbuds in place, their arms pumping, and their eyes set on finishing their laps.

"Don't you know I just about ate Gerald for breakfast with the way I just chewed him out," Monroe says.

Aria laughs, her breath pouring out into the cold air in a white cloud.

"I don't know who he thinks he is sending me demanding emails on a Sunday morning, but I set him straight."

"He's following up on the album already? It hasn't even been two weeks."

Monroe sighs. "I totally agree. But technically, the contract stipulated that it should be delivered today."

"Since when have my deadlines ever actually been deadlines?"

In the past, Aria churned out songs with ease, and representatives from the label reviewed them as the initial versions were complete. They loved all of them, so even when she went over her formal deadline to wrap up the last few songs—the ones that gave her the hardest time but often ended up being her greatest hits—no one batted an eye. In fact, the lack of true deadlines was something they've all previously joked about.

"You just have to start feeding them stuff. Gerald's obviously getting nervous that you're blocked somehow, that you're not going to be able to deliver."

Aria grunts. "How rude."

In truth, he's not *that* far off. Sure, she's come up with a few songs like the football player–theater girl one. Plus a couple she has muddled together into something passable—good, not great—something that Gerald might rubber stamp, but something she would despise performing on tour. But she *has* tried. It's simply that when Aria attempts to write the songs they're asking for, it's as if her body just won't comply. Like her soul has decided that she's ready to evolve, so it won't let her fingers run over the piano in the same melodies it has for years. It won't let her voice sing a song that doesn't also come from the heart, one that it tells her she's already done before.

"So, what do you say? When can we get something over? Nothing fancy, just something raw to show them you're working, that they will be able to put out the album on time."

"I'll get them something by Wednesday."

"You're a queen," Monroe says, then hurries off the line.

Aria slips her phone back into the deep pockets of her sherpa fleece coat. Bailey looks on curiously from beside her.

"Gerald starting nonsense already?" Bailey asks.

"No rest for the wicked."

Aria picks up the pace, and Bailey matches her, the trees surrounding them left only with the barest of leaves, the ground firm below them. The sky is overcast, no hint of blue, despite the lack of rain predicted.

"How *is* it going down there?"

Even though it's Bailey asking, Aria keeps her work close to her chest until it's ready to share. She doesn't like giving play-by-plays or talking too much about the work. Maybe it's a fear of "jinxing" it or maybe it's the desire to allow herself to change her mind on things, but Aria prefers to wait until a full raw version of a song is ready before sharing it.

It's another reason it was so unusual to have Griffin by her side that time in the studio.

"Not as well as I would like it to be going. I feel like I'm caught in between. In between what they want from me and what I want to do. But even what I want to do feels fuzzy."

"I'm sure it only helps to have Gerald nipping at your heels."

"*Exactly*. My voice is evolving—I *know* that. But I need time to fully find it and mold it. Worldwide Records just wants me to be a pop music factory."

Bailey rubs Aria's back, and when their eyes meet, she presses her mouth into a concerned line.

"I feel like I'm starting to disappear." It feels like a relief to admit it out loud. "Like I'm being lost inside this Aria Wilder persona that was once a version of me. The persona that fits me less and less the more time passes."

"Surely there's a way forward."

Bailey doesn't push, and in the quiet that follows, Aria wonders for the first time if maybe moving forward with music *isn't* the way. Maybe all of this struggle is proof that she should quit while she's ahead. She'd have to return certain payments that she received from the contract, but it wouldn't make a dent on her lifestyle. Financially, she's already set for life. It would mean creating a rift between her and the biggest music label in the country, however, and she's constantly reminded that there are thousands of aspiring artists who would be more than happy to take her place.

Aria tries to imagine a life for herself without music, and the only thing she can see is a blank slate.

Admittedly, her heart does pinch at the thought of leaving the industry behind, never again feeling the roar of the crowd, the buzz of a new album release, the beautiful exhaustion of a tour completed. But then again, decoupling from the industry wouldn't preclude her from making music. In fact, historically artists have gone off the map, then reemerged when they were ready to redefine themselves—some more successfully than others.

Aria can't make sense of it, and even as her feet pound the dirt below her, she doesn't reach any clarity.

She can't help but think of "Until You Came Along" and Griffin. At two o'clock this morning, Aria awoke and had such a moment of clarity about the melody, she typed her idea into her phone. New lyrics poured from her, and she jotted everything down. That song is a light in the dark for her right now, but it's also unlike any of her other hits. Those she could readily put together, shine up, and send off to Gerald and his cohorts with confidence. All of those were about an imaginary person, maybe who she thought she should be, maybe who they wanted her to be. Maybe they were just open-ended enough to let the fans superimpose themselves as the main character.

But this time, the song about Griffin is as good as the script of her heart read aloud. Aria says she wants to do this, be real and raw in her music, but it's still not easy. She's lived with walls around her for a reason—because when she's let people close enough to all of her, they've hurt her. Not to mention Griffin is still MIA, and Aria hasn't received so much as a text back. Maybe he doesn't feel the same way, but is that reason enough to hold back?

Aria keeps walking. Considering all of these new and risky things is sending jitters through her, and the ground below her is a comfort. She breathes in the fresh air and reminds herself that she'll find her way. Even if it takes a bit of fumbling around first.

Chapter 47

Griffin

If asked to estimate his aptitude for event planning and organization months earlier, Griffin would've chosen the lowest possible rating. He'd attended more than his fair share of events, but all of those were organized by true professionals—and often with the financial backing of major brands. But the South Shore High School football program, which fell so unexpectedly into his path, seems to have brought out the event planner in him. In only a week, Griffin has set up a picture-perfect senior luncheon in the high school gymnasium.

Along one side of the gym, a buffet sits atop long tables covered with linen cloth, two attendants helping to serve and refresh the platters. Griffin chose barbecue from a popular local place—a favorite among the team, according to Coach Pete—and the sweet scent of smoked meat has already permeated the place. Iced tea and fresh lemonade sit chilled in glass pitchers, and the cake has its own table at the end.

Griffin didn't go too frilly on the decorations, and instead he had the senior portraits of each player printed in large scale and set up on a stand. Alongside, a table has been set up with memory books for each player—a collection of pictures the coaches gathered from the years—for each to sign for one another. The books were the trickiest component of the day to pull off. Getting them put together and printed on short notice wasn't easy, but Griffin enjoyed the feeling of being tired from something—*anything*—other than his injury.

Between the food and the photo hall of fame, round tables have been set with quality linens. As centerpieces, Griffin set out footballs signed by the entire Wardens team, and there are enough for each player to take one home as a souvenir.

Griffin stands back to admire the setup, his knee now in a brace that allows him to move around more easily. He smiles to himself. The guys are going to love it.

The gym doors open, and Coach Pete enters, his eyes immediately going wide.

"Griffin! This is too much!" He stops and looks around, massaging his beard as he admires the setup.

"If I'm doing it, I'm doing it *right*."

That's the way Griffin approaches everything, the way he has since he can remember. He might not have followed in the footsteps of his parents, but he did absorb their lessons about hard work and dedication.

"You sure did. The guys are going to flip."

"Just wait until I reveal my special guests." Griffin grins.

Coach Pete doesn't have a chance to reply before they're interrupted by the opening of the door and the students and their families and guests enter. Their excitement spills over in animated chatter, and it's the final piece to the puzzle of the event.

Griffin shakes hands and takes pictures. Then he points everyone to the memory books to sign before lunch is served.

Before long, Griffin feels a familiar slap on his back, and when he turns, Elliott stands with feet planted, his hands on his hips. "Nice work on this, man. I never got a thing close to this growing up."

A couple of the defensive linemen spill through the doors, and both of the quarterbacks follow close behind.

The Wardens players gather over by the senior portraits, take pictures, chat, and sign autographs. Before long, the food is served and the players—the guests of honor—are sent to join the line first as each Warden finds his assigned table. Plates are loaded, tables are filled, and the room grows noisy as lunch chatter commences.

Griffin sits back and enjoys it. It was work to put this together, but it wasn't anything outrageous. The impact it's having on the seniors and their families far outpaces anything he put in. Hopefully Coach Pete is right: This will be a memory that stays with them.

Honoring someone's hard work is always worth it.

After plenty of time is allowed to eat and visit, Coach Pete takes the mic and makes a speech. He talks about the football season as well as seasons past. He spotlights each player, noting his contribution to the team, progress, and quality of character. A few tears are dabbed away by emotional parents.

Every player is called up and presented a commemorative plaque.

"And finally, none of this would be possible without the incredible Griffin Hayes from the Chicago Wardens, who stepped in last minute and pulled off this whole thing like he'd been a professional event planner all along. Griffin, could you come up?"

Griffin is caught off guard, not planning on being called up for anything. He snags his crutches and makes quick work of propelling himself over.

"On behalf of the South Shore Eagles, we'd like to present you with this honorary player plaque." Coach Pete holds out a plaque like the one the seniors received. "In only a very brief time, you have made a significant impact on these young men, who are now even more confident as they graduate and head out into the world for the success they're due."

A thickness gathers at the top of Griffin's throat, and he swallows it down. He blinks rapidly at the swell of emotion inside him—another surprise.

Griffin takes the plaque. "Thank you, Coach Pete. I have to say this means a lot. Maybe more than getting awards from the pros. It's been an absolute honor to get to support you, even if just for a little while."

The crowd claps, and a few players let out cheers of support.

Griffin makes his way back to his seat, the flush in his cheeks warm. He doesn't blush when he gets accolades from the media or reporters—those compliments feel rehearsed, transactional. He doesn't blush when he gets pulled into celebrity photoshoots.

He *does* blush around Aria Wilder.

Maybe, Griffin realizes, he blushes only when something really touches his heart.

If how he feels today is any indication, it shouldn't be too much longer before he's in good enough shape to reach back out to Aria. He thinks of her all the time.

Griffin settles himself back at his table, and Elliott at his side gives him a celebratory slap on the back.

"With all the business out of the way," Coach Pete announces, "we'll get to the cake. Mrs. Smithfield would like to take a group picture beside it, and then she will begin to cut the cake. Oh, and Mrs. Flinn will help too."

A few of the mothers get up and head toward the cake, phones at the ready to snap their own picture.

In the pause, Elliott leans over. "Dang, man. You know you're killing it, right?"

Griffin shrugs. "It really wasn't much. But thanks for connecting me. It's been nice to be helpful while I'm out of commission."

Elliott's eyes turn serious—a rare occasion. "But you know what else you're doing, right? You're showing these kids—and the rest of us—that there's still life after setbacks. Not a one of these kids are going to the league, but they see you stepping up and making an impact even when you've been sidelined."

"I hadn't thought of it like that."

"You're offering everyone way more than the entertainment of being a top player on the field. We all know players come and go; all of our time is limited. But you're a living example of the fact that there's life after football."

Griffin's mouth hangs slightly ajar.

This whole time, Griffin, though thoroughly enjoying it,

had framed this work as a distraction, a stopgap. He's felt a pulse of pride and fulfillment that he didn't let himself examine too closely. Doing so would only risk extinguishing it somehow, overthinking it into oblivion. The injury had already created far too much time for Griffin to be alone with his thoughts. But now Elliott's perspective makes sense of it all.

He's right—this is proof that there is life for Griffin after football.

He's just been too preoccupied to open his eyes to it.

"Thank you," Griffin tells Elliott. "That helps in ways you'll never know."

A moment passes between them, and as the skin at the corners of Elliott's eyes creases as he draws his face into a tentative frown, Griffin knows Elliott's been thinking the same thing as him: This injury is most likely the end of his career.

The Wardens team—Griffin's team—is supportive of pushing as hard as he wants to get back into game play shape. But Griffin is in the driver's seat. He gets to make the call on what happens next.

Griffin isn't a young buck anymore. There is no better comparison than being among these graduating seniors. Guys only a few years older than these boys wearing sport coats a size too big over their fathers' ties are entering the league fresh and in their prime.

Now that Griffin believes for the first time that there is life for him beyond football, a good life where he can thrive, it becomes clear.

It's time for him to hang up his cleats.

And not with resentment over the injury or with hard feelings over being cut, but with gratitude for the honor of getting to play in the league. And with a new zeal for the next chapter of his life.

One in which he hopes he can do more of this—supporting youth athletes.

Chapter 48

Aria

This evening Aria is the headlining performer at the music festival that's been raging throughout the city since late Thursday, and she welcomes it as a break from the studio. The stage is a temporary structure built of steel beams on the largest field in Roxbury Park, and it's complete with a band and lights. No special effects, no dropping in from the ceiling or rising from the belly of the stage like Aria tends to do at her arena shows.

From the wings, she can actually *see* the crowd. A group of young women decked out in rhinestones and cowgirl boots are twirling one another to the music of the opening band. They sip their tall beers and have eyes for only their best friends. Beside them, a few couples stand close, arms slung around one another. A smattering of people are bobbing their heads and singing along. All of them, real people. People in varying dress, coming from different places, watching from their unique viewpoint.

It reminds Aria that her fans aren't a homogenous mass of sameness. They are all individuals.

Aria tries to imagine these people hearing her new music. She's not overcome by horror. In fact, she wonders if the folks at Worldwide Records are terribly mistaken about what her fans want. As she's come to do frequently while wrestling with her music making, Aria thinks of Griffin. Of that day in the studio. His smile is etched onto her mind so clearly that she hopes it never fades. In it, all of his belief in her shines. The buzz of his quiet presence, supporting her as she lost herself in the work.

Griffin might not be as frequent a visitor in her life as she wishes—although they did end up getting their social media posts up together, which has momentarily quieted the rumors—but Aria can't help but count herself lucky to have had the closeness with him that she did.

Just this morning, Griffin made his own post on social media, one that's since gone viral in its own way. He announced his intentions to launch The Griffin Hayes Foundation for Youth Sports during his recovery period, a foundation focused on raising funds for programs in underserved communities, as well as for student athletes seeking higher education. Griffin spoke from the heart about a recent event, and it inspired Aria so deeply that she can't quite shake it.

Maybe it's because of the way Griffin is seeking to do good—make good out of a bad situation—or perhaps more so it's because the Griffin on that screen was the purest version of himself dialed up to max, but his eyes sparkled, genuinely lit up, and Aria was certain that he'd found magic outside of the game. She cheered for him. Even though he didn't hear it.

A stage manager pulls Aria from her thoughts. "You ready? This act is thirty seconds from finished."

Aria reaches for the guitar she'd stowed beside her. "I was born ready."

She smiles deeply as she says it like it's a joke, but Aria wonders if there's more meaning to her words. What *exactly* does she believe she was born to do?

Aria is announced, and she doesn't miss a beat before marching on in her signature leggy style, waving at the cheering crowd. The core members of her band join her: Marty on the drums, Rochelle and Kay on backup vocals, and Wilson also on guitar.

Once the crowd settles, they break into the first of the agreed-upon set. Aria knows all of her hits so well that even if they surprised her, by only the first few notes, Aria would be able to call the song and jump in. The crowd vibrates, singing, clapping, and dancing as the music floods the park, the city buildings lined up in the background like soldiers on guard.

By the middle of the set, Aria wonders if the fans will ever get sick of some of her music like she's sick of it. From the looks of them, perhaps not, but that also doesn't mean they don't deserve something new.

A sudden lightning strike of sensation runs through her, and with it, an idea: What if Aria gave the audience a taste of her new song?

If Griffin can step bravely outside of the game that he has allowed to define him for all of these years, why can't she take a risk on herself too?

The song winds down, and before Marty leads the band

into the opening of the next song, Aria speaks loudly into the mic and calls for a pause.

The crowd stills, attention glued to the stage, as this unplanned quiet leaves them waiting for the next boppy hit. A few crew members poke their heads out from their hiding spots to assess for issues.

"Chicago! My dear hometown. Thank you for being here with me tonight. As a special token of my appreciation, I wondered if you might like a sample of something new I've been working on."

The crowd erupts. Aria glances over her shoulder, and the band looks shocked and confused.

"It'll just be me on the guitar. The band is as surprised by this announcement as you." Laughter rises from the crowd, and when Aria glances back at the band, they're freshly relaxed. "You guys with me on this?"

Whoops and cheers come from the crowd, and one of the crew brings Aria a tall barstool. She whispers her thanks. It'll make it easier than doing it standing as she had planned.

Aria slips onto the stool, and her body hums with excitement. It feels like her very first performance, the state fairs, the dive bar stages, lived all over once again.

Before her hammering heart talks her out of it, she strums the chords she put her lyrics to and sings them, her eyes closed to the world, the words bringing her back to a time when Griffin was by her side. When she came alive in the most remarkable way. When he paved the way for this very moment.

"Until you came along,
I was living in slow motion.

Playing pop star like they wanted,
For them and their devotion.

But in the dark of night,
I tossed and turned, all wrong.
It started to make sense,
Only as you came along.

In trying to be perfect,
All I did was make me small.
You told me, more than once,
Go ahead and give your all.

Things started to go right,
Me letting go and staying true.
But then you left me in the dark,
And now I know something new.

It wasn't just the music,
Not the hope you sparked in me.
It was everything about you,
I'm like a lock, and you the key.

You're a flame lit inside me,
And I ask you please come home.
Everything is brighter by your side,
Together, not alone.

I don't care about the music,
Or about the final score.

All I know is that without you,
I will always be wanting more."

The words don't come out perfectly, the melody isn't polished or smooth like the songs she knows so well that she could perform them in her sleep, but despite their imperfections, Aria delights in every second of the song. For the first time in a long time, Aria feels alive. Truly and fully. Like she's a creative, a person, not just a brand. Like her music has meaning.

Like maybe being vulnerable isn't such a bad choice after all.

When Aria finally opens her eyes as the final chord ends, the crowd erupts. Phones are held up, recording, and Aria stands and takes a bow. Tears threaten at her eyes for a million reasons, but mostly because she's proud of herself. Because she's shown her real self, her raw but real music, and for once she's not holding back. Before long, her phone will be ablaze with calls once the clips of the performance start making their rounds online.

Gerald will—with absolutely zero doubt—have something to say.

After Aria finishes her set and exits the stage, she stows her guitar back in its case, slots herself between her security team, and heads for her ride. Inside, she feels like she's glowing, like the thrill of that moment is something that shouldn't be contained. Like it needs to go somewhere, be shared with someone.

The only problem is, the person she wants to share it with most won't pick up the phone.

Chapter 49

Griffin

After Friday's event for the South Shore senior football players, Griffin can't stop thinking about ways to continue the work. Within hours he's decided to create his own foundation, and first thing Saturday, he gets a meeting scheduled with the head of the Wardens' philanthropy department for Monday morning. In advance he makes a list of his ideas and his questions, and with every step of progress, Griffin feels like he's waking up.

Griffin's knee still aches occasionally, and he takes over-the-counter pain medication as needed, but while it used to make him wonder if his career was over, it's now only a minor inconvenience to getting around, an unwanted distraction from the efforts he's locked into.

Monday morning, Griffin wakes with optimism, preparing for his day in the very same way as if he were going to practice—eating a nutritious breakfast, his single cup of coffee for the day, stretching and hydration. He parks in his usual spot at the stadium, but instead of heading to the locker room, Griffin walks over to the administration building. Beverly Anderson's office boasts a small waiting room with an administrative professional, so after he announces himself, Griffin sits and waits. He crosses his hands over the leather billfold he sets in his lap, his written-out list inside. Before long, a woman wearing a matching skirt and jacket walks in with a large leather bag slung over her shoulder.

"Well, I know from the TV, you must be Griffin Hayes," she says on the way to what's presumably her office door. "Come on in."

Griffin hops to his feet and crosses the waiting room. Beverly flips on the overhead light and drops her bag on an extra chair in the corner before unpacking a laptop, notepad, and phone.

She pauses by her desk chair. "Have you had coffee? I'll be honest, I didn't expect you to be so . . . timely."

Griffin smiles. "I've had my morning cup, but don't mind me if you want to grab one."

Beverly sighs, then speaks quietly. "I'll just ask Madison if she'd do me the favor. I hate asking my assistants for coffee; it just seems so cliché."

She dips out of the room, and Griffin hears the low murmur of her request peppered with unnecessary apologies.

Beverly reenters the room and settles behind her desk.

"I hope you don't mind, but I have to ask—why didn't you expect me to be on time?"

Beverly's cheeks turn pink. "Honestly? A lot of guys from the team get the inspiration to do some charity work—often around the holidays—but the follow-through isn't always as robust as their commitment to practice or training." She raises her hands as if to deflect argument. "Not that I'm saying it should! I understand they're getting paid to play. It's their job."

Griffin sits taller in his seat. "Well, I'll have you know off the bat that when I commit to something, I take it seriously. Whether that's training or, right now, creating a foundation, I hate it when things are done halfway."

Beverly claps. "Excellent! We're birds of a feather."

Madison slips in and sets a coffee mug on the table. Both Beverly and Griffin look up and smile in acknowledgment.

"So give me a sense of what you're trying to do." Beverly lifts the steaming mug and blows on it.

Griffin pulls in a breath and launches into a description of his vision. Hosting celebrity events to raise money for programs like South Shore so they don't have to choose between a safe field or a senior reception. Helping programs buy new uniforms, send players to summer camps for extra training. Establishing a scholarship program for players who won't qualify to play college ball but will need an education for their future. Eventually establishing his own summer camp program for recreational players as well as professional hopefuls.

"That's the heart of what I want to do here, but I know I'm a rookie at this, and I want to get the opinions of people like you who have been doing this for a while."

Beverly raises a brow. "You're already way ahead of most. Your vision is clear—and more importantly, attainable. You're thinking with logistics and business in mind."

Griffin nods. "Being connected in this celebrity world is a

great starting point. A lot of those folks are happy to make an appearance to help the kids, and if I make it easy on them to donate, even better."

"Player-led camps are a hit. Some families bar no expense to send their children to a highly rated camp, and you could parlay those profits into scholarships and your foundation. Even with you as the head of the camp, designing the programs and teaching, it would be popular."

"What's the best place to start?"

"You need to get a clear and concise mission statement put together. Some basic branding, a website, email contact, etcetera. Then I would start by throwing a fundraiser party of some kind and inviting all of your famous friends. That's a great way to start getting the word out and bringing in the first donations. Oh, and you'll need to officially apply for tax status—in general, you want to hire a finance person to manage that side from the start."

Griffin nods as he takes notes. "All very manageable. I think I have most of a mission statement already."

"Excellent! And yes, of course it can be tweaked over time. You just want to commit to the purpose of the foundation."

"I'll invite a lot of players to the first fundraiser, so it won't be anything too fancy."

Beverly grins. "Some of the guys love a glamorous event! You've got quite the mix over there in the locker room."

Griffin laughs. "You're right about that. I guess you've worked with a lot of them on Wardens events."

She nods. "Overall the players are great sports."

Griffin asks Beverly a round of questions focused on details, and she answers with ease and in depth. She offers him her personal phone number for questions, noting his commitment and focus. "You're really putting your all into it."

Griffin gestures to his knee. "This might end up being it for me." Despite having made peace with the reality that his knee injury will prevent him from getting back in the game, nothing has yet been officially arranged with the team, so he has to remain tight-lipped.

Beverly shrugs. "We're all cheering for you either way. And this"—she points to his notes—"is an incredible and worthy endeavor."

"I couldn't agree more."

By the time Griffin gets home, he decides he's going to rent out a local brewery to soft launch the foundation, maybe hire a local band if he can find one on short notice. Of course his mind goes to Aria.

What if he invited her? Griffin will have to think about it. He wants to be in good shape the next time he gets close to her—nothing like that ghost of a person he was when she surprised him on his doorstep—and the moment needs to be right.

His first event, and when he's still figuring the foundation out, might be too soon. Griffin wants nothing but the absolute best for her—*him* at his best too.

Then again, Aria is going on a tour in the new year, so Griffin can't put off the launch *too* long.

A call from Elliott interrupts his thoughts as he pulls into his condo building's parking garage.

"Hey, hey," Elliott says. "Free tonight?"

"Eh, maybe," Griffin says. "I'm still trying to take it easy on the knee, and I was out today meeting with Beverly from philanthropy."

"Yeah? You transferring departments?" Elliott laughs.

"Well, maybe, sort of! I guess I caught the nonprofit work bug after the South Shore thing."

"For real? Man, that's awesome." The genuine enthusiasm pours through Elliott's words. "To be honest, you sound better. Way better."

Griffin lets out a pressured breath. "It got bad there for a second, didn't it?"

"Yeah, man, it did. I'm glad you found some footing, though. There's so much more life to be lived off the field."

Griffin notes a wistfulness in Elliott's voice he hasn't noticed before. "If you were in my shoes, how would you be filling your time?"

"I have to tell you, I've got the itch for fashion. After Fashion Week, I'm reading the magazines, watching the releases. And I don't mean in a bootleg celebrity mash-up product line. I mean like starting my own thing, for real."

It's clear from the quickness in which Elliott lands on the well-developed idea that this isn't his first time thinking about it. Griffin has always assumed that all of these players have been just like him: singularly focused. But in reality, all of them are just humans at heart, and humans are never just one thing at a time.

"I'm lucky to get a second act," Griffin says, genuinely meaning it. "Thanks for helping me see it."

"I'm always here. And when it's my time to bow out of the game, you'll be able to help me find my way."

"Just say the word, bud."

The reception grows spotty as Griffin progresses into the underground portion of the parking garage, and he ends the call before it drops. How surprising life can be; it certainly has been for him as of late.

Aria coming into his life was one of the brightest, most shining surprises.

And now in the light of his fresh start, a new longing for her blooms within him.

For better or worse, he decides to invite her to the foundation kickoff.

Chapter 50

Aria

Aria leans on the kitchen island on her forearms, looking at her laptop, and Bailey squeezes in beside her for a closer look. Aria squints as she tries to decode some unwritten meaning in the email invitation, one she's most likely conjuring into existence.

"Here, let me just see it," Bailey says, like there should be an obvious answer to be found.

Aria silently slides the computer in front of her sister. "It's obviously an email blast."

Bailey scrolls up and down the message, then checks the sender details. "You're right."

"So how am I supposed to take this? Am I just on Griffin's contacts list and was accidentally sent this? Or does he actually want me there?"

When Aria checked her email this morning, the last thing she was expecting was an invitation to the soft launch of The

Griffin Hayes Foundation for Youth Sports. The graphics are sleek but bespoke, a rounded font that's soft but powerful. The color scheme is slate gray and red—a nod to the Wardens, Aria can only guess.

All in all, it's impressive for a foundation Griffin announced to social media only a week ago.

Nevertheless, the email comes without personalization and notes only that Griffin is inviting his network in hopes of kicking off his foundation with gusto. Obviously there will be a fundraising component—as there should be for a celebrity guest list—and Aria is always more than happy to contribute to organizations doing good work. She would happily write a check.

She doesn't care about the money; she cares about Griffin.

"I just wish he would've texted to ask, you know?" Aria says, dropping her head onto her propped-up palm.

Bailey nods. "Agreed, but also—he's obviously throwing this together pretty quick. He's still physically recovering, and this brewery venue holds a lot of people."

Aria sticks out her bottom lip, letting herself be pouty in only the company of her younger sister. "They're all reasonable points."

"But I get it. It would've been nice to know that he really wanted you there. Not just to blast it to every connected person he knows."

Aria wonders if Griffin saw the clips of the song that's gone around online—the song about him she performed off the cuff. Surely fans would've tagged him. Singing the song itself was impulsive, so it wasn't quite like she'd mapped out the consequences beforehand. Nevertheless, when the reality dawned on her that the song would eventually make its way to Griffin, she quickly made her peace with it.

Aria wants him to know how she feels. It's why she called. It's also why her heart still stings when she reminds herself of the fact that he didn't call back.

"So, what do you think? Are we going?" Bailey asks.

Despite the rumbling inside her mind, her lingering questions, her fragile hope that maybe he feels the same way, Aria is certain about the answer to this question. "Of course."

A grin spreads slowly over Bailey's lips. "So why are you stressing?"

Aria pulls herself upright from the counter. "I never said I was going in a relaxed manner. I care too much to be entirely relaxed about this."

"You're going there to get your man."

Aria pulls her expression upward into a hopeful smile with a hint of a grimace. "If all goes to plan."

She won't know exactly how Griffin feels until she can pin him down and talk to him, but there was never any question about whether Aria would try.

If she's learned anything from him coming into her life, it's that being vulnerable is required for all the best parts of life—the best music, the deepest friendships, and even possibly for love.

Aria walks into the brewery with flawless makeup, wearing a cheetah-print maxi skirt paired with a silver sweater and burgundy boots. She followed her pre-event routine—glam squad plus stylist visit—so not a curl will be out of place. Only she can feel the thumping of her worried heart and the damp on her palms.

Bailey snakes her arm into the crook of Aria's. "Are we mingling first or finding the man of the hour?"

"Let's stop by the bar first, enjoy the band, then we'll find him."

A bluegrass band is playing on the small stage tucked into the corner on the opposite side of the massive box of a building. The bar is outfitted with a mind-boggling number of beer taps, but for the event, a branded menu sits propped in plastic display cards on the surface. A specialty cocktail is available, as well as several wines.

A starry-eyed bartender delivers Aria a glass of red wine and a specialty cocktail for Bailey. The pair strike up a casual conversation with a few Wardens players in their vicinity, and Aria feels proud to be able to discuss the last few games in detail.

"I never would've taken you for a football fan," one player tells her.

"Just a perk of being friends with Griffin," Aria says.

His eyes go wide, and he points as if to confirm that he's placed her reference. "That's right."

Eventually a few more players join their conversation, and one in particular seeks out Aria.

"Hey! I'm Elliott, wide receiver and best friend to Griffin."

Aria smiles at his sincere use of the term "best friend." "It's great to meet you. I'm Aria Wilder." She pushes out her hand and they shake.

"You seen him yet?" Elliott asks.

"Not yet. We came to the bar for a drink first, and I guess we just got carried away chatting with everyone."

In truth, Aria hasn't forgotten about Griffin. She's been thinking about a smooth way to exit the group conversation and make her way over to him without it seeming awkward or rude.

"Now that you mention it, I definitely want to say hello before the evening gets away from us."

Aria gives Bailey a friendly wave, knowing she'll get the message, and looks to Elliott. "So nice to meet you."

Only once she's turned and making her way through the crowd does Aria stop and consider that perhaps she could've asked Elliott if he knew where she'd find Griffin. As she and Bailey had assumed, the venue is full of people, many of whom she recognizes from the music and arts scene. Aria waves and nods at folks she recognizes but stays the course through the crowd.

Through a break in the mass of people, Aria spots Griffin standing close to the band. When they break after finishing up their last song, a playlist begins to float through the speakers in its place. Aria's pulse races as she nears him, watching him talk animatedly to a man dressed in a sport coat and checkered pants—a businessperson by the looks of him. To her luck, the man says goodbye right as she closes in, and when Griffin turns, his gaze meets her own.

"Aria." Griffin's face goes still.

Aria stops before him, her breathing rapid and shallow. Before she can speak, Griffin continues.

"I didn't think you'd come."

"Oh."

Aria feels herself deflate. Does that mean *he* didn't want her to come? Or that he didn't think *she* would want to come?

"Sorry." Griffin squeezes his temples, his cheeks turning pink, then flashes her a sheepish smile. "I think with all the time I've spent laid up, I'm a little rusty. Can I try again?"

Aria's shoulders settle, a spark running through her veins like adrenaline and hope wound up together. "Sure thing."

Griffin closes the gap, pulls Aria into a hug, and when he steps back, he keeps ahold of her upper arms. "Thank you for coming. I didn't know if I'd see you tonight, but it seems I'm in luck."

Aria's face breaks into a smile so deep it begins to hurt. For a moment she considers holding back, pretending like those words don't wrap her heart in fuzzy warmth. But she already took those walls down, brick by brick.

"I was looking forward to seeing you. And this"—Aria whirls around with hands held out—"is amazing."

Griffin looks around at the event, nodding. "It's saved me really. Getting going on something else."

Reflexively, Aria glances at his knee.

"Yeah." Griffin leans closer, and the piney scent of his aftershave sends a shiver across Aria's skin. "Between us, I have a good feeling it's shot."

Aria's eyes go wide. "*What?* You're *serious?*"

Griffin shrugs. "Never say never, but also, I don't want to go back and be less than my prime."

Aria pauses for a moment. She might've become fluent in basic football by watching on television—and hearing jargon from her time alongside Griffin—but she's no sports medicine doctor. It's tricky to know what Griffin may be over- or understating.

"How're you feeling about all of that? Like you said, football's been your life—"

"You were right." Griffin looks at her with true affection. "About there being more to me than the sport."

"It's obvious to the rest of us. Has been all along."

He lets out a tight breath, and his shoulders drop. "It's hard to see from the inside. But now I'm excited about the rest of life. About *this*. About the whole prospect of my life having a next chapter—then maybe even more chapters after that."

Aria smiles. It's impossible not to be happy for him. Objectively, he knew football wasn't a forever thing, but the change in him is undeniably clear: He's realized that a busted knee won't be the end of him.

"I'm so proud of you, Griff. This is a tough hand to be dealt for any player. You're navigating it in true golden-boy style."

Griffin laughs. "Eh. I wouldn't speak too soon. I'm only at the beginning of this, and you didn't see everything behind the scenes."

The comment lingers, trapped between the two of them. Aria would've seen the rest had she been allowed. If he had opened the door, Aria would've walked in. She wanted to stay as long as he needed her.

"I'm sorry, by the way," Griffin says. "For shutting you out. Not only was it the least smooth move of my life, it was a terrible idea. I hope I didn't mess anything up."

"I understand." Aria chews her lip as she fumbles for the right words to say next. She wants to ask what he's referring to when he says "mess anything up." Does he mean the actual relationship between them—what they agreed to keep a friendship? Or was he talking about their fake friendship partnership deal? "Do you—"

"Griffin, hey, sorry to interrupt." A dazzling young woman with dark brown hair and olive skin grazes his upper arm with her freshly polished nails. "It's time to start the presentation. We don't want to miss out on anyone if they're making it a quick stop."

Griffin glances over apologetically. "Sorry, Aria, can we catch up later on? I meant it when I said it was great to see you."

The assistant gasps. "Aria Wilder? Griffin, you're holding out on us! I'm a mega fan!" She squeaks in a manner that makes her endearing.

Aria smiles. "I see an invite from my Griffin, and I do my very best to make it."

The assistant begins to physically ferry Griffin away but calls over her shoulder, "You don't have to tell me twice! I foresee many a Griffin Hayes Foundation event on your calendar."

They disappear into the crowd, then up a set of stairs to the roped-off second level that acts as a balcony. Up there a microphone is set up, and the assistant stops Griffin before he takes it, probably coaching him on his talking points.

A small fire flickers in the very depth of Aria's belly. She's tried to talk to Griffin multiple times at this point, to tell him how she feels, and every time his injury or, now, his foundation work gets in the way. Since when was she a person who lets life get in the way? Since when was she willing to take no for an answer?

The assistant calls the crowd to attention, and Aria sees the opportunity.

It's now or never.

Aria hops onto the low stage at her side, the one vacated by the band and turns on the microphone. A horrendous feedback echoes around the hard surfaces of the concrete and chrome brewery, and like a choreographed dance, hands cover ears, and groans escape the crowd.

Oops.

Aria pulls in a breath, sidestepping the impulse to be deterred, and taps on her mic. When a muffled thud sounds back, she speaks into it.

"Hi, everyone!"

The crowd turns to her, and up on the second level, Griffin and his assistant wear quizzical looks. He runs a hand through his hair.

"Some of you may already know me. My name is Aria Wilder, and I'm a friend and fan of Griffin Hayes. I'm here today to support his brand-new foundation that we're all so excited about. In addition to writing a check before I leave today, I came with a new song."

Excited murmurs slink around the clusters of guests, the offensive microphone feedback forgotten.

"I performed this song for the first time recently here at the music festival in Roxbury Park, and a few videos made it to the internet. Something I know a little about."

The crowd laughs.

"I haven't spoken publicly about this song yet because it's the most personal thing I have ever written. It might not be that surprising to hear, but growing up inside the music business means that for a long time, other people are deciding your career—the persona you go onstage with, the type of music you make, even the clothes you wear. For a long time I have been wanting to try something new with my music, but only once I got to know Griffin Hayes did I finally gain the courage to do so."

The crowd is quiet, and Aria looks up to the second level where Griffin leans over the railing.

"This song is for you, Griffin Hayes."

By the grace of God, an acoustic guitar has been left behind by one of the band members on break, so she won't have to sing a cappella. Aria takes the guitar, then dives right into the song.

"Until you came along,
I was living in slow motion.
Playing pop star like they wanted,
For them and their devotion.

But in the dark of night,
I tossed and turned, all wrong.
It started to make sense,
Only as you came along.

In trying to be perfect,
All I did was make me small.
You told me, more than once,
Go ahead and give your all.

Things started to go right,
Me letting go and staying true.

But then you left me in the dark,
And now I know something new.

It wasn't just the music,
Not the hope you sparked in me.
It was everything about you,
I'm like a lock, and you the key.

You're a flame lit inside me,
And I ask you please come home.
Everything is brighter by your side,
Together, not alone.

I don't care about the music,
Or about the final score.
All I know is that without you,
I will always be wanting more."

Once the crowd finishes their cheers, more than one member pulling an endeared hand to a chest or dabbing at the corner of an eye, Aria speaks into the mic. "And now that I've as good as confessed the depths of my adoration for Griffin Hayes, I'd like to welcome him to the floor to tell us about The Griffin Hayes Foundation for Youth Sports. And don't forget—don't leave without making a donation."

Aria's heart hammers in her chest, and she feels so exposed she might as well be nude. Nevertheless, she watches as Griffin takes the microphone up on the second level. Even from this distance, she detects a pinkness in his cheeks.

He stumbles over his opening words, then resets. "What can I say? I'm a little stunned—in the best sort of way—from that Aria Wilder original, so bear with me if I miss something."

Griffin is adorable as he explains the impetus for his foundation, his injury and personal journey—one that's still underway—and eventually finds his footing as he talks about his vision for what the organization will bring to youth athletes across the country.

Bailey snakes through the crowd to Aria's side, and as Griffin is wrapping up his final comments, she whispers in Aria's ear, "There's no way he's not in love with you, sis. It's obvious in the look on his face."

Aria reaches out and squeezes her hand.

She certainly hopes that's true, but for now she's forced to wait to hear it straight from him.

Chapter 51

Griffin

Griffin is confused at first when he hears Aria's voice on the microphone. He wonders momentarily if Michaela, his event lead, planned a surprise performance from her as a bonus for the guests, but undoubtedly she would've needed his personal connection to make the booking. Since he disconnected—mostly—from the online world and the snarky remarks from commentators, the rambling about his career or lack thereof, Griffin has been feeling more grounded and in no rush to get back online. Only now does he realize that he also hasn't heard about any new song from Aria.

She didn't send it to him directly or he would've checked it out.

He remembers not answering her call, and his gut drops. In his stewing, he never called her back, promising once he got himself to a better place he would. Of course she wouldn't continue to reach out when all she got in response was silence.

The music plays, the lyrics sung in a voice so very Aria—not the one overly synthesized or drowned out by the special effects of the stage—one perfectly accompanied by a simple guitar, simply her. She is everything she spoke about wanting her music to be: real and true. Aria, herself.

Then her words unwind and with them a delightful understanding. Griffin is flooded by a sudden impulse to hold her, to kiss her, to love her.

While Griffin was holed up feeling sorry for himself and berating himself for not being enough for this woman, she was writing a song about the inspiration he brought to her. While he is consumed with improving himself for her, Aria says he's already enough. While the world hypothesizes about his next steps, examines the hit that blew out his knee in slow motion, monitors his appearance in public, she says he's transformed her world.

Aria Wilder says she wants him as is. After the injury. Before the foundation. The mess in between.

When Aria completes her song, she sounds flustered as she introduces him. All Griffin wants is to rush to her, pull her into his arms, and tell her everything. But he has to stick to the script for the event, the foundation, and even for Aria. They deserve to talk things out in private, a cherished rarity for both of them.

Griffin pushes himself to remember what he planned to say. He fumbles words, forgets things, and backtracks more than once, but he can't help it. Pictures of Aria and all their moments together dance through his mind. Griffin knows how to buckle down and perform, and he's grateful for the muscle memory. Without it, he might've jogged down those stairs, picked Aria up into his arms, and carried her out of here, event and all forgotten.

At the end of his comments, he makes a clear ask for donations as Beverly coached him to do.

"Be real clear about what you want. People will come expecting to make a donation—especially the wealthy ones—but they won't come asking you how if you don't make it nice and clear for them. QR code on the tabletops. Have a help table for the older generations where they can handwrite a check and chat with a friendly representative of the organization."

Guests take out their phones and begin scanning the codes, and within moments the band is back. From the balcony, Griffin scans the crowd in search of Aria, whom he spots slipping out onto the back patio where there are firepits set up.

Griffin barrels down the stairs, his focus so keenly locked on Aria that he slides through the crowd efficiently, to the back doors, and onto the patio. Outside, surrounded by the dark night, the noise of the party fades. Aria and Bailey are huddled together beside a firepit, head-to-head, talking.

Griffin clears his throat as he approaches to signal his arrival. "I hope I'm not interrupting," he says as the pair turn to look at him in unison.

"Oh no, no," Bailey says. "In fact, I was just saying how much I wanted a second cocktail, so I'm going to head inside and grab that. Anyone want something from the bar?"

"No thanks, but I appreciate it," Griffin says.

"I'm good, sis," Aria says. "Watch out for number 99. I think he has the hots for you."

Griffin laughs. "AJ? He's harmless."

"We already bonded over a shared love of macramé and *Antiques Roadshow* earlier, so I think we'll be just fine."

Bailey slips inside, and Griffin and Aria are left alone in the light of the fire. Maybe it's the afterglow of the song, but Aria looks even more stunning tonight, her skin glowing.

"The song," Griffin says. The words come out in a deep rumble that falls out of him like a confession.

"I'm sorry if it was too much. I tried to call you to talk to you. I showed up before, and I needed—"

"It was perfect."

Griffin steps closer, and Aria looks up into his eyes. "I wanted to tell you how I felt for a while now, but I also wanted to give you the space you wanted."

"I was an idiot." Griffin looks to the dark sky for support, then back to Aria. "I was so focused on my injury, on how it left me with nothing—*as* nothing—that I shut you out. Things got dark. I worried that you would think less of me all beat up and incapable."

"So is this you beat up?" Aria looks him over methodically as if searching for something elusive.

"This is me well on my way to recovered. This is me finally seeing the bigger picture." Griffin reaches down, puts a finger under Aria's chin, and raises her head gently. "This is me saying I'm really sorry for leaving you hanging. I meant that kiss in the studio, and I never really wanted friendship only. I was willing to settle for it because it made sense—and because that was what you wanted—but what I wanted was more. All of you."

"I was too scared to go for it—like I was with so many things—but now I'm here. I'm ready."

"Well, let's not waste any more time."

Griffin presses his lips to Aria's, and he slides his hands down to the small of her back. She falls into him, and he pulls her close. Aria pulls back after a breath, then she kisses him again, her fingers in his hair sending a sensation like fireworks down his back.

Aria holds his face between her hands and hovers right before Griffin. His legs are like jelly.

"I love you, Griffin. I have for a while now."

His lips curl into a grin. He's known it too. Probably for longer than she has. "I love you too."

Chapter 52

Aria

The brewery event is beginning to wind down, and when Bailey reappears, she's stifling a yawn. She stops in her tracks when her eyes land on Aria and Griffin, holding hands where they sit close beside the fire. Aria gives a wink that tells her sister it's good news.

"I'm going to call a ride and head out," Bailey says, grinning from ear to ear.

Aria doesn't argue it. She's buzzing with energy, and the last thing she wants is to leave Griffin's side before it's absolutely necessary.

"Be safe and text me when you get home."

"Will do, *Mom*," Bailey teases, then slips back into the building.

Griffin looks through the glass doors Bailey has just passed through. "I should probably show my face again, say goodbye to whoever is left."

Aria squeezes his hand. "Do you *have* to?"

When Griffin glances down at her, she grins, betraying her playfulness.

"My first choice would be to stay. You know that."

"Why don't you make the rounds, then make one last stop out here. We'll linger till they kick us out."

Griffin glances at his watch. "Technically, I have the place until midnight."

"Music to my ears." Aria pats his back, encouraging him to go, and Griffin reluctantly gets to his feet.

"I'll be quick."

Griffin leaves Aria smiling, and as she waits, the crackling fire glows before her and she pulls out her phone. Texts from Bailey are already waiting for her.

Bailey: OMG TELL!

Bailey: You're clearly doing couple stuff.

Bailey: Is it official? If so, WHAT is official?

Aria's fingers glide over the screen wistfully as she replies.

Aria: We said "I love you" and we kissed again.

Aria: More than once, of course . . . We have more to discuss, but it feels like we're coming back together.

Replies from Bailey ping in rapid succession.

Bailey: You THINK? Duh! You're IN LOVE!

Bailey: Yay, Aria! You snagged your prince. Or is it that he snagged his queen? I think I prefer that.

Aria: I like any and all of the above.

Bailey: I'm so happy for you, sis. I'm going to hit the hay as soon as I get home, but I expect a detailed play-by-play at breakfast.

Aria: You betcha.

Griffin really does hurry back, and when he pushes through the doors back onto the patio, he seems almost out of breath. Aria waves him over playfully, then pats the seat beside her. Griffin sits down, and his tall, broad presence envelops Aria as he slides an arm around her shoulder.

He looks down at her and grins. "This event turned out way better than I initially expected."

"Yeah? Lots of generous guests?"

"Oh, I have no idea. They haven't shown me numbers; I'm not sure we'd have them yet."

Aria's cheeks heat, and her eyes bat of their own accord.

"You, Aria. That song. Man, I'm a lucky guy."

Aria turns to look at the fire. "You might feel lucky, but so do I. The words in the song, I meant them. *Mean* them. I've been struggling for a long time, feeling pulled between my desire to try something new, to be genuine, and my fears of what that could do to my career—a fear of failure, really."

"*You?* Failing?" Griffin says the words so incredulously that it's as if there's a scoff hanging on the tip of his tongue.

"From the outside, everyone sees the strong, powerful woman who dominates the stage, but everyone forgets that I—a regular person—came from nothing. I didn't have wealthy or connected parents. I didn't have expensive vocal or guitar lessons. I had a dream, a cheap guitar my parents saved up to get me for Christmas, and a high school music teacher who believed in me. All this time, all these years, I've been striving to become the woman everyone now believes is me. Of course I'm afraid of it all falling apart, because only I know how much brute force and persistence it took to put it together. I know I'm not invincible."

Griffin nods. "I see. And you're right." He taps his knee gently. "I know a little something about the ease of things falling apart too, but I've learned that shifting and changing aren't necessarily failing."

Aria looks over and smiles at him. "How you believed in my music inspired me to believe more in myself, and honestly, even if Worldwide Records hates this stuff, I'm still going to write it. Even if my current fans leave, I will get scrappy and find the people this is for."

"You were incredible tonight."

"And you know what? The two times I've performed that song now are the times I've felt most alive while performing in years. It brought back that pure electricity that had me knocking down doors as a twenty-year-old. No pyrotechnics, no elaborate light displays, just me, my guitar, and my heart in the words."

"As I got to know you, it did dawn on me that all of the

production took away from you. The real you is so much more interesting than the overproduced one."

Aria narrows her eyes playfully. "Was this before or after you ghosted me?" She waggles her brow victoriously.

Griffin's head drops and he massages his temples. Then he looks to her. "I'm really sorry about that. Here in this moment it makes no sense, but in the darkness of my injury, I convinced myself that I would be letting you down, that I was too broken for a woman like you."

"Oh, Griff." Aria slides a hand up his chest and leaves it there.

"I thought I was worthless without the sport. Sure, I'd been doing my best to figure out what my 'life without football plan' was, but I hadn't figured much out yet. It happened sooner than I expected, and it was so bad."

"But you're working through it?"

Griffin's chest rises, his shoulders settling back as he nods. "This work has brought me to life. I'm not sure this wasn't more what I was built for than being on the field. Sure, I'll miss it. I know when the new season starts I'll be feeling some sort of way. It'll be fresh hurt every time I miss something. But I'm confident that the new life I'm building is just as valuable as the last chapter."

"And does the new chapter have room for us?" Aria gazes up at him, and he meets her eyes.

"When I pulled away, it was never my plan for it to be permanent. I just wanted to get my head on straight first. It was so shortsighted."

"Sometimes we have to figure things out on our own first

before we're ready for the next thing. I would've waited longer for you."

"I think we're stronger together." Griffin cups Aria's cheek and strokes her jaw with his thumb.

"Next time something falls apart, don't shut me out?"

"Next time, you're my first call."

Aria lifts her head, tilting her lips toward his. "I like the sound of that."

"And me? Am I your first call?"

"Yes. Well, after Bailey."

Griffin laughs. "Fair enough."

He presses his lips to hers, and it fills Aria with a lightness that feels like floating. When he pulls back, she leans into his chest, and Griffin wraps his arms firmly around her.

"I want you to know that being with me won't be easy," Aria says. "The media is ruthless, and even the smallest thing is dissected. When I go on tour, it takes over everything—the months leading up to it, the actual travel dates, all the media and press that happen around it."

"I don't think either of us are ones to take the easy route."

Aria's shoulders release. He's right. Both of them have endured constant challenges as part of their careers, part of fame, and they're not the type to retreat from a bumpy road they want to traverse. In fact, perhaps their shared experiences of jumping through hoops for privacy, playing the public figure game, and finding peace in uncertainty will equip them to navigate the hard times when they come.

"I think we're cut out for it. And I think we're worth it—our love is worth it."

Griffin sighs. "I'm all in, Aria. Us. The good and the bad, I'm here for it all."

Aria isn't sure how long they sit there warmed by the shrinking fire, but she feels her body relax into Griffin in a way she hasn't known in a long time. Maybe ever. Griffin might've started out as a business arrangement in her life, but from her current position, that fact is laughable. He became her first true friend, one who rooted for her sincerely, who wasn't thrown off by her fame, who always kept her best interests at heart. Even if it would've stopped there, Aria would've been lucky to know Griffin Hayes.

But she trusted him, and she let down her walls. She knows she can trust Griffin with her heart, and his is safe with her.

Despite singing about love stories and happy endings for years, now for the first time, Aria Wilder believes it's her chance to live out her own love story.

Chapter 53

Griffin

Griffin pins back the door to his condo while a crew of movers roll in furniture on a dolly to the room that used to be his guest bedroom. Over the past three weeks, The Griffin Hayes Foundation for Youth Sports has landed on several major news outlets, and the calls for collaboration have been so great that Griffin has hired a personal assistant to help him manage the communications. Griffin doesn't need a guest bedroom—visiting family always choose a hotel stay anyway—but now he absolutely needs a home office.

The movers secure thc legs to the base of the desk, then rip off the protective paper layered around the other parts, and finally set it in place. Next, shelving is brought in, Bubble Wrap shed, and Griffin directs the movers to place the pieces where he's planned for them to go. Finally, a black leather desk chair is rolled in. Griffin has ordered office supplies that'll come at a later date. This will be headquarters for the foundation while his assistant works remotely.

Over the three weeks since the brewery kickoff event, The Griffin Hayes Foundation has boomed. Griffin has completed several virtual news features, and he's been invited to partner with a sports clothing brand on a gala that will raise funds for his foundation. He put together some social media sites—ones that have since gained tens of thousands of followers. The basic website is Griffin's handiwork, and he himself manages the correspondence with schools and athletes applying for assistance. Beverly suggested establishing a protocol for accepting applications and reviewing them in batches at set times so that reviewing isn't constantly in flux. For now, Griffin will track and accept new applications, but no decisions will be made until the new year. Beverly is connecting Griffin to some local business executives as well as he works on establishing a board of advisers.

Griffin isn't holding back. Rather than waking up thinking about his nutrition and exercise for the day, he wakes up thinking about his foundation work for the day. Sure, he still eats mostly the same diet and works out—either at home or at the gym he recently joined down the street—but that routine has shrunk to become a piece of his life, not the be-all and end-all.

Griffin has been stopping in at South Shore to check on the players and coaches. He's also visited several other local high schools for practice, stepping in to coach briefly, talking to players to inspire them, taking questions from hopeful players. *That's* the work Griffin wants to spend his time doing, which is why he's already hiring staff to make the gears move behind the scenes.

He can make the biggest difference in front of the players, on the field.

And he'll show his face at whatever event is necessary to help raise the money to keep things flowing smoothly. It's all about playing to everyone's strengths, and the foundation will make the greatest impact possible.

The movers begin balling up the discarded packing materials, then carry the trash out to the chute in his hallway. Eventually they present him with a clipboard to sign for the delivery, and they depart. When the elevator arrives, the movers stand back to allow a passenger to step out. One mover eyes Aria as if he's trying to place her, but they load on without fuss and disappear.

On Griffin's threshold, Aria flings her arms around his neck and dots a peck on his lips. "Sorry, I'm sweaty, and definitely not smelling my freshest."

"They got you flipping tires today?"

Aria laughs as she pushes past him. "I'm sure they'd love that, but not today. I just had to come by and see your new office after all the chatter about it."

Griffin stands back and admires Aria as she marches toward the office. She wears workout leggings, a long sports bra, and tennis shoes. Her trainer has her working out religiously in preparation for her long back-to-back shows. In some ways, they've switched spots—Aria sweating in the gym, and him squirreled away in a home office, concocting magic.

Before Griffin can join her down the hallway, her gleeful scream rings out. "It's wonderful! You're doing it!"

Aria practically bowls him over when Griffin makes it inside the room. "And here I was thinking I was the excited one."

Aria looks up from where she rests, leaning into his chest. "I'm just so happy for you. It's what it represents. And it's also just nice stuff."

"Well, thank you for helping me pick it out."

Aria winks. "Anytime."

"And thank you for the rest—"

"I didn't see any other furniture." Aria's brow wrinkles in an adorable way that only comes out when they're together.

"No, I meant the help. Getting to this place."

Aria whacks his chest lightly. "Oh, you did the hard part. I just nudged you along a little. Plus, my adoration of you, gimp knee and all, helped."

Griffin laughs. "And you keep me laughing."

Aria shrugs. "Any chance I can drag you away from work for lunch? I swear I cannot eat enough with how much they have me working out."

"Do I need to start meal prepping for you?" Griffin asks.

Nowadays, he makes time to cook—unless he and Aria are going out—a few times a week, and it's brought a new joy to life. Turns out food can be fuel *and* enjoyable. All it takes is a little personal flexibility.

Aria cringes. "I appreciate the offer, but I will firmly pass. I'm willing to do the gym program because I don't want to expire onstage, but I need a little more variety in my diet."

"Fair enough. And yes to lunch—as long as I'm back for a three o'clock call. I'm hoping to hire the woman I'm meeting with to join the board."

Aria pulls back and walks with purpose from the room. "Easy peasy."

Griffin follows, and Aria calls over her shoulder, "Have I told you that I love this version of you?"

A smile cracks over Griffin's face, and his cheeks heat, presumably turning red like always. Yes, she has, but yes, he still wants to hear it. He will probably blush over Aria's affection, her attention, her care, forevermore, and he's okay with that.

"Luckily for me, you have. And have I told you I love this version of *you*?"

"The sweaty, stinky one?" Aria scoffs. "You're sweet, but we can be honest."

Griffin rushes up behind her, turns her around, threads his arms around her waist, and lifts her with ease into his arms. Aria lets out a shrieking laugh, then throws her arms around his neck.

Griffin presses his mouth deeply into hers and keeps it there until he has to pull back for air. "Yes. This version. Regular, everyday you. Stink and all."

Griffin's arms are like steel, holding her in front of him, and Aria slides her hands to cup his cheeks. "I'm the luckiest." She pecks his lips. "Now let's get me fed before I turn into a far hangrier version of the me you claim to love in all states."

Griffin lowers Aria gently to standing, then quickly gathers his phone and keys from his kitchen counter. "Your wish is my command."

Aria starts telling him about her workout and the plans for the new show she'll debut on this tour—one that includes their song—and they ride the elevator down to the underground parking garage.

Griffin can't help but hang on the words he last spoke to her. He genuinely does want to make her wishes come true. Never before has he felt so deeply connected to someone, his own personal interests so intrinsically woven with hers. Griffin feels alive when he's with Aria, inspired and challenged, but also accepted as is. Her quick wit is charming, her depth enchanting, and her everyday antics a complete delight.

There is no better feeling than being with her, and he'll hold on to this for as long as she lets him.

Chapter 54

Aria

The week after Griffin's brewery event, Monroe called Aria as she was leaving the gym, and the first words out of her mouth were "I'm not sure I've ever had more fun than I did listening to Gerald eat his words."

Aria felt like she'd entered a conversation somewhere in the middle. "Huh?"

"After weeks of me trying to be diplomatic about letting you do your thing, promising him the fans would follow you in a new direction, explaining how the new direction was more an evolution and not a rebrand, reminding him of all the money you've already made them, the victory was sweet."

"Was it the video?" The one of her performance at the brewery went more viral than any previous Aria-Griffin post.

Aria could've sketched the smirk on Monroe's lips, she heard it so clearly in her words. "Probably. But I'm still taking full credit."

Aria said no more than a handful of words during the whole conversation as Monroe took the lead laying out Gerald's backtracking in great detail.

"We didn't realize that it was more a tweak than a pivot."

"Aria is such a stellar musician, of course the fans are connecting with it."

"Everyone wants a real recording of 'Until You Came Along.' How soon can we make it?"

"We trust her, but we need the music ASAP."

Aria had left the call with a new freshness, like a mustiness following her around had been aired out by a good spring cleaning. Like finally the weight that Gerald was insistent on tying to her ankle had been released. That afternoon she worked four straight hours and wrote three songs. It was as if the music had been inside her all along, and all she needed was the breathing room to let it out—like she'd been able to with Griffin.

Beyond the practicalities of making the new album, Aria felt like herself again. Like the green but hopeful young woman she once was when she first embarked on this journey had finally meshed with her experiences—good and bad—her new perspective, and a new softness. And the music that sprang forth was precisely what Aria had in mind.

In the weeks since, the rest of the album came together remarkably quickly. Aria even invited the band over to help her get the musical arrangement right. After working with them for so long, she trusted their instincts and feedback. They, too, wanted to play music they enjoyed every show.

Worldwide Records had no issue moving earth and sky to get the songs professionally recorded and produced in record speed, considering that the internet was on the verge of revolt with their demands for a real version of "Until You Came Along."

Today is Aria's new album drop, and Aria sits at her kitchen island, reading the emails her publicist has sent over with critics' reviews and early impressions from the fans:

> "Deeply vulnerable, rich, and expansive."
>
> "No one thought Aria needed a glow-up, but girl, did she ever! Dang. I mean, where do her superpowers end? At this rate I wouldn't be surprised if she pivoted to rap in a few years!"
>
> "Aria Wilder's magic knows no bounds. All the stars."
>
> "Don't mind me. I'll be calling in sick for the next three days so I can listen on repeat."
>
> "The songs no one asked for but everyone wanted."
>
> "'Until You Came Along' was just the beginning! Worth the wait."

Bailey walks into the room, begins filling a coffee mug from the pot, and says, "Everyone's obsessed."

Aria looks up, her face creasing into a smile. "I am too. It's my favorite album yet, and I couldn't be happier that the fans are loving it."

"And just think—you knew it all along." Bailey nestles the mug between both hands and sips.

Aria agrees, but Bailey doesn't address the whole picture. There's a difference between thinking something might be true and knowing it. Aria isn't psychic. What she needed in order to truly believe it was someone who helped show her that being vulnerable isn't giving away your superpower; it can become your superpower.

And for Aria, that was Griffin. He didn't write the songs, but without him they never would have existed. Aria wouldn't have found the courage to break out of the Aria Wilder public persona box and try something new.

"I think there's always a lot more hiding inside us—all of us—than we can see from the surface."

Aria sits back and allows herself to soak in this moment. Not only did she produce a record at breakneck speed, a task that was only possible because of how honest the music is, but she did it in a way that feels more like her than anything she has produced in the past three years. She's still proud of that work, and she will never abandon or criticize past versions of herself. But she wouldn't ever go back. She has evolved and grown, and her music has now caught up.

All without having to suffer a messy split with Worldwide Records, the very folks who took a chance on her back at the beginning.

In some ways it's like making her debut as a mature woman onto the music scene, leaving the one-size-fits-all love stories behind and embracing all of her. What the doubters—Gerald, specifically—worried would be an end has become a promising beginning. This is Aria's first album embracing all of her, and she can't wait to make the next one.

"You're the best, and I'm so happy for you. Sister walk this morning?"

Aria frowns. "My glutes are still on fire from the gym yesterday. How about we go out for pancakes instead?"

"Sounds just my speed. Carb-o-loading for tonight." Bailey laughs.

This evening, Worldwide Records is throwing an intimate record launch party—the small guest list was Aria's request—and Aria is looking forward to having Griffin at her side. The world may have warmly embraced them as a glitzy celebrity couple, but few understand his role in this album coming to fruition.

Aria counts every lucky star that Griffin Hayes walked into her life. Or perhaps it's more accurate to say he "sang" his way into her life.

She likes that version even more.

Chapter 55

Griffin

Griffin couldn't miss the kickoff of Aria's new album tour, so he flew out to Los Angeles for the show. He's ushered through a backstage entrance—one heavily guarded—and a VIP badge is looped on a lanyard around his neck. Griffin chitchats with the staff he encounters back there, remembering a few faces and names from the Chicago show crews. He's planning on sticking around—in Aria's life, that is—so making friends with the crew is only a natural extension of his plan.

The show starts, the crowd abuzz and screaming, and Griffin watches from the wings. At Aria's request, the special effects are pared down, and there are more moments of only her and a few layers of accompaniment from the band. "*It's about the music*," Aria always says. Griffin has told her countless times that it's also about her—that if it was another person singing it, the effect wouldn't be the same—but Aria brushes off the remarks. She's serious about the music. Her commitment to it comes to life in the songs themselves. But she's slightly blind to the unique way only she has, the way she can make music that's close to the heart—all hers—but also speaks to millions of fans.

Griffin dances from side to side when the quicker songs come on. He cheers along with the crowd, even being asked twice by crew members to "keep it down." Griffin can't help it; he loves her music. Lest they forget: His fandom was the start of this whole thing between them. If Griffin Hayes had never sung his heart out at Aria's concert, they'd still be going about their separate lives. Missing out terribly.

He knew "Until You Came Along" would be the last song of the night, but when he hears the accompaniment music quiet and Aria take the mic, with slightly heavy breaths from her intense dance routine in the previous number, his cheeks heat. Even now that Griffin and Aria are in a committed relationship—one that's far more than friends—and the public is in on it too, she still makes him blush. Maybe it's simply part of who he is. Or maybe it's her special effect on him.

Aria takes an acoustic guitar from the band setup and slings it over her front as she returns to the microphone stand at the front of the stage.

The opening chords sound resonantly, and from the crowd come a few cheers of delight. The song has exploded in popularity since Griffin and Aria officially debuted to the public as a couple, even further since they shared the backstory of the song to fans on social media.

Griffin's chest opens wide as he watches Aria perform, filling him with a lightness that comes only when he focuses on her. She shines not only as a performer, but in a way that awes him. Not everyone sees the work and dedication that happens behind the scenes, the way she wrestles with her songs until they're just right, the way she holds her fans' opinions as highly as her own. All of the thought and planning required to make any of this work. Aria is an absolute wonder, and Griffin is lucky to behold her.

Especially here from the wings, out of sight, he can adore her undercover.

She knows the depths of his feelings for her, but gazing at her as if she's a miracle becomes a little over the top at certain points—well, at least that's what he's been told. Even if things between them are so effortless it's easy to forget they were ever once apart, he doesn't want to scare her off. But here and now as she sings the lyrics that reeled him back into her life, just as he'd found his footing after his life fell apart, he knows that Aria Wilder might just be the most precious gift he'll ever receive.

Eventually Griffin's cheeks cool off, but then they begin to ache. It's from the smiling. He can't help but smile when he looks at her.

Aria speaks his name into the microphone, and it pulls him out of his daydreaming.

"Griffin? Griffin Hayes, I know you're back there. Get your butt out here!"

The crowd goes wild.

It's not his first time being called out onstage, and he hopes it won't be his last.

This time he grabs a quick sip of water from the bottle he holds, sets it down, and walks confidently toward the woman of his dreams.

The crowd cheers for him warmly, but under the glare of the bright lights, it's only Aria he can see.

The perfect view.

Chapter 56

Aria

Aria turns to the crowd. "I want to thank you all for being here tonight. The great city of Los Angeles always feels like home away from home, and I'm thrilled we could kick off the tour together."

Aria waves with both hands, and the crowd cheers. The set is complete, and her first tour performance can officially be checked from her list.

Griffin slips his hand onto the small of Aria's back in support but hangs back. Aria loves how happy Griffin is to support her without needing the spotlight himself. Not because she's not willing to share it; in fact, she's always trying to rope him into joining her under the lights, and she's often left to call him out publicly like she just did. Once a homebody, always a homebody, it seems. But the real reason is how it reflects his own deep confidence. How he's grounded.

Aria turns and winds her fingers into his, then looks up into his eyes.

She loves being onstage, performing solo, but Aria also loves the feel of Griffin at her side. Especially as he's thrown himself into his foundation work, she's had a front-row seat to a special sort of blossoming, a second act that might just eclipse the first. He's astounding and inspiring—which bodes particularly well for song inspiration. If she's not careful, the next album might as well be named *Griffin Hayes*.

Aria waves to the crowd. She pulls Griffin into her side and drops her head on his chest. The band fires up the final walkout music, a synthesized medley of all the songs Aria just performed, and the houselights start to turn on. Aria disentangles from Griffin to return the microphone to its stand, but as soon as she's back within arm's reach, Griffin pulls her into his arms.

"You are amazing. That show? It was next level." Griffin is beaming, and Aria feels like her insides are glittering. Her face breaks into a deep smile.

"Thank you for playing along at the end." Aria rests on Griffin's chest.

"Anything for you."

Aria had planned to ask Griffin if he thought they should add another song to the lineup, a surprise backlist hit played for each performance, but in his arms, the urgency she'd had fades.

"Thank you for coming."

Griffin grins. "I wouldn't have missed it. Not for the world."

"Can you believe we almost didn't get this?" Aria knows she doesn't need to clarify—she means *them*, not the album that also once lived on shaky ground.

"I almost messed it up. Well, I did mess up, but then you put it back together."

"Eh. We both did. I wouldn't have had the courage to go for it without you."

Griffin runs a hand up Aria's arm, and it sends a shiver over her that radiates to the tips of her fingers. "We do make a pretty good team."

Aria once thought her team was fully loaded with every best professional with connections to every best service. So much so that the suggestion that her team might be incomplete would've been laughable. What a surprise it is that today Griffin Hayes, stuck right in the middle of her life, has become such an integral part of her world. A cheerleader, a friend, a support person (giving much-needed relief to Bailey), and more than everything else combined, a real chance at love.

Aria reaches up onto her tiptoes and presses her lips into Griffin's. The roughness of his skin to her softness is just like each of them to each other. Imperfect alone but perfect complements to each other.

"I love you, Griff."

Aria closes her eyes, and the arena, the crowd, the lights all fade, and it's only the two of them. It's funny how often that happens nowadays. How quickly life shrinks to the two of them, all of the extras falling away.

Griffin snakes his palm around the back of Aria's neck and pulls her into another kiss. "I love you too. Thank goodness I just couldn't hold back during 'Glass Heart.'"

Aria giggles. "Even if that last song was written about you, 'Glass Heart' will always be you."

"As long as it doesn't become us."

Aria shakes her head vehemently at the idea of a breakup song pertaining to them. "Never."

"Glad we're on the same page."

"I mean, who else am I going to call out onto the stage with me? There aren't a lot of willing partners." Aria sings the words with a playful smirk on her lips.

Griffin barks a laugh. "I can promise you there'd be a line around the block if you were looking. But unfortunately for those guys, the spot's already taken."

"Yeah? I like the sound of that. Here to stay?"

"As long as you'll have me."

Aria takes in Griffin under the lights, and she's certain that choosing him—to not let him slip away—is one of the best decisions she's ever made. Her world has grown and expanded with him in it, and Aria is no longer chained by the impulse for perfection or limited by the walls she built years ago.

It's difficult to remember the time before Griffin—like he's been tethered to her by some invisible string all along—but Aria feels the echoes of her old life, the smallness, the fear wound around her. Even if from all appearances she was living large, her heart was locked away, her body wound tight with perfectionism. Griffin helped her break free from that, and in this new place there are so many more possibilities.

It's like opening all of the windows in the house after winter, a fresh breeze carrying the promise of warmer days.

Life together is so much more beautiful. Boundless.

"I'm hoping you'll stay," Aria says, wistful eyes set upon him.

"That was my only plan."

Even when the stage lights shut off, leaving them in total dark, Aria doesn't want to go. Here in this moment with

Griffin is all the best parts of her life tied into one. When she glances out, the venue is almost empty, only a few hardy fans waiting to witness her and Griffin's entire encounter.

"I guess we should go," Griffin says. "You know, before they physically kick us out."

Aria smiles slowly, unhurried. "If we must."

Griffin releases her from his arms, and Aria pushes away the swell of disappointment at pulling apart. He takes her hand, and when their eyes meet, they look at each other exchanging unsaid words, promises, and plans.

This was what all of those songs were about, all of those boy-meets-girl love songs.

One look at Griffin, one deep flutter of the heart, and Aria knows.

They just didn't do the feeling justice.

Epilogue

Six Months Later

Aria meets Griffin at his condo that afternoon, guitar case over her shoulder, writing notebook tucked into the front pocket. Usually she would work in her studio where she has all of the equipment to make it easy, but Griffin had a foundation meeting at the Wardens stadium, so it makes better logistical sense for the pair to meet here.

Aria knocks at the door.

"It's open," Griffin calls from inside.

Aria walks in, pulls the door shut, and flips the lock. She walks down toward the kitchen, talking. "You know, you really shouldn't leave it open. A famous football player doesn't need just anyone walking in."

Griffin rounds the corner and snaps Aria up into his arms.

She yelps, then cries, "Mind the guitar!"

Griffin shuffles her to a single arm, then plucks the instrument from her with ease. "I used to be a football player, you know. Of course I know to mind the guitar."

Aria laughs. "I just said that. *Verbatim*."

Griffin drops a tender kiss on Aria's nose. "I'm not sure what this is about intruders. Again, I'm probably twice the size of the average burglar."

"Burglar? What is this, 1920?"

Griffin spins her around on the way into the living room. "It was your idea, not mine. The penthouse is safe. I added the elevator code because now that I'm dating you, suddenly people care where I live."

Aria stares into Griffin's eyes, a lazy smile tugging at the corners of her mouth. "And what's to say I'm not selling that code on the black market?"

Griffin gasps in fake shock. "You would never!"

"You're right." Aria kisses him slowly and deeply. "I would never willingly share you with anyone—burglar or not."

"Phew." Griffin delivers Aria gently to the floor and hands back the instrument. "Your magic maker."

Aria takes back the guitar, grateful for his care with it. Griffin gifted her an upgraded version of her very first as a tour gift. It's almost identical to the original, but minus the dings and the scratches and the siding that was starting to fall off and distort the sound. By the end of the tour, Aria had developed a new affection for this instrument.

The tour itself was an incredible success, and Aria's latest album has come to be described as her "best work yet" almost unanimously among critics. The long hours put in at the gym helped her make it through the grueling series of high-intensity performances, and Griffin tagged in to help her with some meal prepping and low-key fun on her down days. He ended up traveling to far more of the destination cities than they initially planned. It turns out distance and new love don't mix.

Not that Griffin hasn't also had a lot happening in his own schedule. The Griffin Hayes Foundation for Youth Sports has also taken off with its own explosive success, bringing in several million dollars of donations in its first six months of operation. The foundation is now employing five staff and a couple of agencies for specific support work. Their online presence has gained great attention thanks to the new graduates taking the lead on social media. Griffin is rotating through guest coaching roles for a selection of high school football programs, and he is partnering with the league to do a specialty summer camp this year. Griffin plans to establish his own camp—a longer-running version with more than one session—next year, but he counts it as great experience to work with the league this summer. Especially now that they have reached an agreement to allow him to bring on students from the foundation schools free of charge to the Wardens camp.

Aria sets the guitar case on the sofa, opens it, and begins tuning the instrument.

"Already sounding good in there."

Aria smiles to herself. Griffin is so encouraging, some days she thinks she could sneeze and he would applaud.

Griffin reappears in the living room holding a spiral-bound notebook. He holds it high. "I come with ideas!"

"Yeah?" Aria drops onto the couch beside him.

Griffin nods as he scans the pages with searching eyes. "Here. It's not actual lyrics—I'm leaving that to you—but it's ideas."

Aria's face folds into a deep smile as Griffin looks to her for assurance as he reads. "Okay, forgive me if any of this is super dumb. I'm a newbie, but you said we should write a song together, and I'm obviously taking it seriously."

"Did you meal prep for it?"

A laugh escapes Griffin. "Actually, I did. Maybe I shouldn't admit it, but I prepped dinner last night so I could have a couple hours blocked for uninterrupted brainstorming time."

Aria slides closer and leans into him. "You're quite in demand these days."

"But never too busy for an Aria Wilder moment."

"Well, aren't I the luckiest."

"Funny you say that, because one of my title ideas is"—Griffin holds up his hands, reaches over to the coffee table, and attempts a drum roll—"'When Luck Walked In.'"

"Ooh, I sorta love that," Aria says.

"I was thinking about us and how we got together and about how lucky the timing was. Like for me, if I hadn't known you when I got injured, things might've turned out really differently. And for you—what if you'd never made your own mark on the music? Or your 'glow-up' as the press loves to call it. I mean, if you ask me, not a thing needed to glow up; it was more like stepping into your own power, but here I am rambling." Griffin stops and whips his head to look at Aria. "What do you think?"

She leans up and kisses him. "I think I love it. I think I'm the luckiest woman in the world, so the song should write itself."

Griffin slides his arms around her, letting the notebook fall momentarily to the side. "Well, that's funny because I fancy myself the luckiest man in the world."

Aria melts into laughter and Griffin pulls her into him as she does. They leave the notebook behind. They're just talking about them after all, the story that only they know best.

How they tell it will be up to them. It'll probably go through several drafts.

They won't miss the important things: taking the swing, embracing the bumps in the road, opening up to every new adventure life offers.

It won't be perfect—not the song, or them together.

But it will be wonderful.

And that's enough.

Discussion Questions

1. Both Aria and Griffin struggle with identity outside of their careers. How does fame shape the way they see themselves? Where do you see each of them questioning who they are beyond their "brand"?
2. The book explores the idea of a staged friendship. What moment shifts their dynamic from PR strategy to something more genuine?
3. Griffin initially resists stepping outside his comfort zone. What fears are driving him? How does his perspective begin to shift over time?
4. Bailey plays a grounding role in Aria's life. How does their relationship influence Aria's decisions, both personally and professionally?
5. Both characters wrestle with the idea that their careers won't last forever. How does this awareness shape their choices and emotional journeys?
6. Which moment in the book felt like the most significant turning point for Aria and Griffin's relationship? Why?

7. The book critiques the pressures of fame. Do you think the portrayal of celebrity culture felt realistic? How would the story change if Aria and Griffin were not famous?
8. What was your favorite scene or interaction between Aria and Griffin? Why did it stand out to you?
9. How do you imagine Aria and Griffin's lives unfolding after the book ends?
10. If *Pop Stars and Playbooks* were adapted into a movie, who would you cast as Aria and Griffin? What kind of soundtrack would best capture the story's tone?

About the Author

Juliet Rhodes is a hopeless romantic with a soft spot for slow-burn love stories and swoon-worthy heroes who fall first. When she's not writing, you can find her binge-watching rom-coms, obsessing over celebrity gossip, or cheering on her favorite teams (while secretly imagining the players in love triangles). She lives in a cozy apartment with her two rescue cats, Hemingway and Zelda.

Don't Miss These Other Sweet Romances

AVAILABLE IN PRINT, E-BOOK, AND DOWNLOADABLE AUDIO